Note:
Sale of this book without a front cover may be unauthorized. If this book was purchased without a cover, it may have been reported to the publisher as "unsold or destroyed". Neither the author nor the publisher may have received payment for the sale of this book.

This book is a work of fiction. Names and characters, places, and incidents either are products of the author's imagination or used fictitiously. Any resemblance to actual events or locales or persons, living or dead, is entirely coincidental.

Published by
La' Femme Fatale' Publishing
9900 Greenbelt Road
Suite E-333
Greenbelt, MD 20706
www.LFFP.net

For Information regarding special discounts or bulk purchases, please contact La' Femme Fatale' Publishing at (866) 50- femme and info@lffp.net

Library of Congress Catalog Card No: In publication data
ISBN:
Copyright: © 2007 by La' Femme Fatale' Productions

DC Blood Brothers

Written by: Viyo Lance
Edited by: BE'N ORIGINAL
Text Formation: BE'N ORIGINAL for UMA Marketing
Cover Graphics: BE'N ORIGINAL for UMA Marketing
Concept Design and Layout by: UMA Marketing
Submissions Team Coordinator: Dj Holmes

All rights reserved, including the right of reproduction in whole or part in any form.

DEDICATION

I dedicate this book to my two beautiful daughters Dominique Lee-Martin and Kayah Martin, whom I love more than life. They inspire me every day and keep me strong. To my grandmother, Annie May Cinada who always had my back, and inspired me by proving to people anything is possible. To my father, Kenneth Martin, Sr., and my mother, Gail Martin, who always kept it real with me, uncut and raw with no chaser. To my Aunt Sue, may she rest in peace. Aunt MiMi, Uncle Angelo, Leroy, and Mike (RIP). To all my street family regardless of beef's, City got love everywhere and I love y'all for that. KDP, 103, Glass Manor, 6th Street, SE, Oxon Hill Village, Oxon Run, 202, Columbia, S.C., B-more, Philly, and New York y'all keep it moving.

To all my soldiers on lock down, males and females you're in my prayers. Let's change these drug laws. To all my enemies who made my motivation strong from your hatred, keep hating. To Michele Fletcher my author and publisher, along with the entire LFF Family. Thanks for giving me a chance and making my dreams and yours come true. We're going to Hollywood, baby! -Viyo Lance

preface

"Oh Franklin, I'm so scared I can hardly breathe. You'll be fine Millie," Franklin reassured his wife as he patted her right hand. It bothered him seeing his wife of two years go through so much pain and not be able to help. "Nurse, when will the Doctor get here?" He asked growing impatient. "Dr. Wilson will be here momentarily Mr. Jenkins..."

Franklin looked down to his wife, who was squeezing his left hand so tight it was turning numb. Beads of sweat appeared on Millie's forehead out of nowhere. "Here, let me get that baby..." A smile came to the nurse's face, as she watched the twenty five year old couple go through the miracle of birth with their first child. A slight beep, constantly repeating itself could be heard along with the rain that just started tapping the window.

"Franklin, I can't believe we're about to have a child. How do you feel, do you feel nervous?"

"A little, just a little," he lied, with his stomach already in the air.

Franklin hated hospitals, the cold air, the sterile smell, beeps and too much metal. Like a human garage of some sort, he thought.

"Well folks!" Doctor Wilson said loudly as he clapped his hands together entering the room, "Let's get this show on the road. "Nurse, how far are Millie's contractions?"

"Every two and a half minutes now Dr. Wilson."

"Okay Millie relax, we've talked about this numerous times, just do your breathing exercises."

Millie nodded in agreement, and then looked to her husband.

"Franklin, can you say a silent prayer for our baby and me?"

DC BLOOD BROTHERS

Franklin's eyes closed as his heart and soul made a request to God. "Lord, please give us a healthy baby and please comfort my wife, in the name of Jesus, Amen." When his eyes re-opened, Dr. Wilson was positioning himself between Millie's legs.

"Alright Millie, your contractions are a minute apart, I want you to begin pushing now. Push, push... "

Millie felt like she was about to have the world's largest bowel movement!

"Good Millie, keep pushing" the Doctor coaxed.

Millie gasped for air.

"Keep pushing Millie," said Doctor Wilson, you're doing great; I can see your baby's head crowning!"

Franklin's mouth went dry as he witnessed his wife's body tearing and a tiny skull coming out of her.

"I've got it, I have him" the Doctor said as he realized the sex of the child. "Would you like to cut the umbilical cord Franklin?" Without answering Franklin took the scissors and cut the fleshy cord. The tiny baby boy cried after the Doctor slapped his butt.

"Here nurse," Dr. Wilson handed the baby off to the nurse. "Well, hate to deliver and run but I have another couple waiting. I don't know what was in the air last November, but I've broken a record this July with births.

"Thank you Doctor, thank you."

"Here you are Millie, your handsome healthy son, what's his name? "

Millie looked up at Franklin. "We're naming him Jason Parcell Jenkins," Franklin stated with his chest swollen with pride. July 3, 1974 was now the happiest day of the couple's lives.

"Hi baby, hi Jason." Franklin just watched as his wife spoke to their son. "Thank you God for giving us a healthy baby" Franklin silently prayed.

Four days had gone by and Franklin moved with a frantic pace through his apartment, picking up clothes to carry out containers that had accumulated since Millie had given birth to Jason. It had been a rough four days without his wife. She didn't know he had been fired because he called out from work the day their son was born. But, he had good news. He had found a new and better job.

He looked to his watch. 12:45pm, he had almost an hour until it was time to pick up Millie and the baby.

After washing the dishes, vacuuming, and spraying Lysol all over the two bedroom apartment, he walked the garbage down the hall to the trash shoot and he was done. He grabbed his car keys and stepped out of the door.

He pulled into Columbia Hospital for Women's parking lot. After parking Franklin rushed inside to his wife and new born son.

Millie was patting Jason's back as she held him over her shoulder.

"Hey baby and little man, ya'll ready to go home?" Franklin asked poking his head through the slightly opened hospital room door.

"You know I am, the food here is so bland, and it is terrible."

The nurse appeared in the door way with a wheel chair, "are we ready to go?"

DE BLOOD BROTHERS

"Yes, we are, but what's that contraption for.?" Millie asked anxiously.

"Oh its hospital policy Millie, don't worry, everyone gets this treatment," replied the nurse.

"Franklin, you go get the car, we'll meet you downstairs, we're going home baby Jason, yes we are," she cooed.

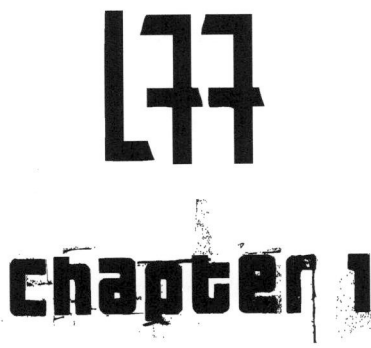

Chapter 1

Five years had passed since the birth of their child. Franklin navigated his brand new white 79' Coupe De Ville down busy Georgia Avenue through the Sunday traffic.

"Daddy, can we stop at McDonald's?" Jason asked after seeing the all too familiar golden arches.

"Not today son, you know Mommy cooks every Sunday. What you been all quiet for today anyway?"

"No reason" Jason answered his father.

Franklin periodically glanced at his son as he continued Downtown.

"So, you are keeping secrets from your old man?" He joked with his son as he ran his hand over Jason's scalp.

"No, I'm not keeping secrets."

"Well what's wrong little man, because you are not normally this quiet?"

"This morning when I got up, Mommy was throwing up."

Franklin looked at his son, "are you sure?"

"Um huh," was Jason's answer.

She didn't mention anything about being sick he thought. Georgia Avenue turned into 7th Street and Franklin got an idea.

"Hey little man, you want stop and get Mommy some flowers."

"Yeah" Jason shouted.

Franklin put on his right blinker once they made it to Giant Foods parking lot. The two welcomed the air conditioned store as the electronic doors swung open. "Hey fellas!" They heard a female voice yell. They turned and saw Mrs. Gladys.

DE BLOOD BROTHERS

"How are you doing today, Gladys?"

"I'm fine Franklin" she answered as she squatted to Jason's height and began pinching his cheeks.

"Hi Jason."

Jason's head turned in embarrassment.

"Look at him; got the nerve to be handsome and shy, going to be a heart breaker I tell you."

"Ah, Mrs. Gladys, did Millie seem a little under the weather today?"

"Why, no, at least I don't think so. I hope she isn't because she's supposed to cover my shift for me tomorrow, it's me and Howard's anniversary."

"Well congratulations! I'm sure it's probably nothing."

"Okay guys I have to go, tell Millie to call me."

"Alright, bye Mrs. Gladys," Franklin waved her off.

After picking out six of the prettiest red roses, they made their way to the express checkout line. The store was packed as usual, but Franklin's eyebrows rose as he watched the old lady in front of him, putting more than fifteen items onto the conveyer belt. Franklin couldn't remember the young cashier's name at the register because she was new. The way her mouth just dropped opened and her eyes rolled as she counted the merchandise, it was obvious that she's livid.

"Excuse me miss," the cashier began as she pointed. "I'm sorry but I can't ring all this stuff. This is the express lane for fifteen items or less."

"You mean to tell me," the old lady began, "I've been standing in this line for 10 minutes and now I have to go to another one."

"I'm sorry ma'am, but as the sign up there reads..."

"Fuck that sign!" The lady cut her off. "I want to see the manager!"

"Fine," the cashier said as she picked up the phone called for a manager.

"You can come on" the cashier said, gesturing for the old lady to step upside.

"Aren't you Millie's husband?"

"Yes."

"How are you doing?"

"I'm fine."

She rang the flowers up. After getting his change, he and Jason squeezed around the old lady and made their way to the door. The father and son were temporarily blinded by the sun for a few seconds then their eyes adjusted. Franklin now saw everything he wanted to get his son away from. There were drunks in raggedy clothes clutching bottles of liquor approaching everyone that passed them for money. A few dope fiends were either nodding off in public or scratching themselves while the drug dealers surrounded the pay phones as if they owned them. If the sights were not bad enough, there was a constant stench of body odor and urine that lingered every hot day.

Suddenly gun shots rang out. Without thinking, Franklin snatched Jason off the ground and ran to his car and sped out of the parking lot. Driving pass the Immaculate Conception high rise, he saw a group of people huddled over a body heard an older lady screaming.

DC BLOOD BROTHERS

MILLIE

"Oh my God!" Millie said aloud as she almost dropped the spoon she was stirring the mash potatoes with. "Crazy fools, don't they know once you take a life, you can't give it back." Dinner was almost ready, rice, string beans, mash potatoes, and BBQ chicken. The Mrs. Smith apple pie for desert was thawing on the counter top. She put her hand on the counter to brace herself suddenly feeling dizzy. What is going on with me?, She thought. If I didn't know any better I'd swear I was pregnant, but I didn't have symptoms like this with Jason.

After turning the stove off and oven down to a simmer, she went to her purse, pulling out her check book to locate her calendar. Her menstrual cycle, which has never been late for 18 years, was due in six days. She hurriedly shoved her check book into her purse as she heard Franklin's keys unlocking the door. He walked in, "Hello my beautiful wife."

"Hello to you too, husband, but if you don't tell me how you left out of here with my son and came in here alone, we're going to have serious problems."

There was a light knock on the door. "I think it's for you," Franklin smiled. She opened the door. "Surprise" Jason yelled as loud as he could. Her hand going to her heart, "Aww, What's this ... a wonderful surprise?" She asked smiling.

"Well, Jason said, you were sick this morning; we thought the flowers might help you feel better."

Her smile disappeared. Damn, I didn't know Jason saw me this morning, she thought.

"So, do you feel better? Even Mrs. Gladys wants you to call her."

Millie could barely hear what her husband was saying as the loud sirens drowned them out, probably rushing to save an already lifeless body.

"What were you saying?"

"Gladys said call her. Is dinner ready? Jason and I are starving, we could eat anything."

"Oh yeah," she raised the roses as if she were going to hit him upside his head.

"What did I tell you about insulting my cooking Mr. Jenkins?"

"I was only joking."

"Whatever Franklin... You take your son and go wash your hands."

After dinner, Franklin rubbed his stomach back and forth as he lay stretched out on the Sealy queen sized bed. "That dinner sure was good tonight baby." Millie just looked to her husband rolling her eyes.

"If you're going to try and compliment my cooking now thinking you going to get some loving from me, you might as well keep on." Both of them fell out laughing at Millie's remark.

"I love you Millie."

"I love you too, Franklin but now I have to ask you what's wrong because you never call me by my name unless something is wrong."

DC BLOOD BROTHERS

"I just wanted to ask you if you'd mind if I started putting in a lot of overtime."

"Franklin, if this is about me wanting my own car you don't have to kill yourself."

"Well actually it's more than that. I just want to move you and my son out of this neighborhood. Gibson Plaza and Immaculate Conception used to be decent buildings. Look at the Kennedy playground; it was an entire block that was designed for children, now it is one humongous shooting gallery for fiends. I'm scared to let our child come up in this environment, I want better for Jason. We deserve better and I'm going to get it for us."

Mille loved her husband, she was his best friend. He didn't hang with buddies. He didn't want to be or need to be anywhere his wife wasn't. Franklin didn't drink, smoke, or gamble, she was his only addiction. She smiled as she realized he gave her yet another reason to know she made the right choice marrying him. She answered, "Franklin, you're the man of this house and whatever decisions you make, I'll support you. Now come here to Mama."

Franklin began kissing, licking, and fondling her everywhere that usually made her hot. And although she responded, and was extremely wet when he entered her, she knew he would be the only one to reach a climax this evening because she had too much on her mind to be comfortable. Thinking how she could be pregnant was weighing heavy on her, especially now that she knew of his plans to move.

Nearly a week had passed. While Jason was playing in his room, Millie watched the five o'clock news. A disappointing sigh was the only response she could make after hearing the murder rate was 310, breaking last year's record of 308 and summer wasn't close to being over yet. She wondered why they kept tabs on murders as if they were bragging or something. She picked up the phone and dialed her sister's number but it was busy as usual. She can't get that many calls; she has to be taking the receiver off the hook, she thought.

Millie was trying to stay busy and not worry about her period not coming for almost two months. She wondered what Franklin was doing. There wasn't a lot of overtime at the Washington Post so he got a part time job at Ever Fresh delivering juices.

"Jason!"

"Yeah, Ma!"

"Boy didn't I tell you when I call you to come see what I want, not to scream back yeah?"

"Yes ma'am. Don't do it again, now come here and give mommy a hug."

She squeezed him tight, and then gave him a kiss on the cheek. Boy you look just like your Father. He smiled; "Can I go back and play now?"

"Sure, you don't have to worry about Mommy; I'll get some of those Oreo cookies to keep me company."

"Can I have some cookies?"

"Come on, I'll give you a few and you can take them in your room."

chapter 2

Franklin was almost finished with his route with two more stops, Jefferson liquors on Georgia Ave and the 5 & 10 on Kennedy Street. He double parked, put on his hazard lights and loaded his dolly. "Hello Mr. Jenkins," The store owner bellowed as Franklin entered.

Franklin was surprised Mr. Lee remembered his name. "How are you doing, Mr. Lee? You want these in the refrigerator, right?" The store owner nodded.

After making three trips to his truck, the delivery was finished. The only thing Franklin needed was a signature on the invoice. Mr. Lee took the clipboard and signed it, "Here you go, Daffy Duck." Franklin looked at the board then fanned it bye to Mr. Lee as he laughed walking out.

Franklin was glad to be getting the over time, but today was brutal. He not only did his route but someone else's. Usually he would be on his way home instead of in the thick of rush hour traffic. He finally pulled in front of the 5 &10 store on Kennedy Street. He loaded his hand-truck with boxes then entered the store.

"Hey," Mr. Anderson greeted him. He probably didn't remember Franklin's name.

"How are you doing Mr. Anderson?"

"I'm doing alright but I'll be doing a hell of a lot better if the Redskins can beat the Cowboys next week."

"You and me both."

The door bell went off indicating that someone had entered the store.

"Hold on for a minute Franklin."

Mr. Anderson walked to the front of the store and looked to the mirror in the upper left corner. A little boy came from out of an aisle and walked to the door.

Mr. Anderson grabbed his arm. "Get off me! Get off me!" The little boy yelled as he tried everything he could to break free of Mr. Anderson's grasp.

"Now look here Bones, I told you about coming in my store stealing. Now the next time I see you I'm calling the police. Now get out of here."

He caught his breath before talking to Franklin. "If I could Franklin, I'd put all my merchandise behind the bullet proof glass but I can't afford that." Franklin nodded, sympathizing with the store owner. After getting his invoice signed, Franklin drove back to the warehouse to clock out.

MILLIE

Millie stepped to the door as she heard her husband's keys. "I thought you forgot where you lived," she joked. Franklin smiled, though she could see the weariness on his face.

"Come on in here, I'll start your shower water, and by the time you come out, I'll heat up your food and bring it to you."

Franklin's eyes closed as the hot water sprayed from the shower head. He reached up and turned the shower head from spray to massage. Then put his back to the water and let it beat on his shoulders until he started to relax. His mind's eye pictured his goal, his home, somewhere nice in P.G. County.

Franklin heard a soft knock on the door. "Daddy, mommy said to check that you didn't drown in there." Franklin laughed until his eyes watered. "Tell her no, son. I'm coming out now."

After eating dinner, Franklin read Jason "The Cat in the Hat," and then sent him to bed. Afterwards, he watched a movie with his wife but they couldn't find out the title. Franklin's eyes closed and he began tossing and turning to get comfortable. Millie scooted over until her body touched him then closed her eyes. For a long time she just laid there.

Suddenly, she was dreaming of their two story house in Largo or Waldorf, MD. There was a German shepherd running around their yard, and her kitchen was just how she wanted it. Then her dream changed, now she was holding hands with her husband walking through Hanes Point. "Come on baby, let's go fishing" he said. Next, they were on a boat and there were so many fish in the water she could reach down and grab one out the water. Hold up, she thought, FISH!

She woke up with a light sweat all over her body. Today's the day, she told herself as she went to the bathroom hoping she was at least spotting. Nothing. Maybe it'll come later this month. I've probably worked myself into making my

DC BLOOD BROTHERS

body think it's pregnant. But if I am, we won't be able to move like Franklin wants. She felt a little guilty though she knew it was not her fault alone. It takes two to make a baby.

The next day Millie looked to the clock when she heard Franklin's keys. "Hi baby, these are for you." He walked up to his wife and kissed her, handing her a dozen roses.

"And I heard somebody been doing real good learning their alphabets and numbers."

Jason looked to his father wide eyed as he walked to the door, then stepped back in with a new BMX bike.

"Thank you Daddy! Can I go outside and ride?"

"We'll do better than that, son. You and I will go up to Bannaker grounds across from the McDonald's."

Millie loved it when her family shared times like this, she called them Kodak moments. She waved goodbye to her two favorite men, "See ya'll when you get home."

Once Franklin helped Jason get on his bike, he felt an instant sense of gratification seeing the smile on Jason's face. Jason peddled as hard as he could up and down the walk way, falling once into the sticker brier bushes resulting in just a few scratches.

Everyday Franklin thought of how he was closer to getting his family off 7th Street. He wanted to save and protect the innocence on the face of his son. "Lord," he began silently, "please give me the strength to bring my son up; and be a positive role model."

The five o'clock news was about to come on, so Millie plopped her body in her favorite part of the sofa and ripped open a big bag of Utz Sour Cream & Onion potato chips. She put one in her mouth then licked her fingers before picking up the remote control to turn up the volume.

As soon as her arm reached toward the coffee table, her head became very light. She sat there on the sofa very still until the dizziness wore off. Millie took the dizzy spell as a sign that she's been straining her body too hard. She went to get the box of chocolate doughnuts and the bag of candy corn from the cabinet. While watching the news, it took her a while to notice that after every bite of a doughnut, she would eat some chips followed with some candy corn. This is crazy she thought and reached for the phone.

"Hello, this is Mrs. Millie Jenkins. I need to see Dr. Fandell. Yes, tomorrow... two o'clock... thank you."

After dropping Jason off at day care, Millie flagged down a cab to get to George Washington University Ambulatory Center. She sat fidgeting by flipping through a pamphlet on HIV and AIDS. "Mrs. Jenkins, the doctor will see you now."

"How are we feeling Mrs. Jenkins? What do I owe the pleasure of this visit?"

"Well, for one my cycle didn't come, and two, I'm having dizzy spells."

"Well, let's take a pregnancy test first and see what's going on."

Millie took the test then waited for the Doctor.

DC BLOOD BROTHERS

"I have good news Mrs. Jenkins, you're pregnant" he said smiling until he noticed her face didn't seem happy to hear the news."

"You alright Mrs. Jenkins?"

"Yes," she answered looking as if she were about to cry. "It's just," she started to explain then changed her mind, "I don't know".

"Look Mrs. Jenkins, I'm going to give you a number to a counselor here, that way if you don't want this child; you can always have the option to give it up for adoption or abortion."

Millie almost took offense to the doctor even suggesting abortion, but what's even crazier is now she's considering it. She was a God fearing church woman, and the church frowned upon abortions, but something inside was telling her not to have this baby.

"I need to talk to my husband," she said and walked out of the Doctor's office.

She sat silent in the back of the taxi on the way to pick up Jason. Millie decided to have the cab driver pull over and walk the two blocks to the day care; she needed the air.

"Mommy," Jason screamed as she walked into the door. Jason began reaching to hug his Mother. How could I entertain the thought of aborting a child? If it's half as loving as Jason ... I want it.

chapter 3

Franklin sang and whistled as he drove home. He was happy that after five years with the Washington Post, they just gave him a $1.50 raise. Looking out of his window after he parked he thought how happy he's going to be when he pulls up to his own home and wouldn't have to witness the madness that was going on around him now. Both elevators were out of order as usual so he walked up the stairs.

"What's up Daddy?"

"Ain't nothing son. Where's your Mommy?"

"She's been in her room all day."

Franklin just noticed how Jason seemed to be growing every day, looking like his split image. Chocolate brown complexion, light brown eyes, bow legged, and since Franklin was six feet two inches he knew the boy would be tall.

"Let me see how Mommy's doing and I'll come back to play with you after I eat," he rubbed his hand over Jason's head like he always did and walked to his room.

"Hey Baby, you feeling okay? I got some good news for you" Franklin said excitedly.

"What's the good news?" Millie asked.

"I finally got a raise at the Washington Post, we'll be out of here by next year tops," he smiled.

Damn, she thought, how can I tell him? She decided to get it over with.

"Franklin, I'm pregnant!" she yelled.

He stopped smiling as the words set in.

"You're not happy about it, I knew it." Her head dropped.

"Hey girl, come here and give me a hug, of course I'm happy."

And he was, but his feelings were torn as if he found out he'd won a million dollars and his best friend died at the same time.

"But now we can't move yet like you've been planning."

"It doesn't matter Millie, as long as our family is safe, I'm fine. We may not be able to move as soon as I'd like but we're getting away from here. Knowing that we have another bundle of joy coming just fuels my motivation. Thank you for making me another child."

Over the next few weeks Franklin saved more money out of his checks, opened a new bank account for his unborn child, realizing he would soon be thirty one years old. He took out a life insurance policy on himself. Every day that passed he was becoming more excited at the prospect of having another child.

Millie promised that she would work as long as the pregnancy would allow her, but it wasn't easy on her. If she wasn't sick all the time; she was having dizzy spells or headaches. Franklin took over the chore of cooking. She loved how he spoiled her when she was expecting. Jason seemed more excited than the both of them that he's about to get a little brother or sister; that's all he talked about.

Six months had come and gone. Franklin drove up Georgia Avenue to Jefferson liquors as he felt his pager go off. He read *911 and knew instantly that Millie's water had just broke. First he called her back and told her he would meet her at the hospital. Next, he called his job and informed his boss, which he was glad they more than understood the situation.

After dropping off his truck, he headed to Columbia Hospital for women. He was glad that traffic was at a minimum, as he pulled into the hospital's parking lot. This has to be easier the second time around, he thought.

After scrubbing and putting on his hospital gown he walked into the delivery room. She was soaking wet with sweat, and panting as if she was gasping for air.

"I'm here baby, I'm here," he consoled his wife knowing once again the situation was out of his control. As her half opened eyes looked up to him, her dry chapped lips cracked a smile. The nurse came into the room.

"Mrs. Jenkins since you're in so much pain we're going to give you an epidural. Now it's important you restrict your movement because the needle will be placed in your spine."

"Okay," Millie nodded.

Dr. Wilson entered the room joking. "Haven't we met before? How are we feeling Millie?"

"I hurt like hell but I'm ready."

"How far apart are her contractions, nurse?"

"Every three minutes."

"Page me when they are down to a minute and a half."

"Doctor!" Millie called as he headed out of the room.

DE BLOOD BROTHERS

"Yes, Millie."

"Can I have some water or something please? My mouth is so dry."

"The best I can do is let you munch on some ice chips."

"That'll be fine, thank you."

Once Millie's contractions were down to a minute and a half Dr. Wilson was paged.

"Alright Millie I want you to push for me."

Suddenly a concerned look came over Dr. Wilson face.

"Wait, stop pushing Millie!"

"What's wrong doctor?" Franklin asked in almost a whisper.

"Your baby is positioned to come out feet first. I'll try my best to turn him around, and if that doesn't work we'll have to do a C-Section."

For the next hour Franklin watched Dr. Wilson fail at every attempt to turn his child around. "Nurse, I'm about to do a Caesarian. Please start prepping her for me... thank you". Franklin nearly passed out at the sight of his wife being cut open. Millie began sweating heavily. "Dr. Wilson, her fever is rising," the nurse said, trying to remain calm.

"How's her pulse?"

"Alright but fluctuating."

Franklin's ears became familiar with all the noises the machines were constantly making, but suddenly a loud sound nearly sent the room in to a panic.

"She's going under nurse! Code blue! Code blue!"

The nurse called the code, then ushered Franklin out of the delivery room as other doctors rushed in.

Lord no, he thought, then immediately prayed. "Lord I hope this isn't a sin, what I'm about to ask you. But that's my wife in there, Lord Jesus. Please, please, I beg you Lord, don't take my wife ... just don't take my wife, Amen."

The next two hours felt like two days. A little relief came once the doctors walked out patting each other on the back. That's got to be a good sign, Franklin thought to himself.

"Mr. Jenkins," the nurse called. He got up and walked into the room. Another nurse was holding his new born, his wife was still unconscious. He stood over her, and after 15 seconds her eyes opened.

"You passed out honey."

"What about our baby, is our baby alright?"

"Millie, your baby is fine but you better calm down before you go back under," the nurse explained as she placed her baby in Millie's arms.

"He's cute. What's his name?"

"Anthony," Millie said, "Anthony Kenard Jenkins."

Franklin was taken aback; Millie had just named their son without even consulting him. Since he named Jason, he assumed he would name this child. For a split second he wondered if she had chosen their second child's name a long time ago. He then realized that with everything that transpired, he should be glad that both his wife and Anthony survived the birth.

Chapter 4

"Mommy, can we go outside?" Anthony asked. He was now nine years old, but already had the determination of a teen.

"Yes, as soon as I go over your homework."

"Aw man!" He grumbled with disappointment.

"Ant, come here."

"Yes ma'am."

"Do I look like a man to you?"

"No ma'am."

"Then don't say that towards me anymore, you hear me?"

"Yes."

"Now get that homework done."

"I told you we got to do this first," Jason told his brother.

After finishing their homework, Millie let them go outside. "You get your key to the security doors downstairs, Jason?" Millie questioned. He felt for the key on the shoe string around his neck.

"Yes ma'am."

"Okay, have fun, but don't go too far!"

There was a chill in the air, but not as cold as it could have been for February. The boys crossed the street and entered Kennedy playground. Normally they would have played on one of the large toys, or at least rolled down the giant four ramp sliding board. Not today, Ms. Jackson was having a ping pong tournament in the recreation room and everyone was going to be there.

DC BLOOD BROTHERS

When they walked in, they saw their friends and neighbors battling on the ping pong table. It was so crowded everyone was standing elbow to elbow. Most eyes were on a kid named Red from 5th Street who was playing Sam from 1512.

"What's up, Jay? Hey, Ant!"

"What's up, Black?" Ant replied, recognizing one of his friends from the playground.

"Ain't shit."

Suddenly, a fight broke out at the far side of the room. Everybody ran to the door to see what was going on. Red was beating up one of Sam's friends for accusing him of cheating.

"Stop it! Stop it right now," Ms. Jackson yelled as she rushed to separate the two boys. Ms. Jackson was at least 60 years old but she was a big woman.

"Come on, Ant. Let's go." Jason demanded, "We aren't supposed to be over here anyway."

After getting their sandwiches from the O Street Market, they rushed to get back to the small playground behind their high-rise. A few minutes, the boys heard loud music playing in front of their building. It was almost deafening. They came from behind the building and saw Smiley get out of his 190E Benz and everyone flocked to him. "That's my car," Ant said as he pointed to the money green Mercedes.

The following morning Millie woke the boys up for school. Ant ran to the bathroom to brush his teeth as he heard his Mother's footsteps coming down the hallway. She stuck her head into the small bedroom they shared.

"Jason Parcell Jenkins! Get your butt up; I didn't beg the principal to allow you to attend Shaw Jr. High School so you could walk in late. Get up I said!"

After getting dressed and grabbing their books, both sons were on their separate ways. Jason walked out the front door of the lobby and Anthony, who was still in elementary school, went through the back. Jason walked past the O Street Market and cut through Giant Foods' parking lot to 9th Street. Deciding since he had some change he would stop inside of Shiloh Baptist Church and buy a couple donuts.

"Two chocolate glazed, please," he requested from the lady behind the counter.

"Hi Jason!"

He turned around. "Hi Shana, how are you doing?"

"I'm doing fine."

Shana was one of the prettiest girls in school, and also one of the only ones already developing a woman's body but not fast or hot in the behind as his Mother would say.

"Ah, you want a donut?"

"Sure," she smiled. "Thank you; I love these chocolate glazed donuts."

Jason stared at Shana's hazel eyes. She looked up and for a moment their eyes locked.

"Your hair looks nice, he complimented her. "

DC BLOOD BROTHERS

"Thanks, my Aunt did it. You finished?" She asked.

"Yeah, then I think we better be getting to school. You know how the security guards are, especially the one going bald, Mr. Baldwin."

They walked outside and Shana opened the pink umbrella she had after feeling a couple sprinkles of rain. They began walking towards Rhode Island Avenue. Suddenly a car slammed on its brakes.

"Shana, what's up baby?" A boy yelled out of the car.

Shana turned, seeing Ortega, who was 15 years old driving the new 300ZX. Without speaking she turned her head straight and kept walking.

"Oh, I see. You still on them bammas, huh?," He screamed then sped past them.

ANTHONY

"Ant, wait up!" Someone yelled.

Ant turned around to see his friend Jamal from 5th and O Street, running to catch up with him.

"What's up?" He asked mimicking the older guys around his way.

"Nothing, you want to cut through Bundy's baseball field?"

"Yeah come on." Jamal answered.

"Hey Ant, you know that girl Lisa in our class likes you."

"Who?" He asked, knowing exactly who Lisa was. As a matter of fact, since she was put in his class his grades had gone from B's to C's because he spent most of his time staring at her.

"Lisa, you know, the light skinned girl with long hair that sits by Tiffany."

"Oh her, okay," Ant played it off.

They looked down the street and saw four guys approaching them. As the older kids got closer, both boys realized there was going to be trouble. While passing, Tyrone, the shortest of the four, intentionally bumped in to Jamal.

"Hey, what you can't say excuse me?" Jamal screamed.

"Who you talking to, Jamal?," Tyrone barked.

"I'm talking to you nigga. You the one who bumped into me."

Tyrone laughed and turned as if he was going to walk away, then punched Jamal so hard in the eye it instantly began closing and turning purple.

"Hit 'em back Jamal," Anthony screamed, seeing his friend was scared. Jamal managed to punch Tyrone back, but the offensive didn't last too long. Tyrone was simply way too strong and quickly countered, dropping the smaller kid to his knees. All Jamal could do was ball up, trying to shield his head and torso as Tyrone kicked him over and over again.

"Leave 'em alone" Anthony yelled, jumping on Tyrone's back trying his best to choke him. Though Tyrone was small for his age, he still considerably larger than both of Ant and Jamal and easily threw him to the ground. Even though they didn't have a chance of winning, Anthony and Jamal continued to fight until the other three boys started to get bored and pulled their friend away.

DC BLOOD BROTHERS

"You okay?," Anthony asked Jamal as Tyrone walked off with his three friends laughing at him.

"Yeah I'm alright. Thank you for helping me, man."

"You're my best friend, I'd never let anything happen to you." Ant replied.

FRANKLIN

Franklin loved the rain so he enjoyed his lunch at Eddie Leonard's in N.E. Staring out the window while eating. A young couple walked into the restaurant and he smiled. Remembering how he and his wife were inseparable in their early twenties. Next year, they would turn forty, and celebrating their 16th wedding anniversary. Time really does fly he thought. Then, he thought it again as he glanced at his Citizen Quartz seeing his lunch break was over.

His next stop was a local strip club, the Foxy Playground. He never cheated on his wife in all their years of marriage but he wouldn't dare tell Millie it was one of his stops.

He delivered to two 7-Elevens before finally arriving at Jefferson liquors. After a few trips going from his truck to refrigerators, he was glad to be at his last stop for the day.

Getting out of his truck to open the back door, he saw the boy he'd heard Mr. Anderson call Bones, so he spoke.

"How are you doing today, Bones?"

"Fine, sir. Do you have any spare change?"

Franklin reached in his pocket, handing the boy a dollar.

"Thank you," Bone's yelled as he took off running.

"Hey Franklin, how are you feeling today?," Mr. Anderson greeted him as he walked in.

"I feel Okay, Mr. Anderson, what's the lesson for today?"

"Balance!"

"Balance?" Franklin repeated.

"Yes, balance. See Franklin, everybody wants to be on either this side or that side. People thrive off competition, so we feel we had to have a team, or favorite color, or even a religion. And we stress ourselves out to make a stand for this or that when it really doesn't make a difference. We give ourselves too much damn credit, Franklin. We fool ourselves into believing we have to be heard or noticed when we're merely a grain of sand at the beach."

"So in all that, what do you propose we do, Mr. Anderson?"

"I propose instead of thinking a woman is a woman because of how she carries herself, and a man by his actions, that we finally realize it's nothing we can do to justify our existence. It's already justified, we just need to simply be. "

Chapter 5

Jason looked to the clock and smiled when it finally was at 2:59pm. Mr. Thompson was a cool teacher, but he just talked too much. Turning around he saw Ortega leaning over his desk talking to Tina. Ortega was mixed with black and Spanish, and everybody knew his family members were big time drug dealers. He probably made more money than his Mother and Father put together. How could I think I can get a girl like Shana when O can't even get her?

The school bell sounded at three o'clock. Jason put his book bag over his shoulder and walked to the stairwell.

"Jason!"

He turned around, seeing Shana.

"Wait for me outside by the front door; I just need to run to my locker."

Jason's heart was beating faster by the second. He waited outside the front door; most of the students had exited the building. Cars were pulling up, some parents picking up their children, others were older guys with cars picking up their young girlfriends. It was ten minutes after three o'clock now, and he started wondering what's up with Shana until she came out the front doors with a baton in her hands.

"I'm so sorry Jason; I didn't know I had band practice."

"And you know Mr. Hoove don't be playing."

"Are you going to wait for me, we'll be finished by 3:45pm.?"

"Alright."

Watching as Shana high stepped and twirled her baton, Jason finally realized he could probably get punished for coming home late. She's worth it though.

ANTHONY

"Jamal! You coming or what?" Ant yelled to his friend over the crowd of students exiting Scott Montgomery Elementary School. Jamal was talking to Lisa, and Ant wanted to know if he was the subject of their conversation.
"Ant, Lisa gave me this for you." Passing him a folded piece of paper, Ant opened and read it.
Do you want to be my boyfriend?, the top box had yes and the bottom was no. Jamal read the note over Ant's shoulder.
"I told you she liked you. "
"Man, did you see the new Michael Jordan sneakers that just came out?"
"Yeah, I saw Benjamin had a pair. The black and red ones right?"
"Yeah, are you going to be at Kennedy playground later on?"
"Probably, you know my mother be tripping about me leaving the block."
"Well," Jamal turned to give his friend dap, "I'll see you later. Thunder Cats and He-Man is about to come on."

JASON

"You ready?" Shana asked tying up her off white Ellise tennis shoes.
"Yeah." Jason answered nervously.
"I told you practice wouldn't be that long," she smiled.
They walked slowly up 8th Street. Jason basically listened while Shana chattered on. "I was like Oh my God; I am not putting on anybody's old majorette uniform…"
Noticing Jason had barely talked to her since they seen Ortega that morning she said "I hope you're not still bothered about Ortega this morning, are you?"
"No" he lied looking to the cars that passed instead of at Shana.
"Look Jason," she stopped walking, "this is my house." Shana pointed to a green painted row house across from Shiloh Baptist Church.
"Jason I want you to know, I don't like Ortega. I like you!"
Shana gave him a peck on the cheek then quickly turned and ran up the few steps to her door, opened it and disappeared. Jason stood there in shock, she kissed him, his body and emotions were stirred in ways he never knew existed. He couldn't explain it if he had to, but he knew he felt good.

chapter 6

A few years later, Jason and Shana stood side by side on the cement wall outside of Shaw Jr. High School taking their 9th Grade class picture. Jason stood looking like a splitting image of his father, only younger. He stood at five feet eight inches tall with a brown skinned complexion. He had his father's high hair line, long nose, and chinky eyes.

Graduation was in two weeks and everyone was excited to either be attending Dunbar, Coolidge, Cardoza, McKinley Tech, or Duke Ellington School for the performing arts. Shana had been Jason's girlfriend for two years now and everyone knew it because they never left each other's side.

A midnight blue Range Rover, sporting dark tinted windows and chrome crash bars on the front and back of it, pulled up blowing its horn. Ortega turned, then stepped out of the crowd and began walking towards the truck.

"I wonder how much he paid for that sweat suit" Jason heard three girls next to him talking about the black and brown Louis Vuitton sweat suit that Ortega wore.

"I'm going to miss you when I go out of town," Shana whispered in Jason's ear. She was going to visit her Aunt and cousins in West Philly for two weeks.

"I know it's only for a couple of weeks, right?"

"Yep, then I'll be back."

"I'm supposed to get a summer job with that new Marion Barry summer youth program."

"My Mother and Father wanted me to sign up then they changed their minds." Jason said with a bit of disappointment.

"They'd rather I stay home to watch my little brother and pay me. They said they're going to be working a lot because they want to move away from 7th Street."

A car horn blew.

"Well, there's my Mom Jay, I got to go. I'll call you later."

FRANKLIN

"You feeling okay today, Franklin?"

"I'm alright, Mr. Anderson. I just want to move. Every time I save money it seems like one thing after another happens and I'm back at square one.

"I've been talking about moving since I met you. Do you know what really pisses me off? Here I am forty one years old, I've never smoked, drank, robbed, sold drugs, shot anybody, stole or beat on women; but these street niggas run through D.C. doing all of the above, are half my age and drive new Beamers, Benz's and Jaguars. Just makes me think, what's the point?"

"Franklin, it's like this; now I'd be lying if I said I never committed crimes, because I did. I have sold drugs, I've even hurt people, and it was all around me from my family to my environment so it lured me in. I've been locked up in Lorton. I know what it's like to put your family through the drama. You may think these people have more than you or better than you, but they don't. And I'll tell you why. What they have; the big cars, fancy clothes, and jewelry can all be taken away as fast as they got it. You, my friend have stability and peace of mind. That's priceless, Franklin. No one can take that from you."

"You're one of the finest gentlemen I ever met in my seventy three years on this Earth, and now that I've come to know you, I have to tell you I'm proud of you. I'm seventy three and you're even a good role model for me."

Franklin smiled as Mr. Anderson slapped him on his back.

"Just budget your money Franklin. If you don't need it, don't buy it. A penny saved is a dollar earned, you know."

Franklin nodded; glad he came to talk to Mr. Anderson on his day off.

MILLIE

Millie danced around the small living room with her favorite record on by Minnie Ripperton. She was singing her heart out, snapping her fingers while bopping from left to right. She was so into her song that she couldn't hear Jason's keys unlocking the door. With her husband in mind she closed her eyes and moved her hips with the groove.

After spinning around, she opened her eyes and saw her oldest son smiling from ear to ear.

"What you laughing at boy, get over here and dance with your momma."

Jason took off his Madness Shop Bucket hat. It was all white bearing his nickname Jay in different color letters on the hat, and green on the underside of the brim. He sat it on the card table, which was used as their dining table, before joining his mother.

ANTHONY

"You want something out of here, Mal?"

"Why, you got some money?"

"No, I'm just asking to tease you. Yeah I got some cheese, what you want?"

"A pack of grape Now & Later and a bag of sunflower seeds …Oh and a Cherry Smash soda."

Ant bought himself a bag of Doritos, a candy bar and an Orangina soda.

"Where you get money from, Ant?"

"Found it," he lied. He'd stolen it out of his Mother's purse that morning.

"Ain't that Molinda up there?"

Ant looked, "Yeah; didn't she transfer to Seaton Elementary?"

"Yup, and she still got that bamma Jerri-curl."

"I'll meet you behind Gibson Plaza tonight."

I'll see you later then, alright.

FRANKLIN

For the next week Franklin started budgeting as Mr. Anderson suggested. He and Millie had sat down one night and discovered how they were wasting a lot of unnecessary money. They even joined the new store called the Price Club, where they started buying everything from toilet paper to washing detergent in bulk. He was happy they had already begun taking serious steps to saving money.

Traffic was light as he made his usual stops. Franklin was looking forward to seeing Mr. Anderson so he could thank him for the pep talk and good advice. He drove up Kennedy Street and double parked in front of the 5&10 then turned on his hazard lights.

"Hi, do you have any spare change?"

Franklin looked down to the thin young man Bone's, who couldn't have been more than thirteen or fourteen years old. With all the scratches and scars on the boys face, it was evident that he had already lived a hard life. And as much as he wanted to, he couldn't give the boy any money as he had done for years. And, he had two boys of his own to worry about.

"I'm sorry Bones, no I don't have it."

The little boy ran off mumbling under his breath.

DC BLOOD BROTHERS

Franklin walked into the store, seeing a young woman instead of Mr. Anderson behind the bullet proof glass.

"Is Mr. Anderson here today?"

"No he's not, you must be Franklin," she said with a smile.

Franklin noticed how the young woman favored Mr. Anderson. "He's my Grandfather and he got sick last night. He has sugar diabetes but he usually keeps it under control."

"Well, will he be OK?" Franklin asked with deep concern.

"He'll be fine" she assured Franklin. "I've seen him a lot worse than this. "

"Well I'll pray for him, he said as he gave her a copy of the invoice. Enjoy your day."

The following week Millie and Franklin were all smiles as Franklin snapped picture after picture of Jason at his junior high graduation. The way the parents were screaming and cheering when their children's names were called, you would think they were graduating from college.

"I'm so proud of you son!" Franklin yelled as he opened his arms to his son.

Just three more years now, he said, as he brushed his hand over Jason's head like he's been doing since he was five.

"Dad, can you take a picture of Shana and me together?"

Franklin's right eyebrow rose as he said sure.

Shana and Jason put their arms around each other's waist and smiled for the 35 mm camera. "Well, that's the end of my film" Franklin said after taking four pictures of the graduating couple.

After the graduation Franklin took his family to Jason's favorite restaurant to celebrate, The Hot Shop in Marlow Heights, MD. After eating Franklin pulled his son away from the table, leaving Millie enough money for their meal. Together they stood outside of their car; Franklin popped the trunk, pulling out a Wilson's Leather bag.

"Thanks, Dad!" Jason said before even inspecting the bags contents, knowing it was the $150 jacket he wanted. He looked in the bag and saw his jacket along with a card. He opened it. Happy Graduation it read and there was also a hundred dollar bill in one of the pockets.He hugged his father.

"So son..." his father smiled before asking. "What's up with you and Shana?" Jason's face had turned more serious than Franklin had ever recalled.

"Dad, how do you know when you're in love?"

Franklin took a deep breath before answering.

"Son, you know you're in love when you have someone that the thought of being without her makes you feel as if your entire world could end. That's how I feel for your Mother."

Jason merely nodded his head. Franklin noticed how mature Jay seemed. My boy's growing up, he thought.

Chapter 7

Three years later, Franklin pulled in front of his last stop and saw Mr. Anderson standing in front of his store. For the past few years, Mr. Anderson had been in and out of the hospital. His eyesight had gotten so bad that his grand-daughter had been running the store.

"How you doing, Mr. Anderson?"

"I guess I'm getting better Franklin, when you get my age, you don't have much to complain about."

Franklin smiled as he loaded his hand truck. Mr. Anderson held the door open for Franklin and followed him in.

"So, how's the wife and kids Franklin?"

"They're great, my youngest starts junior high school and Jay graduates Dunbar in a few months. He is thinking about attending college. He's thinking about maybe P.G. Community College or Morgan State University; somewhere not too expensive or far."

"Well Franklin, you can't put a price on education; it's wonderful no matter which school he attends."

"I told you" Mr. Anderson said as he shook a finger at Franklin

"Told me what?"

"I told you, your kids would turn out good. I'm happy for you Franklin, what are you and the wife going to do after your kids are grown up and move out?"

"Well, I think we have a while before that."

"Oh you do, huh Franklin. Let me ask you this, how long we known each other?"

"Over ten years."

"And it seems like we met each other yesterday right?" He had to agree after catching on to Mr. Anderson's point.

"Well, Franklin, before you know it, your kids will be grown." Franklin had never thought of it that way.

"When I realized I was getting older Franklin I started making plans." He laughed before continuing; "even my grave and funeral are already paid for. I don't want to burden my family when they'll already be grieving, you know."

Franklin nodded with a smirk on his face.

"What's so funny young man?"

"Nothing, I just want to tell you thank you Mr. Anderson because you've just proven to me how fast time flies. I didn't want to miss a chance to tell you that."

ANTHONY

"Man, I can't wait until we start Jr. High next year."

"I know," Jamal agreed with his best friend as they took turns shooting a basketball through the middle hole of the monkey bars behind Gibson Plaza. Chris walked up and spoke.

"What's up ya'll?"

"Hey Chris, what's up?"

"Ain't nothing, ya'll little youngin's about to graduate ain't you?"

"Yeah, we'll be going to Shaw next year," Jamal answered.

"Ah-ight I'll holler at ya'll!"

Chris ran off to a car, sticking his head through the passenger window, digging in his pockets. Suddenly a police siren went off as it pulled behind the car. Black saw cops and took off running. One of the officers pulled out his gun, aimed it at the driver and ordered him to shut the engine off. The second officer, a female, ran after Chris.

"Damn," was all Jamal could say as the situation unfolded. Chris continued running down the narrow sidewalk, digging in his pocket then throwing something in the bushes. The female officer slowed down, realizing she couldn't catch him and she snatched the pack of baggies off the ground.

"Hey! Do you two kids know that boy" she asked, pointing in the direction Chris ran.

"No Ma'am" Ant answered, then looking to Jamal.

"Uh ... no, Miss. We didn't know him," Jamal answered.

Her eyes narrowed, and then she walked back to her police cruiser. There was a crowd now, buzzing with conversation as they speculated what happened. The police cruisers pulled off slowly, shutting off their lights. Smiley walked out of the crowd of spectators.

"You two come here," he called to Ant and Jamal.
"What did she ask ya'll?"
"She asked us if we knew Chris," Ant answered.
"You didn't tell her did you?"
"Hell no" Ant yelled, insulted by his question.
Smiley cracked one of his famous smiles that earned him his nick name. "Ah-ight youngin', I believe you" Smiley said as he dug in his pocket and he handed each of them a twenty dollar bill.
"That's for keeping your mouths shut. Your name's Ant, right?"
Ant nodded.
"If you ever need anything youngin', come see me."
"Okay" Ant answered.

TWO WEEKS LATER

JASON

"I'll be testing you all Friday so study over the weekend, class dismissed." Ms. Lawrence excused her English Literature class. Jason was glad it was Friday, in a good mood as he gathered his belongings.
"What's up Jay?" Jason turned and saw Ortega staring and replied "Ain't nothing much. What's up? You got a problem?"
Ortega merely shook his head no.
"It's just you know I get money. I just wanted to tell you if you ever need to get put on, holler at me."
"Thanks, but I don't want to sell drugs" Jason answered throwing his backpack over his shoulder and stepping around Ortega.
After stepping out of the front doors of Dunbar High School, he scanned the crowd for Shana. He spotted her talking to some guy hanging out of the driver's side window of a Pathfinder truck. Jason's entire body felt as if it had caught on fire as he watched his girlfriend smile at the driver. He started cutting through the crowd of students, getting closer he suddenly realized he didn't know what his next move would be but his jealous rage had already overtaken him. He grabbed Shana hard by the elbow, spinning her around.
"What the fuck are you doing?"
He yelled so loud he never heard the truck's driver door open. Collapsing to the ground, it took a few seconds for his mind to register that he had been hit with something heavy. As his vision cleared, he saw a large .45 caliber handgun pointed directly to his face.
"Troy no!," He heard Shana screaming. "Please Troy... Please don't shoot him, that's my boyfriend that I was just telling you about."
"This him," Troy asked pointing the gun at Jay. "Shana, I'm going to ask you

DC BLOOD BROTHERS

one time... has this nigga ever hit you."

"Fuck no, he ain't never hit me. He probably thought you were some dude trying to rap to me and I was all up on your truck. If I was your girl, how would you have responded?"

"You right. My bad, little cuz. Tell your mutherfuckin' boyfriend he better start asking questions before he try some shit like that again."

"Okay Troy, now get out of here before the police come. You just got out."

"That was your cousin?," Jason whispered while wiping blood off of his forehead.

"Yes, that was my cousin."

She crossed her arms over her chest. "I thought you trusted me, Jason."

"I do..."

"You can't" she cut him off, "how could you think I would be flirting with someone. Didn't I tell you I'd never hurt you?"

He just stared at her knowing she was right.

"You know, you promised me you wouldn't hurt me either, but you just did. Don't call me no more." She ran off crying leaving him still sitting on the ground.

ANTHONY

"Hey youngin'. Come here!" Smiley yelled out of his new cranberry colored 300 Benz with his cell phone to his right ear. "Take this to Boo or Dre over there. Come back when you finish," he said while handing Ant a grocery store bag. "I gave it to him Smiley."

"Here, take this, thanks slim."

Ant just opened his hand and took the balled up bill. Deciding to go buy a slushy from the O Street Market, he ran across the street.

"Mix my drink up with all the flavors" he told the Chinese lady. Ant wondered if he had enough, he unfolded the bill. His eyes got big as he turned it front to back. It was a hundred dollar bill.

MILLIE - FRANKLIN

"Franklin, what are we going to do about Jason's tuxedo for the prom?"

"Millie, I'll take him tomorrow, what's with you today anyway, your memory of things is on overdrive. We need to get you on Jeopardy so you can win us some money."

"Shut your mouth," she yelled as she playfully pushed her husband.

"Oh Franklin, we're getting old."

"No, I'm getting better" he corrected her.

Her hands went to her hips, "so I'm not?"

"I didn't say that" he defended himself. "You didn't say otherwise either."

DC BLOOD BROTHERS

"Seriously though Franklin, our baby is about to graduate high school. I remember when I was changing that boy's messy diaper. Now he got a girlfriend. We know she still ain't gave him none 'cause he still a little goofy. But...I don't want to let go of my baby."

Franklin saw the tears forming in the wells of her eyes.

"Come here Millie" he embraced his wife. "We've raised one hell of a son. We've done all we can do. And another thing pretty lady," he lifted her chin with his index finger until their eyes met, "we're not losing our baby, we're gaining another man in the family."

The next couple of months were a learning experience as always for the Jenkins family. Jason did everything he could to get Shana back. He endured an entire month of being hung up on and ignored in the school hallways. She had erased his face and their memory from her mind until the day he screamed in front of a hundred or more students "Shana, I love you!"

She made him promise to never doubt her again, which he did. She even made her cousin apologize for hitting him with the gun. Things were pretty much back to normal with the couple.

Every Friday, her Mother came home late and that have them two hours to kiss and fondle each other. They had kissed until their jaws were sore but still they couldn't get enough.

Millie and Franklin had budgeted their money well enough to be able to rent Jay's Tuxedo, buy him a Seiko watch for his graduation present, and a new Cannon camera to take pictures of his graduation.

The next time Ant was called by Smiley, he refused to take a package to anyone. He told Smiley how it would break his parent's heart if they found out. Smiley nodded and told him, "alright slim, I really respect your style little man. You got heart."

Even though the money looked good, he knew that his parents would kill him if they thought he'd even entertained selling drugs.

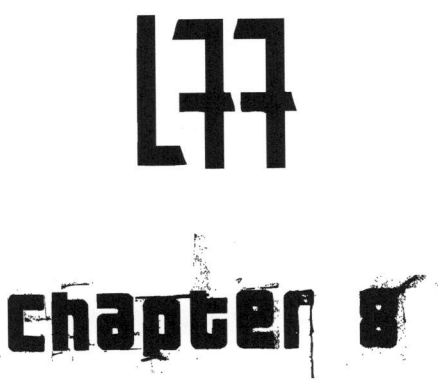

Chapter 8

GRADUATION DAY..

It was a beautiful day, the temperature was 85 degrees. The Dunbar Senior High School Auditorium was packed with friends and family of the class of 1991. The master of ceremonies stepped to the podium clearing his throat. After adjusting the lapel of his suit jacket he began to speak.

"Ladies and Gentlemen, may I have your attention please? I'd like to welcome you to the class of 1991's graduation. I ask that you please hold your applause to a minimum throughout the program. Those of you taking pictures, please step to the side of the stage or kneel in front of it. Please don't stand amongst the audience blocking anyone's view."

After a performance by the Symphony, the emcee took the microphone and began reading names. Jason was so excited he couldn't stop rocking his knees back and forth. Shana was on the left side of the auditorium. They were both smiling already knowing they would walk across the stage together.

"Jason Parcell Jenkins, and Shana Rene Mosley," the emcee called their names. They stepped to the middle of the isle and took each other's hand as they walked to the stage. Franklin was snapping away with his camera while he stood on the side of the stage. He took at least three more pictures as his son held his High School Diploma with his left hand and shook his principles hand with the right.

Millie felt her eyes water as she rambled through her purse for a Kleenex. Ant, who was paying more attention to the young ladies behind him, was slapped on

DE BLOOD BROTHERS

the shoulder by his mother.

"Boy, leave them little fast in the behind girls alone."

An hour later, the ceremony was over. Camera bulbs flashed from all angles of the room as the seniors posed for picture after picture.

"Hey Dad, can you take a few pictures of Shana and I together?"

Franklin pointed his camera at the happy couple. Jason and Shana embraced each other in a hug.

"We're hanging out tonight, right Jay?" She blushed as she asked.

"You know it, Baby. Just let me chill with my parents and we'll hook up later."

"Let them get all their pictures then I'll call you to come pick me up."

Franklin watched the couple as they spoke in whispered tones and made himself a mental note to have a nice Father and son talk later on with his oldest boy.

"Jason, I'm so proud of you boy," Millie said as she pulled her tall son out of Shana's arms and hugged him. Franklin's smile was from ear to ear.

They left, and after celebrating at Red Lobster, they returned home.

"Here, this is for you, Jay."

"What is it, Ma?"

"Just open the wrapper and see."

Jason pulled the paper away from the box and saw the Seiko chronograph watch.

"Thanks, ma."

"Jay, can I have a word with you for a minute in my room" his dad yelled from the hallway. Franklin was standing with his head down and his hands together at his nose as if he were in deep thought as Jason entered the room.

"Shut the door son and sit down."

Jason did as he was told.

"Look Jay, first I want to tell you I am extremely proud of you son. Not only have you just graduated high school, but you have almost made it past your teenage years without putting grey hair on my head, thank you. Even though I haven't been able to move us away from here, along with a few other short comings of mine; I want you to know, I know I couldn't give you everything you wanted, but I did the best I could, son."

Franklin walked to his dresser, grabbed a large envelope and handed it to his son. Jason's eyes spread wide in shock as he fingered through the stack of $100 bills.

"That's two thousand dollars son, one third of my savings, I hope it can help you along with the start of your future."

Now 17 years old, Jason's heart almost pounded out his chest as he witnessed tears falling from his father's eyes for the first time.

"I love you, son."

"I love you too, dad," Jason hugged his father.

"Ok." Franklin said as he took a step back from his son, wiping his eyes. "That's enough with the mushy stuff. Here's your last present," he reached into his pocket then handed his son the box of Trojan condoms.

Jason cracked a smile as he accepted the box. Franklin cherished that moment after seeing how Shana and his son eyed each other earlier, he knew now would probably be the last time he ever saw that innocence in his son's smile.

"Why are you staring at me like that, Dad," Jason asked embarrassed.

"You think your old man don't know what you got planned tonight, huh? I saw the way you two looked at each other. But I'll tell you this, use those condoms, don't come this far to set yours or her life on a different course. We have enough children struggling because their parents were still babies themselves."

"Yes sir," was Jason's reply.

Later that evening...

"Jason, you are wearing that tuxedo," Shana complimented as they walked out of Houston's steak house restaurant.

"Thank you, Baby."

"Oh, that's all I get is a thank you baby after I give you a compliment, where's mine? I am just playing boy," she smiled as she unlocked the door to her graduation present; a green 1986 Ford Escort.

She started the ignition, "so, where are we going?"

"Let's go up New York Ave."

Along the way she talked about anything that came to her mind as she drove. She knew she was nervous, but she also knew she was ready. Jason seemed to be listening intently, but if she had paused one time to ask him something, he would have been lost. His mind was on the Trojan condoms in his pocket, and hoping whatever it is he's supposed to do tonight is done right.

"Turn right here on Florida Avenue" he pointed to his right

"I thought the hotels were a little further up."

"We can't go to those because we're underage. They'd never give us a room. Make a left here."

"This is the Farmer's Market, and it's closed, I'm not losing my virginity this tiny car."

"Make a left here and park."

Jason stepped out of the car, glad he could give his long legs a stretch. Shana followed him up the tiny dark street, turning left into a small shabby looking hotel. After opening the door, Jay felt around for the light switch. There was an old dresser with an even older looking mirror, a twin sized bed with an obvious lump in the mattress. The entire middle of the mattress sunk into the bed frame and there was a slight odor in the air.

The stench of mildew was fighting with a miniscule amount of cleaning fluid that must have been used in a weak attempt to clean the room.

"It's Ok, Jay," Shana said after seeing the disgust on his face.

After talking for what seemed like hours, Jay turned the television off, which was serving as the only light in the room.

"I got to go to the bathroom."

DC BLOOD BROTHERS

Shana jumped off the bed and sprinted to the tiny bathroom.

Jay lay back on the bed after taking off his shirt, with his fingers locked behind his head. A brief moment of light was seen as Shana stepped out of the bathroom, walking to the bed. He watched as she pulled the zipper down behind her neck and pulled her dress over her gorgeous body. She was standing in front of him in her bra and panties while looking down to the floor.

"Come here," Jay reached for her.

Their lips met. He rolled his body over top of hers while trying not to crush her breast under him. He began kissing and sucking her neck and ears. The temperature was rising in Shana's body as Jay's kisses sent shocks through her. She could feel his hardness pressing onto her thigh and the combination made her dizzy with desire. He got up and unbuttoned his slacks, leaving his boxers on as he rejoined Shana who was now under the sheets.

He began kissing her neck as he pulled her bra straps down over her shoulders exposing her young firm breasts. He took her erect caramel nipples, one by one, into his mouth.

It was a different from before, this time he knew that he was finally going to get past fondling for the first time and it made it feel more intense. While massaging her breasts ever so gently, Shana was lost in the sensational feeling of Jay's warm mouth and wet tongue. His moans and groans proved to be equally erotic to Shana who found herself wondering what it would feel like if he were to get lost between her legs with the same enthusiasm that he showed on her breasts.

Her body began thrashing and arching under him as his hand went between her legs, rubbing on the hard knot at the top of her vagina. She moaned as the wetness between her legs grew. He pulled her panties to the side now pushing a finger into her. His breathing became shallow as he felt the heat and wetness. He knew that he must be doing something right. Jay gently stroked her creamy womanhood. Her tight vagina gripped his index finger with each throbbing sensation. Then it happened.

Jay leaned over and positioned his face over his upward open palm and began to lick and suckle on Shana's clit. He worried that his technique was awkward. Shana soon put his fears to rest when she began to breathe erratically and very heavily.

She screamed a guttural scream and began to curse. "Oh shit, Jay, Oh my God, Shit…" Satisfied with her reaction, Jason was more than ready to move on. Reaching over the side of the bed, he grabbed his slacks and took a condom out of his pocket and tore it open. Shana took off her bra and pulled off her panties as she watched Jay put the condom on. Swallowing hard as she imagined the pain she was about to feel as she stared at his penis. Although she was a virgin, she'd heard enough stories to know what to expect.

He positioned himself between her legs. The thrills of being at her entrance made his head spin. He pushed as her knees pressed against his legs. He pushed again and felt a tightness overwhelm him. The wetness and heat engulfed him as he pushed in and out. Shana screamed as Jason penetrated her. The pain hurt so bad, yet felt so good, she was confused. Her hips began meeting his thrusts as if they were possessed.

She screamed as another orgasm soared through her body. He couldn't take her tightness and all the noises combined. Jason felt his balls tighten, his eyes closed as his penis stiffened inside her, sending a hot spasm through him as he exploded.

His head dropped onto her shoulder. A few minutes later he was snoring. She wiggled her body until she was on the side of him and then she began to twirl his hair softly with her fingers. She stared at him, silently praying, "Lord, please don't let this be a mistake. I love this man and I want to spend the rest of my life with him."

Chapter 9

The summer of 1991 was about the fastest the Jenkins family had seen. Ant was now five foot nine inches, 170 pounds, and going through a serious case of puberty. So many girls began calling for him, Millie and Franklin decided to get him his own phone line for his upcoming 13th birthday. Mr. Anderson at the 5&10 store had a different old man joke for Franklin every day, since Franklin was noticeably growing grey hair. Millie was finally made an Assistant Manager at her job.

Jason was doing very well working for a floor cleaning company. In July, he had invited the entire family to Phillip's Restaurant at the waterfront. He pulled a box out of his pocket and dropped to one knee. Jason proposed to Shana who accepted teary eyed. Before they knew it, the summer was over.

ANTHONY

"Hello class, my name is Mrs. Spelling and I'll be your homeroom teacher this year."

Ant paid no attention as he scanned the classroom at his new class mates. Some he already knew from elementary school, but the majority of them were strangers. Lisa, who he hadn't seen in two years because she moved, sat directly in front of him now. She was the finest in the class. The bell rang and the students exited the classroom to go their separate ways to different second period teachers.

"What's up Lisa?" He spoke as they walked up the hallway. Her head looked over her shoulder. She looked Ant up and down and responded, "Hi".

She turned back forward as fast as she turned around.

"You don't remember me, do you?"

"Does it matter" she remarked smartly and started walking faster.

Ant had heard how Shaw Jr. High School was nothing but a fashion show, and how the freshmen girls always go for the 9th grade boys. He figured that was why she was acting like that. Fuck her.

After math, reading and music class, it was finally lunch time. Jamal and Ant stood in line sharing their morning experiences, while wondering why the lunch line was moving slowly.

"Damn, all they got to do is grab a tray," Jamal remarked, finally making it to the door and seeing the huge carousel, loaded with food options.

"Yep, this is far from Scott Montgomery Elementary," Ant said smacking his best friend on the back.

After getting their lunches and finding a table, Jamal pointed, "Ain't that, what's her name?"

Ant turned seeing Lisa smiling from ear to ear at Mike Turner, "yes, that's Lisa."

"Damn, she looks good and those guess jeans she got on looks like they are painted on that ass."

Ant continued eating, deciding not to mention the situation with her earlier. The remainder of the day went by slowly. Ant was used to getting attention from all the girls at Scott, but things were different here. It seems like it doesn't even matter how you look anymore, he thought. Lisa was sweating Mike, one of the funniest looking niggas he'd ever seen. But everybody knew that Mike hustled.

After school, Ant went straight home. Unlocking the apartment door, Ant threw his book bag on the sofa, went to what was finally his own bedroom.

Jason and Shana got their own apartment on 21st off of Benning Road. He lay across his bed, and threw his right arm over his eyes to block the light. He was just glad the day was over.

FRANKLIN

Franklin hummed a tune as he cruised up Georgia Ave, thinking how Ant started Jr. High School today. He was anxious to get home and ask him how his first day went. Franklin put his hazard lights on as he double parked in front of the 5 & 10. He grabbed his clip board off the passenger seat then stepped out of the truck. As soon as his foot met with the concrete he heard...

"Gimme your money, old man."

Franklin's mind raced as he tried to figure out the situation and the hard object that pressed in between his rib cage. He recognized the voice and turned to face his assailant.

"Bones, I don't have much money."

Bones slammed the butt of the weapon against Franklin head. A stream of blood

DC BLOOD BROTHERS

trickled down his face as he fell against the truck.

"Muthafucka, did I ask you how much money you had?" Bones screamed as he pushed the barrel into the side of Franklin's head.

Franklin's hand frantically dug into his pockets, pulling out the $25 he knew he had. He accidentally dropped the loose change he had as he handed the money over. "Here, this is all I got. Please don't kill me."

Bones hands shook as his need for drugs took its toll on him. Franklin had seen his face and knew his name. There was no way Bones could let him live.

"This all you got muthafucka, huh!"

A bullet ripped through Franklin's face, entering his left cheek, shattering his cheek bone before exiting his left ear. Fortunately, he was killed instantly. He never heard the second shot that violently tore through his chest collapsing his left lung and ricocheted as it shredded his internal organs. Franklin's body laid still as his intestines fell through a gaping four inch hole on the right side of his navel.

Bones ran around the corner past the 7-Eleven, looking back as people in cars slowed down to get a description of him. Fuck him, he thought as he ran with the .38 snub nose revolver burning his abdomen, he should have given me that money that day I was starving.

Police arrived on the scene, followed by an ambulance. Two men from the crowd took off their shirts to lay over his face, which barely could be identified as a human, and his stomach where his intestines spilled into his bloody hands.

Chapter 10

MILLIE

Millie unlocked the apartment door, she mumbled as she began straightening out the living room. She sucked her teeth after picking up a cup.

"I told Franklin a million times not to leave food and drinks around, wait until..." she was interrupted by a knock on the door.

She walked to the door squinting, and then straining to make out the two figures through the tiny peep hole. She opened the door,

"May I help you?"

"Hi, Mom." Shana playfully smacked at Millie's hand. "We were just in the neighborhood so we stopped by."

"Well wasn't that nice of you two."

"Have you two set a date yet? "

"We're thinking about this June, Mrs. Jenkins."

"Mrs. Jenkins" Millie repeated, "I liked it better when you called me Ma."

"Is Ant home, Ma?"

"I don't even know, I just came in a few minutes ago," she answered.

Once Millie and Shana began their girl talk, Jason took that as his cue to see if Ant was in. He opened the door to the bedroom they shared not even two months ago. Ant was in a deep sleep.

"That boy must have had a rough day," Jay pointed back towards the hallway.

DC BLOOD BROTHERS

"Oh! My baby is home?"

"Yep, and snoring like crazy."

Suddenly, there was a knock at the door.

"I'll get it," Jay stepped to the door, leaning down to look through the peep hole. He saw two with men in suits.

"Who is it?"

"I'm Detective Nelson and this is Detective Brown, we need to speak with a...," he looked down to a pad, "Mrs. Millie Jenkins."

He opened the door. "What did Ant do?" Jay asked, putting two and two together. He knew Ant wasn't so tired from doing nothing.

"Are you Mrs. Jenkins?" The second detective asked, ignoring Jason.

"Yes, what is it officers?"

"May we step in, please?"

She nodded; unable to talk knowing something was very wrong; she'd seen television shows where this happened.

"Mrs. Jenkins, I'm sorry, it's your husband, he's..."

"No! Tell me he's in the hospital please!" She cut the detective off.

"I'm sorry Mrs. Jenkins, he's been killed."

Jason caught his mother as her body collapsed to the floor after she passed out. He gently laid her across the sofa.

"Are you sure it's my father, officers?" Jason asked with his eyes pleading for some chance of a mistake.

"I'm sorry but we're sure, we got his ID off of him; the owner of the 5&10 store on Kennedy Street told us his name before we saw his wallet."

Jason turned toward the hallway, seeing his younger brother just shaking his head side to side as if he were saying no.

"Detectives, do you know who did this?" Shana asked as she cried as if it were her own father.

"I'm sorry ma'am. No, we have a description and we do have cars patrolling the area, the man fled on foot so we figure he lives somewhere close by. We'd better be going."

"This is a murder investigation so there will be an autopsy, we'll notify you when the body can be released for burial, and we'll keep you up-to-date on our progress as we make it."

Jason followed the two detectives to the door. He and Shana spent the following twenty minutes trying to wake up Millie.

"Oh Shana!" She cried embracing her; "I can't believe my husband's gone."

"I know, I know this, Shana rocked Millie back and forth as if she were a baby.

"I'm gonna go check on Ant," Jay walked down the hallway and opened the door.

Ant was staring at the wall when he entered.

"Ant! Look Ant, say something. Don't hold it in. It's not good. Let it out."

Ant continued to stare at the wall.

DC BLOOD BROTHERS

"Anthony," he began in a whisper, "I know this hurts like nothing you have ever felt before."

"The only reason I haven't broke down yet is because someone has to be strong for Ma."

"Anthony!"

"What Jay? What? What am I supposed to say?"

Ant's body was numb with shock but he still felt the tears about to fall from his eyes, so he ran out of the apartment slamming the door behind him closed.

"Where is my baby going?"

"He'll be alright, Ma. He just needs some time alone."

Ant ran down the steps, pushing the stairwell door open as hard as he could. People waiting for the elevators turned right hearing the loud bang, seeing the tight faced youth coming towards them. Turning left, Ant walked past the mail slots, through the security door then turned right towards the Kennedy playground. He crossed the street, not knowing where his destination was; only feeling the need to keep moving.

"What's the long face for youngin'?"

Smiley asked as he stepped out of the high-rise.

"My Father just got killed."

"What! Come on; take a ride with me youngin'."

Smiley hit his remote, shutting off his alarm and unlocking the doors to his black Acura Legend Coupe. Ant opened the passenger side door and got in. Smiley got in and started the ignition.

They cruised up to Clifton Street where they parked. "Tell the N. O. I. Security your name is Reggie."

Ant nodded, still unable to really speak.

As they walked towards the first building, Smiley spoke to everyone on the steps as they moved out of their path.

The Nation of Islam security guard handed Smiley and Ant a clip board to sign, Smiley explained that Reggie was his little cousin.

Walking up the narrow hallway then turning left to the elevator. After riding one floor up on the elevator, Anthony followed Smiley to the left, then to the right at the end of the hallway, finally stopping at the last door on the left. Smiley unlocked the door and pointed towards a black leather sofa.

Ant sat down, then swallowed hard as the woman stepped into the living room hugged and kissed Smiley. She was beautiful, not only that, all she was wearing was her bra and panties. Smiley sat down beside Ant.

"Bring that open bottle of Remy off the counter with a couple glasses."

She wiggled back into the living room, breast fighting to break free of the confinement of her bra as she leaned to sit the bottle and glasses on the table. She smiled, winked at Ant and walked away. Ant couldn't help but turn around and watch her butt eat up the silk panties as she walked away. Smiley cleared his throat.

"I'm sorry" Ant apologized for staring at his girl. Smiley waved him off with a smile.

"No little nigga, fix us a glass while I roll this."

"I don't care if you look at her ass."

"You don't?" Ant asked surprised.

"Fuck no! Bitches ain't shit, fuck them. Drink up little youngin'"

After three shots of Remy and five pulls of the joint, Ant felt more relaxed than he ever had before in his life. Hearing the woman go back into the kitchen he decided to ask Smiley her name.

"What part don't you understand of what I told you earlier. Fuck a bitch. Say it with me."

"Fuck a bitch!" They said in unison.

"See Ant, us niggas take care of them bitches, buy them jewelry, clothes, cars, give them nice apartments" he explained as he waved around the expensive living room. "But the first time a nigga get locked up or take a fall, that same bitch you took care of will be out to fuck your friends to maintain the lifestyle you gave them."

"And Ant," Smiley leaned closer as he spoke with a finger in the air.

"Never, ever, fuck your man's girl; or no girl tied to a nigga you do business with. It's bad business. The niggas you fuck with, if ya'll get caught up they got your back. Ya'll get locked up, they may do the time with you and don't talk. A bitch, she ain't going to do a day."

He leaned back on the sofa as he took a toke of the second joint he just fired up. Smiley held in the smoke until he choked and coughed it all out.

"So Ant, what we learn today, what was lesson number one?"

"Fuck a bitch!"

Chapter 11

FRANKLIN'S FUNERAL

"Dearly beloved we are gathered here today." The reverend paused as he looked over his congregation. "We are gathered to mourn the death of a good man. A God fearing man. I'd like for the church to bow your heads please. Dear Heavenly Father. Today we come to you Lord. Asking you sweet Jesus to comfort the Jenkins family in their time of need. Lord, a terrible sin has been committed. But we know! I said we know that your word says when Able was murdered by Cain his blood cried from the ground that it be avenged Lord, he whispered. Please Lord; send the Jenkins family a comforting spirit. Let them know, whoever did this will pay for it on the last day, Lord. Amen. Brother Stevens, you may do the eulogy now. Since it was a closed casket funeral, everyone pictured the man they knew lying inside the casket.

Deacon Stevens did a wonderful eulogy on Franklin. He called him one of God's special soldiers. Franklin was the perfect example of a man was right with the Lord. The head nurse of the church Ms. Jordan sat with Millie throughout the ceremony. Shana rubbed Jason's leg throughout the ceremony. They drove no more than ten mile per hour with their head lights on. The procession was over sixty cars long.

Ant sat quiet through the entire funeral, never taking his eyes off the black and silver casket until it was lowered into the ground out of sight. He felt different but he couldn't explain it.

The next few months helped the healing process of the family somewhat. Millie was so depressed she couldn't work, she couldn't find the energy to eat or bathe on some days, let alone pay the rent which was almost three months behind. She received two pink notices saying to pay the rent or prepare to be evicted. She sat in Franklin's favorite chair, his old brown recliner, could even smell his scent a little off the fabric.

Hearing gun shots, she knew she should get away from the window but she missed her husband so badly, she silently wished a stray bullet would hit her and send her to join him. A week before she was due to get evicted, she received a letter in the mail from Allstate. Franklin had a life insurance policy with them and she would receive a check for $90,000. When she received the check, she did exactly what Franklin had worked his entire life for. She put most of the payment down on a townhouse in Largo, Maryland. Ant had moved in with a friend of his, and she stayed worried about him, but her faith had grown in God since Franklin's murder. The killer was still on the loose and that bothered her, but she knew no matter how long it took, he would answer for killing Franklin.

ANTHONY

Three and one half months after Franklin's murder, Ant had joined the ranks of the local hustlers. His father was a good man, but Ant no longer felt that it mattered. He accepted his mortality and plan to do what he damned well pleased.

"What you want?" Ant asked the fiend who cautiously approached him.

"Gimme a forty."

"You got straight $40?"

"Yeah man" the fiend answered fidgeting and scratching.

Ant looked left to right, up and down O Street, digging in his pocket, then handing two bags to the fiend. The fiend held one of the baggies up by the corner and plucked it.

"This shit is all shake; you ain't got nothing better than this?"

Ant snatched the money out of his hands, slapped the man in the face, and then kicked him in his butt as he turned.

"Now get the fuck out of here for I take your money and don't give you shit."

Smiley pulled up just as Ant kicked the fiend and he blew the horn. Ant turned seeing Smiley in the Benz, ran to the window.

"What's up, Smiley?"

"Get clean youngin'. I want you to take a ride with me out the south side."

After Ant stashed his crack in an old newspaper, and tossed it under a car he knew wouldn't be moving soon, he got into the Benz.

"This is nice, Smiley," he complimented as he took note of the white leather seats and wood grain on the dash, steering wheel and console of the S500 Benz. He'd never ridden in a Benz before. Smiley began talking as they went into the

DC BLOOD BROTHERS

3rd street tunnel.

"What the fuck was that all about back there?"

"Oh, the fiend... nothing, he was trying to complain."

"So you kicked the man all in his ass?"

Ant smiled as he nodded yes.

"Check this out slim, you a hustler now, which means if you don't sell, you don't eat. That man that you just whipped on for whatever could have brought you thousands more. I like your style Ant, and it's good that you down to put down a demonstration, but do it when it's called for. Those pipe heads and dope fiends are how we survive on the street. You never know when a fiend will hear somebody plotting to rob you. Or, see the jump outs about to do they thing and you playing front line. They could warn you, but they're not going to if you treating them like they ain't people. Just like those dumb little niggas Joe and Brian. They'll sell a crack head $500 worth of crack, then when the crack head comes to them later broke, asking for a twenty or fifty rock, they tell him no. That's the difference between them niggas and me, fiends love me. Don't be like them, you got to be a thinker," he tapped his right index finger to his temple.

Ant listened intently, whatever Smiley suggested he would try because he wanted a Benz just like the one he was riding in.

JASON

Jason just turned off of Florida Avenue onto Benning Road. Shana looked at him periodically, trying to read his mood to see if now was a good time to talk.

"Is everything alright, Jay?"

"I can't really say baby, I have so much on my mind I wouldn't know where to start."

"Start anywhere, just talk to me."

"Okay, I've been talking to Detective Nelson, and I asked him what I would have to do to become a cop. I don't know what it is, but since my Father got killed that's all I've thought about. I don't know if I want a badge just to hunt down his killer or if I can just keep somebody from going through what my family did. I just want to make a difference from this somehow.

"Well what did he say about you joining the force."

"He told me to fill out an application and recruits would be screened. If chosen, given physical examinations, then they would go to the police academy."

"You know I've always had a thing for men in uniform."

"Since when," asked Jay?

"Since I knew you were going to be a cop. Even though it's a very dangerous job, especially in D.C., I'll support you. I've always told you to trust me Jay, now it's my time to trust you."

"Thank you for your support, Shana."

DC BLOOD BROTHERS

ANTHONY

Another week had passed and Anthony was in school, bored as usual. Ms. Spelling looked at every name on the homework she collected.

"Mr. Jenkins, did you turn in a paper?"

"I accidentally left it at home, Ms. Spelling."

Lisa turned around and looked him up and down then smiled. Class went by fast and the second period bell rang. The students exited the class room and went their separate ways.

"Hi, Ant," he heard the female voice over his shoulder.

"What's up, Lisa?"

"Ain't nothing cutie, I like your outfit."

"Thanks."

"What you doing after school, Ant?"

The question reminded him of a conversation he had with Smiley the day before. "Keep your business to yourself. I don't care if your favorite color is green, you tell a muthafucka its blue". Ant laughed as he recalled the statement.

"Did I say something funny, Ant?"

"No, I ain't doing anything after school."

"Good, you can walk me home; meet me by the soda machines at three O'clock."

After school Ant walked Lisa to her house. Following her into her home, Ant allowed Lisa to take his hand and lead him upstairs to her bedroom. She kissed him, and before it all registered to Ant, they were naked.

He was on top of her grinding his penis into her tight wet vagina as she clawed his back. After three minutes, he started slamming himself into her as he ejaculated. His head was spinning as he tried to keep his composure.

"You want something to drink, Ant?"

He nodded yes, and watched Lisa's red bone body with pert breast and a tight butt, get off the bed and disappear out of her bedroom door. He smiled to himself, proud that he wasn't a virgin anymore.

"Here you go," she handed him a glass of cold grape soda. "So, you going to be my boyfriend now, Ant?"

"I thought you didn't like me?"

"Why you say that" She asked seeming shocked. " You remember how you carried me the first day of school and barely said anything else to me until today? Boy, I been liked you. I was just playing hard to get." She lied, proud of herself because she sounded just like her older sister when she was under pressure.

"Yeah, I'll be your boyfriend."

She smiled then put her arms around his neck kissing him on the lips. How could he say no, Lisa was one of finest girls in school.

chapter 12

One year had passed and Jason sat full of excitement as he looked around the classroom of men and women in navy blue jogging sweat suits.

"Good morning Cadets," a slim older white man greeted them as he entered the room. It was obvious he had his coffee this morning.

"I am Lt. Hawkins and I will be your instructor along with a few others throughout your training. I want all of you to take a look at everyone in this room because a few people you see right now will not make it throughout the day. Your applications were acceptable and you passed your physical, which does not guarantee anyone in this room a place in the Washington, DC police department. When I call your name, please step to the door and begin a single file line. Good luck, ladies and gentlemen.

After a 1 ½ hours of different classes, note taking and tests, the cadets were taken outside where they did a stretching exercise, then they jogged for 5 miles around the academy grounds. Jason thought he was in good shape since he didn't drink or smoke, now feeling like he would collapse if they didn't stop jogging soon. A whistle blew, and everyone stopped, some fell to the ground, others doubled over choking as air continued to fill their lungs in sporadic bursts.

"Okay Cadets," Lt. Hawkins began, you made it, well, five didn't, but you made it through your first day. Congratulations! Now, hit the showers and I'll see you all at 0-500 hours."

The men and women went into the dormitory, and then went their separate ways.

DC BLOOD BROTHERS

"Today was brutal, huh champ?"

Jason looked to his right as he took his shirt off, still breathing a little heavily.

"Yeah, it was, I see you held up alright though."

"Name's Mitchell Green," he extended his hand.

"Nice to meet you Mitch, I'm Jason Jenkins."

"The secret to not being out of breath is that you have to breathe in through your nose and exhale out your mouth as your pace increases. If you're running for a long time, when you intake, hold your breath longer and exhale slower."

"You make it sound so easy Mitch," Jason smiled.

"I guess it's second nature to me now, you'll get it though. Where you from anyway Jason?"

"Are you familiar with the Shaw community?"

Mitchell nodded.

"Well I'm from 7th and O Street"

"Yeah, I used to know a couple girls down there, Ace and Star, I'm from James Creek in South West, though."

"Okay well let me get in this shower so I can call my fiancé, I'll talk to you later Mitch."

ANTHONY

Ant adjusted the charm bearing his nickname on the Gucci link chain he wore. Looking at the clock, it was 2:45pm. Ant heard someone whisper so he turned and saw Lisa trying to get his attention.

"What?"

She sucked her teeth, "Are you going to drive me home after school?"

"I got something to do," he lied.

"Ant it's raining, I didn't bring an umbrella plus you know I just got my hair done."

He knew that because he paid for the hairdo. "Look Lisa, I'll take you home, but I'm telling you now, I'm not dropping off any of your friends so don't bring them to my car."

"Okay Baby, no problem, and you still going to get me the Gucci bag I want, right?"

"What bag?"

"The bag for $350. We saw it at Georgetown. You said you'd get me."

"I'll take you to go get it this weekend".

He turned back to face the chalk board. Her eyes rolled as Ant turned straight in his seat. Little bastard. Better get my fucking bag. I don't give him all that bullshit when he wants some pussy or for me to suck his dick. She grabbed the Gucci link chain Ant brought her and began dangling the charm. Her older sister always told her after a nigga fucked you any way he wants, he'll get bored and start acting funny.

DC BLOOD BROTHERS

The three O'clock bell sounded. Shaw Jr. High School was its usual fashion and car show after school. Ant hit the alarm on his gold Maxima, squatting down to his tires after thinking he saw a scratch on one of his deep dish classic rims. Lisa waved bye to her three closest gold digging friends. Tasha sneaking a wink in as Lisa got in his car. He'd just had sex with her yesterday. It was only a three a minute ride to Lisa's house. She asked, "Can you get my bag tonight, Ant?"

"What I tell you Lisa?"

She looked around desperately. She wanted that bag tonight. Lisa remembered something else her older sister told her. Taking off her seat belt then unzipping Ant's jeans, Lisa was determined to have her way. She dug his penis out of his boxers and dropped her face into his lap.

Ant's head dropped back onto his leather head-rest as the warmth and wetness of Lisa's mouth engulfed him. She was trying to do it better than ever before, with her sisters words in mind. "If you ever want a nigga to do something and he acting like he don't want to, suck his dick, but before you let him cum, ask him to promise he'll do it for you as soon as possible."

Lisa made a pop sound as she pulled him out of her mouth. He looked down to her wondering why she stopped.

"You gonna get my bag today?"

She whined then licked over the head of his penis. She licked him again.

"Yeah Lisa, I'll have it for you in the morning."

She put him back into her mouth and squeezed while she pounded him until she felt him swell in her mouth and hands. He buckled in his seat as he exploded into her eager mouth. She swallowed it all, even after he went soft she squeezed him until a thick clear looking liquid came out and licked that too. Lisa smacked her lips.

"I love you, Ant".

"I love you too, Lisa."

"Can I have some money?"

He dug into his jeans pulling out a wad of money wrapped in a rubber band. Pulling the rubber band off and handing her three 50 dollar bills. She took the bills, kissed him on the cheek and then got out of the car. Ant stared at her, she was getting so womanly, she was thick, hips forming, and a nice gap could be seen between her legs when she wore her tight jeans. Ant pulled off, going to see Tasha again, then to Georgetown to get Lisa's bag. His cell phone rang.

"Hello, what's up nigga?"

"Ain't shit Mal, I'm about to hit Tasha again. You trying to roll with me down Georgetown after I leave her house?"

"But I ain't got any money"

"Nigga I got you, just be ready".

After leaving Tasha's house he headed towards Jamal's neighborhood. Ant pulled into Sergeant Quarters apartments and stopped in front of Jamal's building. Everyone outside turned to the honking horn, inspected the situation then continued their business. Jamal's chubby frame came running out of the building and opened the passenger side door.

"What's up, cuz?"

"Ain't shit Mal, Tasha's sister Kita told me to hook her up with one of my boys, she go to Dunbar."

"How she look, Ant?"

"Well, she ain't all that in the face but she fine as shit."

"For real?"

"Hell yeah. Come on Mal, you my man you think I'd set you up?"

"Just pay attention to the street, you ain't got your license yet and 5-0 is all around here."

"Look," Jamal pointed around the bumper to bumper traffic.

"Did you finish that shit I gave you?"

"Yeah, but I lost most of it in a dice game."

Ant just shook his head side to side.

"Jamal, you hustling backwards. Look, I'm going to give you a half ounce later on. Don't gamble with your money, promise me you won't."

"I promise."

After shopping in Commander Salamander's, they went to Boogie's, then to Polo's exclusive shop, and finally to buying Lisa's Gucci bag. After eating a few slices of pepperoni pizza at the Hawaiian Cafe, they left the area.

They found themselves frustrated with the usual busy traffic of Wisconsin Avenue while they were trying to get back.

"Damn" Ant said as he leaned up in his seat with his mouth open as the cream Infinity Q45 went by.

"Jamal, I'm going to get one of those if it's the last thing I do. Oh! That's what I meant to tell you. Mal, guess what?"

"What's up?"

"My brother Jason is in police academy. My mother told me yesterday."

"Go ahead, you bullshitting."

"I swear to God Mal my brother about to be 5-0."

"So what you going to do now?"

"What you mean, Mal?"

"You can't hustle around KDP no more if your brother..."

"Look," Ant cut him off waving his hand, "don't sweat it, I ain't."

Chapter 13

The next few years flew by quickly. Jason graduated out of the police academy, and was assigned to the 7th district precinct in S.E. He and Shana had gotten married a few months after that.

Jason was even happier after his first partner; Officer Croger retired after his rookie year. His new partner was Mitch Green. They had become good friends after the academy.

Ant was graduating Dunbar High School and Millie was on cloud nine. And even though she wished he would move in with her so he could get out of DC, she understood his need for independence after his Father's death. Millie's shiny brunette hair was transformed into all grey. She wore it well however; all the gentlemen in her neighborhood flirted with her. She actually enjoyed the attention though, especially after being lonely for so long.

There was one man she even found herself very attracted to. He was tall and browned skin, Everett was his name. He was so kind, and Millie didn't notice it at first, but he resembled Franklin a lot.

One night after a nice dinner on Connecticut Ave and a movie at the Marlow Heights Theater, she was going to sleep with him. The minute she had taken off her clothes and he began kissing her neck and fondling her breast, tears fell from her eyes as she apologized while running out of the bedroom. She later explained that she just couldn't do it; Millie said it felt wrong, as if she were cheating on her husband.

"But your husband's been dead for years now," Everett said. "That may be true," she replied, "but he's still very alive in my heart."

Everything was going wonderfully for the Jenkins family until Millie went for her yearly check up, every test she had taken came back fine. This time things were different. She was given a mammogram, and a medium sized lump, about the size of a prune was discovered in her right breast.

The Doctors explained to Millie how the cancer was growing very rapidly, and couldn't be cut out. They would have to amputate her breast. "Over my dead body," she told them.

"If we don't amputate, the cancer will grow and spread until it eventually kills you. Maybe we can try chemotherapy." To this, Millie at least agreed to try.

1994.

Ant was driving in his car with Lisa and suddenly his phone rang. He answered in his deep voice.

"What's up, slim?"

"Ain't nothing big homie. Look, meet me at the Florida Ave. Grill in an hour."

"Everything cool, Smiley?"

"Yeah youngin', just meet me. It's very important; it's 3pm now so no later than 4pm!"

Smiley hung up.

"Lisa, I got to drop you off. I got to do something for my Mom," Ant lied.

"Well, are you going to pick me back up later?"

"I can't answer that now. It depends on when I finish."

Lisa unfastened her seat belt and reached for Ant's zipper.

"Look Lisa, I ain't got time for this shit, I'll call you when I'm finished."

Lisa sucked her teeth as she got out of the new Acura Legend, slamming the door. "I know that muthafucka is cheating on me, he already fucked three of my friends, and he lucky he paid or I would have been kicked his ass to the curb" she was mumbling under her breath as her heels clicked up her steps.

Turning, she saw the forest green Mercedes driving by. She locked eyes with the driver then noticing the girl in the passenger seat. He'll be back though.

After collecting his money from Jamal, Willie, and Shawn, Ant went to the Florida Ave Grill. Unable to find a parking space close to the corner Ant rode by, spotting a space in front of the Children's Hospital Clinic. He got out of his car and saw Smiley's red S-500 parked in front of a black NSX. Ant knew whose Acura was parked there before having read the plates. The tags simply read "O".

His eyes briefly out of focus as he stepped from the sunshine into the dimly lit restaurant. Smiley stood and waved him over to the table where he and Ortega sat. He shook Ant's hand as he walked up and instructed him to take a seat.

"Ortega, this is Ant, and Ant.."

"I know who he is" Ant interrupted.

"Well, you might as well let me introduce you because after today you'll be seeing a lot more of each other."

Smiley leaned over the table so he could whisper. "Listen carefully because I'm not going to repeat myself. As of right now, I'm retired."

Ant's and Ortega's eyes went big with surprise.

"I don't know why y'all looking like that. See, it's like this. I've had a hell of a run. Ortega you know, I watched you run around digging up your nose in dirty diapers. The moral of the story is, I ain't one of the dumb niggas who feel I can hustle forever, because the game was never truly designed for longevity. So...," he clapped his hands together. "From now on Ant, when you need something you call O. Both of you are good dudes, and it would be hell to pay if you ever crossed one another, so handle your business. Ortega, I've already spoke with your uncle about this; it'll be more money for the both of you now that I'm out the way. Ant, you'll pay what I was paying. I'd appreciate it, if you'll discuss any business you need to tend to after I pull off. It's been great knowing you two, I'm about to disappear."

L77

Chapter 14

JASON

"Man, it's a nice day today. Ain't it?" Jason asked Mitch with his elbow hanging out the side of their patrol car as they cruised Alabama Ave. They pulled up behind a tinted 89 Caprice.

"How many heads in that car Mitch?"

"Looks like five."

"They're just asking for trouble. Look, I just saw him pass the blunt to the driver," Jason pointed.

"You want to pull him? Let's check and see if the car is stolen first."

Jason grabbed the CB and called in the tag - District plate RTM-856. One minute later his call came back; the car was clean.

"Let's let them go Mitch!"

Mitch looked to his partner.

"What?" Jason asked, annoyed with his staring.

"I just noticed you don't like to pull too many cars over, or do routine stops. You only spring into action when we get calls, why is that?"

"Look around Green," Jason's hand waved left to right. "What do you see?"

"Projects and slums, that's about all." Mitch answered.

"Exactly, and where we grew up ain't to much better. I didn't become a cop so I can harass young black men. I know why their selling drugs, but I also never seen an airplane or ship land on 7th Street from Columbia, either. If I'm going to arrest somebody for drugs, it'll be one of those crooked politicians that brings or allows drugs to flow into this country. I told you why I wanted to become a cop; I explained what happened to my father."

"I understand, and I agree with you Jenkins. I was just asking a question."

ANTHONY

"Jamal meet me downstairs, I need to holler at you about some serious shit."

Jamal came out of his building and got into the car. Ant told him about Smiley leaving the game. At first, Jamal couldn't believe it, but the serious look on Ant's face changed his mind.

"This is what I need to talk to you about Jamal. I'm about to start getting a lot of money, so I need you to help me put a crew together. One thing though. Mal, once you in and anybody else we pull in, we in this shit to the very end."

"You know I'm with you nigga."

"Mal, let me get out of here. I need to take care of some shit."

After giving his best friend a pound, Mal exited the car. "What's up, Michelle?" He yelled to the girl walking by.

"Hi Jamal" she said flatly.

"Girl, when you going to let me take you out or something?"

"Come on Jamal, you try to holler at every bitch in the Quarters, you a dog."

Walking back into his building he saw Black and Ross shooting dice with a couple dudes he'd never seen before.

"Shit!" Black yelled as the 3-4 came up on the dice.

"Let me buck them again, slim."

Black threw down two hundred dollar bills and shook the dice, letting them go and snapping his fingers. The dice landed on 1-4. "You want to put a ball on the 5-9?," the light skinned fader asked.

"Yeah," Black responded in his raspy voice.

Shaking the dice and throwing them again. The dice tumbled slowly as they finally stopped on seven. "Yeah!" The fader smiled as he snatched the money off the floor. Black's hand went behind his back.

"What the...."

"Shut the fuck up," he cut the boy off waving the Glock-40 from him to his friend. "Nigga set that shit out."

Both the young men began digging in their pockets, dropping their money to the floor.

"Take off that chain and your jackets, muthafuckas."

Ross snatched the jackets and gold chains from the floor.

"Cuz, you got it," the second boy said with his hands up.

"I know I got it, you bitch ass nigga. I wish I would let you suckers leave with my money and you ain't from around here. Now get the fuck out of her before I put something in y'all ass; and don't come around her no more. Y'all barred from

DC BLOOD BROTHERS

the Quarters."

The two boys ran off just happy they weren't shot. Jamal stood there with a smirk on his round face after witnessing what went down.

"Black and Ross, let me holler at ya'll."

"What's up, Mal?" Ross asked as Black gave him a break down from the robbery.

"Y'all niggas trying to make some serious dough?"

"Hell yeah, this drought is fucking me up," Black said.

"Well, give me about a week and I'll do something with ya'll. Once we get it started ain't no getting out though, no bullshit."

"You just make sure you get at us next week Mal."

Three months later, a police cruiser roared with its sirens blaring down Good Hope Road after getting a call for a kidnapping. Hunter Place was packed with people as Green stopped the cruiser.

Walking up, their superior officer was barking out orders. "Knock on doors! Comb the streets, I want this little girl found an hour ago," Sgt. Blain yelled.

"Green, Jenkins, come here."

"This is what's going on. You see that man in the back of the patrol car that's about to pull off? That's Eric Frazier, A. K. A. Hands. He's a well known drug dealer in S.E. He and his cousin and enforcer, Antonio Frazier, aka Tony .T. or Big Tone, beat a murder last year in District Court. It's Eric's daughter who was kidnapped."

Jason, confused asked, "Well why..."

"We had to arrest him," the Sergeant cut him off, "he was unconscious when a neighbor found him and made the call. His apartment door was open. When the first officers arrived on the scene, they checked the apartment to make sure there were no one else injured and found two kilos of heroin. I want you two to ask around and see if anyone knows anything. This is the ghetto; somebody always sees what goes down. And if we don't get to the kidnapper before Eric's people do, I can assure you, we'll be finding bodies throughout next week. Now get on it!"

ANTHONY

Ant sat in his Maxima on the front side of Terrell Elementary School, head lifting to his rear view mirror to see who just pulled in behind him. It was Ortega in an old Volvo. Ant got out of his car and got into the Volvo. Ortega handed him a small tablet and ink pen, Ant took it writing $8,000. O saw the number then tore it off and ripped it to pieces. Meet me in back of Gibson Plaza in 35 minutes.

Ant got out of the car and drove to his building. He had rented an apartment in the same building he grew up in, Gibson Plaza. Exactly one floor above where he used to live. Opening the door to apartment 418, Ant threw his keys on the dining room table; a six seat wooden table that he purchased with a matching china

DC BLOOD BROTHERS

cabinet. His entire living room was in crème and black.

Before he knew it, it was time to meet O so he went to the parking lot. He turned to the right of the lot as he stepped out of the back door. He saw Ortega sitting on a small wooden bench.

As soon as Ortega saw him, he got off the bench and walked off with his usual right hand in his pocket. This is where he kept his Glock 380. Ant walked to the bench and picked his bag up, then walked to his car which was parked on the N Street side of the building. He pulled off, making a right onto 7th Street noticing the two brand new Lexus LS's that were parked in front of the building as usual every Wednesday.

He wondered who owned the cars as he noticed the Maryland tags. Making a right turn down O Street, Ant headed toward Sergeant Quarters.

JAMAL

Jamal leaned with his arms on his new Honda Accord Wagon. Standing at 5'8" and weighing 235 lbs., he repeatedly wiped the sweat off of his forehead with a cold wet rag.

"Michelle, come here," he yelled down the parking lot.

"What's up, Jamal?" She asked as if she didn't want to be bothered.

"Damn, why it got to be like that, Michelle?"

"Look, Jamal it's too hot, what do you want?"

Jamal turned as Ant pulled into the parking lot.

"Who is that, Jamal. I see him come around here a lot?"

"That's my man Ant, why?" He asked with a bit of jealousy in his voice.

"Cause he's cute, and unlike all you other niggas around here, he hasn't broken his neck to make his presence felt." She rolled her eyes and looked back to Ant who was now getting out of his car.

"He got a girl?"

"Yep," Jamal smirked as he saw the look of disappointment on Michelle's face.

"Well," she said, "tell him I'd like to get to know him, and tell him I'm not a home wrecker, I'm a big girl and I'm confident enough to share." And with those words Jamal watched her petite but jiggling figure walk away.

"What's up slim, shorty ain't trying to give you no play?"

"No, she just asked about you though, Ant."

"Oh yeah, give her sexy ass my cell number. Come on, get your fat ass in here and cook my shit," Ant smiled.

"Fuck you, you NBA height Muthafucka who can't make a free throw."

The two best friends laughed as they walked into Jamal's building.

MILLIES' HOUSE

DC BLOOD BROTHERS

"...Pass me those dinner rolls," Shana pointed over the Macaroni & Cheese.

"Girl, your stomach is getting so big," Millie teased. "I was wondering when you two would make me a grand baby."

Ant laughed, almost choking on his BBQ turkey wing. Shana rolled her eyes at Jason as he fought not to laugh with the rest of the family. Millie loved these every other week Sunday dinners they shared at her house.

"So how are you feeling, Ma?" Jason asked seriously.

"I'm doing alright, I hate this chemotherapy but the doctors say it's working."

"Look y'all," she said, "put those smiles back on your faces; I'm not going anywhere any time soon. Ant how is everything going at that warehouse you work at in Fairfax ?" She asked to lighten the mood again.

"It's going good Ma; I just got a raise last week."

"That's good, and you Officer Jenkins?," she smiled.

"Everything is fine at work, Ma."

"How about you Shana?"

"The office is crazy as usual but I cope, Ma. I already told them in a few months I'm taking my maternity leave with or without their blessing. I'll see them in court."

"I know that's right," Millie commented.

"And before I forget" Millie started raising her eyebrow. "Which one of you keeps paying my mortgage, I told you I can handle the payments."

"Ma, you raised us Jason began."

"Yeah, you and Dad took good care of us. Can we take care of you a little?" Ant asked.

"Okay but don't spoil me too much. I might get used to it and start expecting it."

After a four course meal, and a couple glasses of wine, everyone headed to the door. Millie laughed as Shana waddled to the car, "y'all drive safe, I love you."

Ant blew his horn as he pulled out. Jason and Shana followed. Millie stood in her doorway until her son's cars could no longer be seen. She told Franklin everyday in her thoughts, how she loved him, missed him, and thanked him for their wonderful sons.

Walking back through the living room, she looked to the oil painting of Franklin she had made and smiled.

The next day..

"So what did you do for the weekend Jenkins?"

"The usual Mitch, went to Lamaze class with my wife and had Sunday dinner at my Moms. What did you do Green?"

"My usual, had a date Saturday and a hangover Sunday."

Jason just shook his head.

"So what's your take on this Frazier case?"

"I don't know Green, for three armed men to kidnap his daughter; I think he's lying about not being contacted by the abductors."

The traffic was steady as they cruised down Martin Luther King Avenue.

"Get the fuck off me!"

Jason turned and saw the woman snatch her arm away from a man.

Green stopped the cruiser and Jason jumped out of the car, "hey you, put your hands up against the wall."

The man did as he was told and Jason frisked him. "Please don't lock him up," the woman grabbed Jason's arm screaming. "He didn't do anything."

Jason and his partner looked to each other then at the woman as if she was crazy. Jason threw his hands in the air as he walked back to the car. Mitch pointed to the couple, "y'all take your drama in the house, and if I get a call I'll lock both your asses up."

He slammed the door as he got back into the driver's seat. "I can't believe that shit, people are crazy." Green fumed.

THE KIDNAPPERS

"Man, I don't know what the fuck is wrong with this little girl but she act like she can barely breath."

"Move, let me see." Daryl shoved his friend Boe out of the way to inspect the girl they kidnapped.

"I told you I think she got asthma, Daryl," his girlfriend told him as she stood over his shoulder with her hands on her hips.

"Who the fuck asked you, Trish?"

"Fine, if she dies, y'all asses will be dying behind the wall up Lorton."

"She right, Dawg" Jerald, the third kidnapper agreed.

"If this muthafucka hurry up and give us that million, she will be fine, man. I ain't trying to go behind the wall for killing no little girl."

"Well, if you so scared Jerald, go get her some medicine, grab her little ass some juices too."

Jerald walked out of the apartment building making a left out of the Butler Gardens Apartments and walked down to W Street to the corner store.

"Excuse me, do you have any asthma medicine or inhalers for children?"

"How old is the child?" The man behind the counter asked.

"She's five."

"Let me check and I'll be right back."

The man returned with a small box, "this should do it, young man."

"Are you sure that it's safe for her?"

"Yes, you would need a prescription from a doctor to get anything stronger than this. Will this be all?" He began ringing up the medicine and the juices.

DC BLOOD BROTHERS

JASON

"It's too early for the B.S. Jenkins. What do you say, coffee on me?"
"Sure."

Green turned right and stopped at the small corner store. Both officers walked up the steps as a young man was coming out. He looked to the officers and then dropped his head. This wasn't unusual to Jason, Officers always got away with illegal procedures when they said that a suspect seemed nervous; everyone in the ghetto gets nervous when they see a cop.

Green said good morning to the man behind the counter who was smiling. "Good morning officers, y'all have to excuse me but it really touches me when a young father seems to be concerned about their children. That young man who just left out of here had sincere panic and concern on his face as he asked me if I was sure the asthma medicine I sold him would be safe for his child."

"What did you just say?" Jason almost yelled.

"I said it touches me..."

"No, no" Jason cut him off, "did you say that young man just inquired about some asthma medicine."

The man nodded and Jason ran to the door to see if he could see the guy who just left. He saw him at the top of the street. "What is it Jenkins?" Green asked.

"Remember, last week in roll call they said the girl that was kidnapped had a severe case of asthma."

Green started the car and cruised up the street, watching the suspect turn right. Jason told him to drive past him, then slowly circle the parking lot. They watched him walked into Butler Gardens and turned into the first building to the right. Pulling back in front of the building, they looked through the steps since the buildings had no hallway doors, but he had already entered an apartment.

"Hey kid, come here," Green called one of the little boys in the hallway.

"Did you see that man just come into the building?"

The little boy shook his head yes.

"Which apartment did he go into?"

"The first one to the right on the third floor."

"Here, take this dollar and do me a favor. You and your friends go play in another building Okay!"

Ten minutes later, Butler Gardens was flooded with unmarked police cars. Jason's heart raced as he stood in the small stairwell awaiting permission to raid the apartment. The team leader nodded, and then put one arm in the air. As soon as it came down, a rammed the door.

The apartment door flew almost completely off the hinges as the officers rushed in. The kidnappers screamed "Don't shoot! Don't shoot!"

"Get on the ground, look to the fucking ground before I stomp your eyes out!" An officer screamed to Daryl.

"We got her!"

Jason's eyes grew big as he saw the five year old girl, Tiffany.

DE BLOOD BROTHERS

"Everything's okay. Tiffany, we have come to take you home." Jason reassured her after noticing her chest heaving in panic verging on an attack.

"Call paramedics, she's about to have an asthma attack."

"You okay, Jenkins?" His partner asked slapping him on the shoulder as officers escorted three men and one woman out in cuffs

"Good job men, damn good job." The Captain said as he walked into the apartment.

"You guys just prevented a lot of murders, although they will be targets the entire time that they are in prison."

The Captain shook his balding head, "You two make out your reports and take the rest of the day off."

Chapter 15

Ant parked his new black Q45 Infinity on the N Street side of his high-rise. He pulled out the number that Jamal passed him earlier and dialed the numbers.

Ring!

"Hello."

"I'm Michelle, from around the Quarters, you told Jamal to give me your number."

"Oh yeah, what's up with you?"

"Not too much, Ant. Are you doing anything later on?"

"Damn, you cut straight to the chase, huh?"

She laughed, "Ant, don't take that the wrong way, I don't plan on fucking you tonight anyway. Jamal already told me you got a girl, and that's cool. I just like what I see. Your woman is not my concern, she's yours. I just want to spend some time with you to see to get to know you."

"Damn" was all Ant could say.

"Well, Michelle I got some business to take care of tonight. Maybe we can have dinner on The Spirit of Washington tomorrow night."

"Okay, call me."

Ant got out of his new car and circled it while trying to figure out what type of rims to put on it and whether he should darken the tint. He began walking to the front of the building, taking notice that the two Lexus's were in front of the building again.

After entering his code to unlock the security door, he stopped into the semi

DC BLOOD BROTHERS

crowded lobby. The left elevator door opened and two men stepped out.

It took Ant three seconds to notice the jewelry around their necks, diamond pinky rings and Rolex watches. People rushed into the elevator as Ant turned, acting as if he forgot to check his mail.

The two men got into the matching burgundy Lexus's and pulled off. Ant's mind was racing a thousand miles per second. Ring! His cell phone shattered his thoughts.

"Hello."

"Hi boo, what you doing?"

"I'm about to change my clothes Lisa then I'm coming to get you."

"Well, I'm not at home Ant. I'm over Toya's house around 14th and Oak, remember?"

"Yeah, I'll pick you up in about an hour and a half."

Ant hung and dialed Jamal's number.

"Hey-Hey! Hey, Hey," Jamal answered.

"Who the fuck you suppose to be Mal, Re-run off What's Happening?"

"What you want Ant? I'm busy."

"Did you pick up what I told you?"

"Yep. Cream, just like you said, Ant."

"I want you to take it somewhere for me."

A few hours later, Lisa was looking out the window for Ant.

"Do you see him out there girl?" Toya asked.

"I can't believe this nigga is cutting up on my birthday. Let me call him."

Ring!

"Hello."

"Why do you sound sleep, Ant, when you told me you'll pick me up an hour ago?"

"I'm tired."

"You tired, it's my birthday Ant. I can't believe you pulled some shit like this on me. I…"

"Girl shut up," he interrupted, "I already got your present."

"Well a lot of good it's doing me, and I'm uptown."

"Your presents uptown, too."

"Huh?" She asked confused.

"Look, baby I set all this up. Your present is right outside. The keys are in the ash tray and there is a couple grand in the console."

"Thank you, baby! I love you! So we not doing nothing tonight Ant?"

"Nothing, I'm tired. You and Toya hang out, I'll see you tomorrow.
Click.

"Come on, bitch," Lisa ran to the door.

"Where we going Lisa?"

"Right there," Lisa pointed to the Crème 318 BMW with the bow on the hood.

"You like it?" Lisa asked as she opened the door. "Where we going?"

"I don't care, let's go see Rare Essence tonight. We got a find you a nigga anyway."

"Hell yeah, so I can get me one of these little Beamers."

Lisa turned to Toya, "I know who I'm gonna hook you up with."

Within the next two months, Jason and his partner received citations for having solved the Frazier case. They were also given promotions to Detectives and were assigned to Robbery/Homicide. They asked to be transferred back to NW and they were sent to 555.

Millie continued chemotherapy and was doing well. That is until she was getting dressed for church and began to comb her hair and saw it falling into the sink. Shana's water broke while she was shopping for sleepers. Jason and Shana named their first son Jason Parcell Jenkins, Jr.

Chapter 16

"Knock!

"Who is it?"

"It's Lisa."

"Put the money up, he whispered to Jamal, Willie and Nick. After they cleared the table, Ant opened the door for Lisa and sent his men out.

"You look stressed baby," she massaged his shoulders. "I know what you need"; she squatted in front of him, staring into his eyes as she pulled his zipper down with her teeth. She pulled out his penis, licked all over it, then took his balls one by one into her mouth. Ant grabbed the back of her head, and she took him deep into her throat. She gagged as he pushed himself deeper.

"You like it huh?" She teased.

She fondled his balls as she sucked him harder, tightening her grasp on him as she pulled him in and out her mouth. Ant couldn't take any more and he began shooting semen down her throat. She pulled him out her mouth and held out her tongue as she jerked him, making cum shoot over her tongue and face.

"Oh shit!" Ant yelled. "Damn girl, warn a nigga before you start doing freaky shit like that."

Lisa got up smiling and walked to the bathroom, coming out with two wash clothes. She wiped her face with one and cleaned Ant off with the other.

"Baby, can I have three thousand?"

Ant started to curse her out, but Smiley always told him, think before he opened his mouth. Ant smirked before answering her.

"You love me, Lisa?"

"Of course I do, didn't I just show you how much I love you."

"Ah-ight, I'll give you the three grand before you leave but I want you to do something for me."

"What?"

"It's these two niggas with matching LS's that park out front every Wednesday. I want you to be in the lobby this Wednesday and meet those niggas for me. No problem baby, she felt her panties getting damp just hearing about the matching Lexus's.

JASON AND SHANA

"Jay, what are you doing home?"

"I came to check on you and the baby"; he kissed Shana on the forehead.

"We're fine, my breast are so swollen with milk they are throbbing."

"Here, burp your son Mr. Detective."

Jason put his son's head to his left shoulder and began patting his back "How's your day going?"

"Boring, but I hear boring means things are going good when you work robbery homicide."

"I can imagine, when you come home, I need to get some things from the store. Are you going to be back at a reasonable hour?"

"I should, no later than seven, okay. Ma wants you to call her. She wants us to celebrate the fourth of July with her church. They are going to the monument."

"Sounds like fun, I'll call her later."

Jason looked down to his pager then reached for the phone. "What's up Green?"

"We got a stiff off Georgia Avenue, Jay."

"I'm on my way."

ANT'S CREW

Nick looked out his apartment window, and held a finger gesturing he would be out in a minute. Reaching under his bed, he pulled out a Nike shoe box. He lifted the lid and took out the Glock 40 handgun and shoved it into his hip.

"You about to roll Nick?"

He turned, seeing his pregnant girlfriend Kim with their son Kenny on her left hip. "Yeah, why, what's up?"

"Can you bring me some Butter Pecan ice crème and two packs of M&M's?"

"Ah-ight," he kissed her on her lips and left out the door.

"What took you so long, nigga?" Asked Jamal.

DC BLOOD BROTHERS

"Had to get my bitch Mal, you know I don't leave home without it."

"Is Willie ready?"

Jamal nodded as he pulled into the traffic on Alabama Ave.

"So what happened anyway?"

"I ain't sure, Ant just told me some nigga Willie knew tried to brace him, so we all going to meet down by the Market." Twenty minutes later Jamal parked beside Ant's Maxima. He saw Willie in the passenger seat evidently upset. Mal could tell from how red his face was.

"Damn youngin'!" Nick said as he noticed the knot on the side of Willie's head.

Ant began to speak, "Nick I want you to ride with Black and Willie, just make sure shit go smooth. Don't come back to my apartment when you finish."

"Let me drive youngin," Nick opened the driver's side door before hearing Blacks answer, which pissed Black off. Although Black was no sucker, the reputation Nick built over the years kind of made you want to stay out his way.

"Just keep straight," Willie told Nick as he pointed with one hand and held the knot on his head with the other.

"You ready, I'm going to drive through Park Road First, if you see him, tell me and I'll stop."

Nick put on his turn signal then turned into the small street; the block was crowded as usual on a hot day.

"There he goes," Willie pointed, his target had his back turned to the street. Nick grabbed his Glock 40 off of his lap as he heard the duffle bag unzip. Nick slammed on the brakes. The unsuspecting man turned when he heard the tires screech. His eyebrows rose to his forehead as he saw three men get out of the car with guns drawn. The man turned to run.

A bullet ripped through his shoulder, spinning his body. Women and children screamed as they took cover behind parked cars. A few guys on the block drew their guns and shot back at car. Black swung the AR-15 left to right. Nick bit his bottom lip as he ran to the target he just dropped, aiming for his head. Black continued shooting until they all made it to the car. They sped off, three blocks away Nick turned to Willie.

"Feel better now Willie?"

Nick laughed as he looked at Willie through the rear view mirror.

JASON

"What we got here?" Detective Green asked the patrol officer as they walked under the yellow tape on Morton Street.

"Black male, 20-25 years of age, one close range shot to the left side of his head. Somebody got him in his car, when we arrived on the scene, he was slumped over his steering wheel."

"Drug related?" Jason asked.

DC BLOOD BROTHERS

"Could be but the only thing we pulled off the body was a P-89 semi auto hand gun and $350."

"Alright, let us look around," Green said as he pulled a small white tablet from his pocket. First, noting the obvious, the victim was either talking to someone or waiting for someone since he was double parked.

Second, he had to be a regular in the neighborhood because anybody would have known to pay attention to their surroundings on Morton Street.

"You finished, Green?"

"Yeah Jenkins, you ready to hit the morgue?"

" Yeah, I'm ready to go."

Every time Jason saw a dead body he thought of his Father.

Ring!

"Don't tell me," Jason said as he opened the passenger side door.

"Sorry kid, but yeah, we got another body on Park Road."

Chapter 17

LISA

The security guard sat at his desk in front of the rental office. He had been working on a report for the past hour. He couldn't stop looking in front of him. The elevator door opened, Lisa turned around, only seeing two ladies step out with shopping baskets.

She looked down inspecting herself, her dress hugging every curve she had. And, her 4 inch heel on her black 9 west boots gave her ass the perfect lift. She looked out the lobby's front window admiring the two Lexus's while twirling her car keys on her finger. The elevator doors opened and she looked over her shoulder.

Oh yeah! She thought as the two men stepped off.

She looked back to the glass and watched as the reflections got closer.

Then she dropped her keys to the right of her, then, bent over without bending her knees to pick them up. The two men stopped as they watched the Coogie dress rise and the soft fabric stretch around her big round behind.

"You need some help?"

She turned her head over her shoulder still bent over. Standing straight, she smiled, "it's Okay I got them."

She opened her hand to flash the keys. Then she looked the men up and down. The tall one that was talking to her wore an Iceberg History T-shirt with Mickey Mouse on it. The short quiet one wore a Sobiato T-shirt with the matching sweat

DC BLOOD BROTHERS

pants.

"What's your name sexy?"

"Lisa."

"Nice to meet you, Lisa."

"I'm Derrick and this is my man Cedric." Cedric just nodded his head in response to the introduction.

"What you doing later on?"

"I don't have anything planned, she answered in almost an innocent whisper."

"Huh, take my cell number and call me around 7pm. We can go get something to eat then whatever's nice later."

"Okay. I'll call you."

She walked to the elevator in the walk she only used when she wanted attention. It was a switch and a bounce. She looked back and smiled, already knowing Derrick and Cedric were watching her ass.

ANTHONY'S APARTMENT

"Man, you should have seen him Ant. That nigga Willie looked shook when we left Park Road. Nick laughed recalling the situation.

Ant smiled and slapped Willie on his back; "It's alright champ, y'all handled your business. I'll tell you something else," Ant put up a finger as he looked around at his crew, "I bet don't nobody else try to rob one of us for a while."

Knock!

Nick grabbed the AR-15 from the side of the sofa and walked to the door. He looked out the peep hole and saw Lisa standing with her hands on her hips. He unlocked the door.

"Damn girl, you killing them softly with that dress."

"Thanks for the compliment, Nick" she smiled and walked in.

"Did you meet them?" Ant asked.

"Yeah, I got the tall ones cell number; I'm supposed to call him at 7pm."

"Good, this is what I want you to do. Go chill with the nigga, and then later get that nigga alone in a hotel somewhere."

"Okay baby, let me go home and get changed. You know I don't wear the same outfit for over 12 hours."

JASON

Jason phone suddenly ranged. He shook his head as he answered. "Detective Jenkins"

"Hi Jay, I just wanted to know if you were coming home for dinner."

"Yeah, Shana. I should be home in an hour."

"Every time you say that Jay, I don't see you until six hours later."

DC BLOOD BROTHERS

"Look Shana, don't start. I'll be home as soon as I can."
Mitch looked across his desk to his partner.
"Want to talk about it, buddy?"
"Man, we don't have enough hours in a day for this conversation. Shana's just becoming real annoying lately. She wants me to spend time at home that I don't have. Two days ago, Jr. took a couple steps, as soon as I unlock the front door she went ballistic on me for missing it."
"Well Jenkins, being married to a cop is hard on a woman, especially now that we're detectives. They never know when they'll get a phone call saying we've been shot, or worse murdered. Shana's a good woman and she loves you. And you're also one of the three only detectives I know who are still married. Hell, I can't even keep a steady girlfriend. This job has me standing so many women up; half won't even return my calls."
"Okay, I'm getting the message, Green."
"You better get the message; it's a hell of a lot cheaper than getting a divorce lawyer."

LISA

Three hours later Lisa walked to the Lexus, surprised that Cedric was in the passenger seat. "Get in the back" Derrick hollered out of his sun roof.
"So, where we going?" Lisa asked trying to start conversation.
"We going to a little spot I like out in Alexandria, you'll like it."
He looked to the back seat, Lisa turned towards the window as if she didn't notice his eyes get big. Derrick now tapped Cedric with his elbow, pointing his thumb to the back seat. Lisa knew she crossed her legs just enough that her panties could be seen. Cedric looked back to her, she looked back at him, saw his eyes lower then he looked forward. That's right niggas, get a good look at this million dollar piece of ass.
Twenty five minutes later, they were making a left into the parking lot of a restaurant called Captain Johns off of Route one in Alexandria, VA. They entered and were seated immediately. Lisa scanned her menu while moving her French manicured nail down the selections.
"Order what you want baby," Derrick said.
She smiled, although she was beginning to feel creepy because Cedric stared but never spoke.
"Excuse me gentlemen, I need to go to the ladies room."
She looked under all the stalls before pulling out her cell phone.
"Hi baby, we're out in Alexandria at this place called Captain Johns."
"Look, try to get that joker to a hotel, call me back and tell me where and what room."
She returned to the table.
"This is a nice restaurant," she touched Derrick's hand. The restaurant wasn't

small; it had the allure of ambiance with its dim lighting. Lisa sipped her second Long Island iced tea then picked up another shrimp; she peeled it, and dipped it in cocktail sauce.

"This is so good," she moaned before opening her mouth. She was slurping the cocktail sauce seductively off of the shrimp before putting it into her mouth. Cedric and Derrick looked to each other then back to Lisa who was pushing her plate to the center of the table.

"Did you enjoy it?"

"Yes Derrick, thank you."

"No, thank you for letting us watch you eat those shrimp, it was like soft porn."

She giggled then took five big gulps from her drink. "So," she slurred, "what else are you boys trying to get into tonight?"

"You."

Lisa looked surprised that Cedric said something.

"Well what are we waiting for?"

Derrick put up a finger, "waitress, check please."

JASON

"Baby it's so good to have you home for a change." Shana played with Jay's right ear as they watched their rental movie, Jacob's ladder.

Little Jay walked from his Mother to his Father using their knees to balance himself. "Yeah!" Shana screamed and clapped. Little Jay clapped with a huge smile on his face, mimicking his mother. He lost his balance and his smile briefly turned into shock as his butt hit the floor. Then he clapped and smiled again.

"Boy, you are crazy, come here." Jason picked his son off the floor and cradled him in his arms.

"Don't you two look perfect, let me get the camera." Shana darted out the living room in her pink pajamas to get the camera. "Okay, smile boys. Oh hell, I'm out of film."

"I'll bring some home tomorrow," Jay patted the sofa, "come sit that pretty behind down and let me stare into those hazel eyes."

"Who me," she put her hand to her head as she looked behind her to her left then right.

"Oh look, he's sleep," she pointed to Jr., "I'll take him upstairs."

She took him from Jay and walked Jr. to his room. Jason exhaled as he stretched, glad he was spending a quiet night at home with his family.

"Jason," Shana sang from the top of the stairs.

"Yes baby," his mouth slowly forming a smile as he watched her pajama top float to the bottom of the stairs. Then the pants and black butterfly thong he knew she had on underneath. "You trying to tell me something?" He asked as he turned down the television.

DC BLOOD BROTHERS

The only response he could hear was the wet smacking sound her fingers made as she masturbated at the top of the stairs.

"Coming Dear!"

LISA

Derrick pushed the button for the elevator in the lobby of the Ramada hotel, holding the key card in his right hand. The doors opened and the three stepped in. Derrick pressed number four then turned to Lisa, then rubbed his thumb over her pink lips. Cedric followed suit and palmed her butt cheeks.

"Oh, now ya'll want to fondle a bitch huh?"

"This good shit ain't cheap you know," she turned back to Cedric.

"You like how big and soft my ass feels?"

"Oh yeah," he moaned as he continued.

"And you," she looked to Derrick, "you like how my lips feel?"

She took his hand, and began loudly sucking his thumb.

"Oh shit!" He yelled. "How much is this gonna cost us?"

"For you two, give me nine hundred."

Cedric pulled out a bankroll. Lisa cursed under her breath realizing that she probably could have gotten more.

"Here," Cedric said, "here's an extra four."

She smiled, "thank you."

After making it to the room she excused herself to the bathroom.

"Hello" She whispered.

"We're at the Ramada Hotel off by the Rivertown Shopping Center, both dudes are here."

"What room?"

"419."

"Stall them jokers until we get there in about 25 minutes."

She put her cell phone back into her Chanel bag, then began taking off her clothes, thinking of how wet she was since they felt her up in the elevator. Shit, might as well, I never been with two at one time and they paid for it. She took off her bra. Her 34 C cup breast swinging as she stepped out of the bathroom with her red thongs and red heels.

Derrick rubbed his hands together and licked his lips, staring at Lisa's perfect figure. She turned around with her hands out to her sides as if she were modeling. Then she got down on the floor and crawled to Derrick who was sitting on the edge of the bed unzipping his pants.. "Hold up shorty, my runners don't sample shit til I do."

Lisa dropped Derrick's manhood as if it was a dirty rag and crawled to Cedric. She unzipped his pants pulling his manhood out. She licked over it, and put him into her mouth until she felt him at the back of her throat. She nearly choked on Cedric's dick while she felt Derrick's dick penetrate her from behind. Her eyes rolled to the back of her head as her first orgasm shot through her.

"Let's get on the bed," Cedric ordered.

Lisa reached for Derrick's dick as she lifted her butt to Cedric. He rammed into her, pulling her hair. "You like it don't you, you nasty little bitch? Cedric asked as he slammed into her. Smack! He was slapping her cheeks until they were red with his hand prints.

ANTHONY

"Hurry up Black!"

"I am Ant, you know how slow traffic be moving on South Capitol St."

Ant was a little frustrated, realizing now that he may have put Lisa in a terrible situation. I just hope they don't rape her.

"I know what to do," Black grabbed the spot light on the side of the bubble caprice and began flashing the light to cars in front of him; who were now slowing down and pulling over thinking maybe it was a police car.

"Look, these stupid motherfuckas think we 5-0."

Five minutes later they pulled into the Ramada parking lot.

"Sam, you stay in the car," Ant ordered.

"The rest of ya'll come with me."

Ant, Black and Nick took the stairwell to avoid being seen by as many people as they could. They stepped onto the fourth floor.

"Oh Yes!"

Ant heard Lisa's familiar cries of passion as they neared the door, Black and Nick looked toward each other and knocked as hard they could.

"Who is it" Derrick yelled as he continued ramming himself into Lisa's butt.

"It's security, Sir; someone broke into your car downstairs."

"Oh shit!"

He pulled out of Lisa, grabbed his jeans and hopped on one foot to the door while pulling them up. He opened the door.

"Get the fuck back in there and shut the fuck up!"

Nick stuck the Glock 40 to his lips pushing him back into the room. Cedric dove for his gun which was under his T-shirt 5 feet from the bed but Black smacked him with the 45 cal he was holding.

Lisa pulled up the sheets to cover her breast as they walked in, fighting to regain control of her breathing. Ant looked towards her with a coldness in his eyes that made her spine shiver.

"Which one of them the man, Lisa?"

"He is," she pointed to Cedric.

"Bitch you set me up, you dead bitch!" He spat in Lisa's face. Black split his mouth open after smacking him a second time with his gun.

"Tie his ass up Nick. Gag the other one," Ant ordered.

After Nick tied up Cedric and gagged Derrick, Ant walked to Cedric and kneeled close to his ear.

"Look here slim, I ain't here to play. I'm going to tell you what I want."

"I want three hundred thousand within the next hour, or you and your man are dead. Do you have that kind of money?"

Cedric just stared into Ant's eyes, already knowing he was dead because the three wore no masks. Derrick frantically began shaking his head up and down. Ant asked, "Are you saying y'all got that?"

Derrick continued shaking his head.

"Bring him with us, Lisa, get dressed you riding with me. If you make one sound outside, I don't care if you sneeze, burp, fart, I swear to God I'm going to kill you," Ant warned Derrick, "now let's go".

Everyone left the room except Nick and Cedric. After the hotel door shut, Nick pulled out his knife and cut Cedric's throat from ear to ear.

The lobby was empty when they entered through the back door. The apartment was lightly furnished, a couple lounge chairs, a sofa, and one bed in the apartment.

A triple beam and two digital scales sat on the bedroom dresser. Derrick, still gagged and bound led them to the safe in the bedroom closet.

"Cut the tape off his hands, Sam."

Lisa sat down on the sofa, so nervous her knees couldn't stop shaking. She began biting her nails, thinking of a lie good enough to excuse her from having sex with the two men. *That's it, they raped me.*

Ant stood over Derrick's shoulder as his fingers fumbled with the combination. The safe door popped open. Ant pushed Derrick to the side with his knees. Eyes wide, he couldn't believe what he was looking at. Ant pulled the gag off of Derrick.

"How much in here slim?"

"About eight hundred thousand and three kilos of heroin."

Ant smiled then looked to Black. Derrick saw the gesture and stood up, "please man, don't kill me, I gave you what you…" Derrick's brains hit the wall as his lifeless body fell to the floor. Lisa almost jumped out of her skin.

Oh my God, they just killed him, she thought, then realized that they must have killed Cedric too.

"Come on Lisa, let's go."

Ant dropped off Black, then drove Sam to his car to follow him since Nick wasn't around. Sam followed Ant to First St., Lisa glanced every few seconds in Ant's direction, his face was tight and he wouldn't look in her direction.

He pulled in front of her house and he just stared ahead out the window.

"Ant, they.."

"Bitch stop lying," he cut her off.

"Get the fuck out my shit, if you call the police, naw fuck that, if I hear you were even questioned by the police I will kill you, and your Mother, you got me?"

She nodded and got out of the car.

Chapter 18

JASON AND SHANA

Shana dreamed of her and the family at Disney World. With a smile on her sleeping face as her head lay on Jason's chiseled chest.

Ring!

She elbowed Jason until his eyes opened, handing him the receiver.

"Okay, I'll be there in 20 minutes."

Jason drove half sleep down Branch Avenue until he was in D.C. and turned on his sirens, speeding to 7th Street. Twenty five minutes later, he was pushing five repeatedly on the elevator.

It wouldn't light up and from growing up in the building, he knew what to do in case it was broke. As the door opened he saw his partner Mitch sipping a cup of coffee.

"Hey, sleeping beauty." Mitch teased as he stepped out of the elevator.

"What we got here, Ted?," Jason questioned the first officer to arrive on the scene.

"One black male, 30-35 years of age, one gunshot wound to the head, no shells were found, looks like a robbery; follow me."

Jason and his partner followed the officer past the body to the closet. The safe was still open. Green put his hand on the officer's back.

"When the lab boys get here I want them to swipe that safe to see if any drugs were in it, if so, what kind!"

DC BLOOD BROTHERS

Jason kneeled to the body and lifted the sheet, the victims face was so swollen Jason couldn't see how they distinguished an age.

"Here we go again," he said out loud. "I'm going to question a few neighbors, Green."

Jason began stepping out of the room when he noticed something. He stuck his head back into the room.

"What is it, Jenkins?"

Jason pulled a pen from his pocket and kneeled to the floor. Then he raised his arm to show Mitch the casing he found on the floor.

"Might be open and shut after all," he smiled.

A WEEK LATER..

"Dag, you ain't even going to let a chick cook you breakfast huh?" Michelle said standing at her bedroom door, watching Ant get dressed.

"Not today, I got some early business to take care of."

"No problem," she walked up to him, reaching her arms around his neck and kissing him. "I love you," she exclaimed staring into his eyes. "Boy, why are you looking at me like that, like I haven't been telling you I love you for the past week.

"Nothing," he turned around and grabbed his shirt.

She knew when he acted like this not to pressure him. So she walked out of the room. Ant was thinking, how he had just come so close to telling 'Chelle he loved her too. And he did; but more than loving her, he respected her.

They had been involved now for a year, never once did she bring up Lisa. Never once has she cracked on me for money, he thought. She even promised that no other man would touch her. He promised himself that he would do something very special for Michelle. He picked up his key ring off of her dresser and his face tightened as he noticed his copy of Lisa's BMW key.

He stepped out of Michelle's building, took the key off of his ring and threw it as hard as he could down the parking lot. He smiled as he thought of how Smiley had warned him; "Bitches ain't shit!"

MILLIE

Millie adjusted her grey wig in her hall mirror before heading to answer her front door. "Who is it?"

"Jehovah's Witness."

She opened the door. "Oh my, look at my Grand baby, he's getting so big." She took Jr. out of Jason's arms as they walked in.

"Hi Ma," Shana kissed Millie on the cheek.

"I'm going to fire up the grill" said Jason as he walked to the back sliding door.

DC BLOOD BROTHERS

Shana locked the legs on Jr.'s walker and put him in it.

"So, Shana. When are you going back to work?"

"I told them in two weeks but I may start next week. I'm just trying to secure Jr. a good baby sitter."

"That's all, look; you can drop my grand baby off over here anytime, Shana."

"I wouldn't want to trouble you Ma."

"How are you gonna trouble me, that's what family is for. And, I know you'll feel a lot better at work knowing you left him with family instead of a stranger."

"Are you sure, Ma?"

"Yes, and that's the end of that. Open the door for Ant, will you Shana?"

After opening the door, Shana embraced her brother-in-law. "Boy, you getting big, who you got cooking for you?"

"I'll introduce you to her soon."

"Do I here wedding bells?" Millie teased. Ant shot her one of his famous cold stares. "Well, I guess not," she scratched the back of her head. "Who you think you supposed to be scaring with that look, mister.?"

"What you talking about, Ma?" Ant put his hands in the air.

"Where's Jay?"

"He out back on the grill," Shana answered.

"What's up Jr.," Ant squatted to his nephew, "Hey Champ!"

Jr. just smiled at his uncle. Ant walked out the room to the back sliding door toward Jay.

"Please tell me some burgers are done; I'm starving Jay."

After Jason finish cooking, the five of them sat on the small picnic bench in Millie's yard and ate coleslaw, hamburgers, hot dogs, steak, and Millie's special baked beans. The only secret was that she used a mix of Dijon and French mustards in it. For dessert, they ate fresh ripened watermelon and cantaloupe.

"Jay, this was delicious." Ant complimented his brother as he wiped his hands and mouth off with a paper towel.

"Do you mind going for a walk with me before you leave, Ant?"

"Yeah, as a matter of fact, let's walk now because I'm leaving soon."

The brothers walked up and down Harry S. Truman Drive.

"Boy, Ant, look at this neighborhood, it's so quiet, serine you know."

"Yeah, this is what Dad wanted so badly for us."

"How's everything going with you, Ant?"

"It's going good, I'm working hard, I even opened some mutual funds," he lied.

"Oh yeah, that's good, we'll have to discuss that sometime."

"What's been up with you, Detective Jenkins?"

"Oh! Well, I'm really not supposed to discuss this but hell, we're brothers."

"I found a body in Gibson Plaza last week."

"You bullshitting, Jay."

"No seriously, an execution styled killing; the killer almost got away perfectly clean."

"Huh?" Ant said more from reflex than confusion.

"Well, I say the killer almost got away clean because I found a bullet casing..."

Shit! Ant thought to himself. He had told Black's stupid ass to put the gun in a cap to catch the shells.

"...But, it came back inconclusive," said Jay.

"What does that mean?" Ant asked after missing half of what Jay just said.

"The shell, there were no prints on it, so we're at a dead end. If nobody comes forward or the same weapon isn't used in another assault, this murder may go in the cold case files."

"What's the cold files?," Asked Ant.

"They're the files of unsolved murders or other cases, that's where dad's file is."

"Well Jay, it's been real, I'm about to roll. I'll see you in a couple weeks."

Ant drove to Oxon Hill, Maryland and dropped off $1200 to Black's Aunt to rent an apartment. Ant reached for his cell phone as he made a right on Southern Ave.

Ring!

"What's up, Mal?"

"Ain't shit, I been waiting for you to call."

"Tell everybody I said meet me up 7th St."

Ant turned onto Alabama, a few minutes later he pulled in front of Nick's girl's house.

Beep!

Nick came out the door with his duffle bag as always, and got into his tinted caprice and followed Ant back to N.W. Ant looked around the room, from Jamal, Willie, Black, Sam, little Barry and Ricky.

"Look ya'll, from here on out shit gonna get real serious. From now on, I don't want anybody in this room calling me Ant."

"What you want us to call you?" Little Barry asked.

"Don't call me shit until I give you a name to call me."

"Now, Willie how shit going with the blow?"

"It's moving but slow, you know them niggas up by the barber shop? Well, he is giving out extra dope to keep clientele."

"Well, ya'll give out more dope. Look, we ain't out to get rich with this shit. It was a come up, let's use it to build customers, we can always get more shit."

"Mal, you got that for me?"

Mal handed Ant the Safeway plastic bag with $40,000 in it.

"And from here on out, we don't meet here. I just rented an apartment out Oxon Hill, down the hill from Colonial Village in Glass Manor. All of you will have a key, don't go there unless I tell you or you need somewhere safe, and never come dirty. Only straps, don't bring no product.

"As always, keep ya'll little bitches out my face and out your business. Now get out of here and make that money."

DC BLOOD BROTHERS

Everyone left except for Nick, who was not only enforcer but Ant's personal body guard and escort.

One week later, Ant and Ortega stood on the side of O St. Market.

"So how's everything going for you?"

"Everything's cool, O"

"You don't mind the prices going up a little?"

"No, if it wasn't for you I wouldn't be where I am."

Ortega covered his mouth as he spoke. "The next time a car passes, looked down the street and tell me if the two bammas still looking over here."

A car rode past and Ant saw the two men staring. "They probably some new dudes who don't know us."

"Fuck that!"

Ortega yelled as he threw his arms in the air, "what the fuck you niggas keep looking at?" One of the men pulled out a gun. Ant stepped in front of O with his hands out.

"Cuz, we were just playing. We thought you were our man."

"Ah-ight slim but pretty boy better watch his fucking mouth before I down his ass."

"Come on, Chris," Ant heard the second man call the gun man, pulling at his arm. The two men walked off.

"I'm going to kill him, I swear to God." Ortega growled under clenched teeth.

"Don't sweat it O, I promise I'll take care of it for you."

JASON

"I still can't believe that we haven't made any progress on the Brandon or Hollis murders."

"I know what you mean Jenkins," Mitch responded as he made an attempt at cleaning his junky desk.

"It's got to be something we're missing. I mean, as much as the killers went through to get away with these crimes, we could give them all first degree."

"Don't let it get to you Jenkins, we've got years to see a hundred more cases like this."

"Jenkins, Green in my office now," Capt. Moore yelled from his office door. Green followed Jason into the office and closed the door. "Detectives, this is Agent Stevens from the FBI." The short agent shook the Detectives hands.

"Hi gentleman, I'll be as straight forward as I can about this." The Detectives nodded.

"Two weeks ago you found a Derrick Hollis. We have been investigating Mr. Hollis for over 8 months. Him along with the man he worked for, a Cedric Anderson. Mr. Anderson was reportedly found the same night you found Hollis in Maryland." Jenkins and Green's mouths fell open.

DC BLOOD BROTHERS

"That's right gentlemen, we have a double homicide. Mr. Anderson was found with his throat slit from ear to ear. The desk clerk remembered Hollis and a woman checking into the hotel with him."

"Are you taking this investigation from us," Green asked?

"No, but I am going to oversee it, since we know it's a double homicide, I'll be putting together a joint task force, and both you and Prince George's County Detectives will be working together. These men were pretty big heroin dealers, so check your informants to see if anyone popped up with a nice supply of heroin."

NICK-THE ENFORCER

Nick tied up the laces on his most comfortable pair of basketball shoes. He wore his oldest grey sweat suit; it even had a hole in the hoodie. He put on his sunglasses and jogged down the street and walked into the complex of apartments on 6th and O Street. It was a slight chill in the wind with the rain drizzling. He dropped his head as he approached the drug dealer. Not wanting to draw attention until he was close.

"What you need, main man?"

"Gimme a forty."

The hustler pulled out a capsule and opened the top. Nick reached under his hoodie. The drug dealer saw the gun coming out of his sweatpants and ran. The impact from the bullet knocked him to the ground, as the heat shot through his back.

Nick ran down on him, looking him eye to eye as he raised the gun to his head. Nick fired the gun, ran out of the complex and hopped in the stolen Accord he had a fiend get for the hit.

"Oh my God!" Debra Daniels said out loud, as she watched the shooting through her kitchen blinds. She grabbed her cordless and dialed 911!

"911 Emergency!"

"Hello, I want to report a shooting." Debra bit her index finger knuckle as she watched the clock as a crowd formed outside. She knew the victim, and although she hated what he did for a living, she knew Chris didn't deserve what happened. The police and rescue squad arrived on the scene.

Ten minutes later, tears fell from Debra's eyes as she watched them put a white sheet over Chris' body.

Knock!

She jumped, "who is it?"

"Police ma'am, we would like to ask you some questions."

She opened the door after looking through her peep hole and seeing their credentials.

"May we step in?"

She waved them in as she wiped the tears from her eyes.

"I'm Detective Jenkins and this is my partner Detective Green. I'd just like to ask you some questions OK?"

She nodded and Jason pulled out his tablet.

"What is your full name ma'am?"

"Debra Nicole Daniels."

"Did you know the victim?"

"Yes, Chris grew up around here, he moved away a few years ago, and he's just been back for four months.

"We already know you made the 911 call, did you see what happened?" She nodded.

"Can you tell us?"

"A man in a dirty grey sweat suit approached Chris."

"Can you describe the man?"

"He was slim, I couldn't really get a good look at his face because of the rain, but he looked real scruffy, like an addict."

Jenkins looked to his partner with his eyebrows raised.

"Did I say something wrong, sir?" She asked confused.

"No ma'am, it's just we found a trail of crack cocaine from where Chris must have ran from. I don't know too many drug addicts who would have left all that on the ground."

"Oh! I did notice the man wore shades even though it was raining and he had a big nose and a scar on his left cheek."

"Wonderful!" Jason said as he wrote the description.

"Do you think what I've told you will help you?"

"Hopefully."

"Mrs. Daniels, do you think you could recognize the suspect if you saw him again?"

She shook her head yes.

"Do you mind coming downtown with us and look through some mug shots?"

"I'll have to call my husband first."

"No problem, we'll wait."

Two hours later, Mrs. Daniels looked through six mug shot books and she still didn't see the shooter.

"Nope, he's not in here." She closed the last album sounding defeated.

"Don't worry Debra, we'll find him."

"And if we do, would you be willing to testify?"

"Yes, I couldn't sleep knowing that I allowed a murderer to go free."

chapter 19

The day after, Michelle leaned as far back as she could in the passenger seat of Ant's pearl white STS as he stood outside talking to Willie. Nick was standing at the car in front of them with his signature D&G sunglasses on.

"How's it going Willie?"

"Everything is Everything, Dawg."

"I'm down to a half."

"Alright slim, I'll get something to you by tomorrow."

"I'll bring you that bread later, Dawg."

"Ah-ight cuz, call me if shit get crazy."

"I see Warren's men all scoping us out and shit."

"Yeah, it's getting to the point half of them directing traffic to the other end of the corner."

"Don't sweat it Willie, just handle business, and watch your back. If these niggas thought about bringing you a move, I'll turn this part of 7th St. into history in DC."

Ant got in his Cadi, flipped his Washington Wizards cap backwards, and pulled off. "Where we going Daddy?" Michelle asked.

"Why? You don't trust me or something?"

Michelle rolled her eyes, then turned up the volume to the Frankie Beverly CD they were playing. Ant took the 3rd Street tunnel to 95S, riding for forty minutes until he reached Landmark, VA.

Driving past an Acura and Infinity dealer, then pulling into the Lexus dealer.

DC BLOOD BROTHERS

Nick parked behind Ant and stepped out of the car while putting both hands in his pockets. Ant and Chelle got out of the car.

"Tracey, how you doing?" The fat Italian man greeted Ant as he put both hands over Ant's and shook them.

"What can I do for you today, Tracey?"

"I want to test drive the GS and ES."

Ten minutes later, Ant, Chelle, and Nick pulled out the dealership in a red GS 300 Lexus. Afterwards, they decided to test drive a blue ES 300.

"So, which one you like better Chelle?"

"The GS rode better, I think." She answered then crossed her arms looking around the lot.

"Gimme the GS, Giorgio," Ant told the dealer.

"Give me 20 minutes, Tracey and you can pull it off the lot."

Ant winked to the man.

"Chelle, let me holler at you for a minute."

Michelle followed Ant away from Nick.

"Look," he lifted her chin with his finger. "I'm glad you got a job, but I want you to do something else."

"What baby?"

"I want you to go to hair school, learn everything there is to learn, and I'm going to get you a shop."

"For real?" She screamed throwing her arms around him. "Thank you! Thank you! I love you."

"Tracey!" Giorgio yelled just in time to save Ant, "your car is ready, here are the keys, and it already has an alarm and remote for the door."

"Thanks Giorgio."

"No, thank you. It's been a pleasure to do business with you as always, Tracey."

They walked outside and Ant covered Michelle's eyes and whispered, "I love you, too" then took his hands from her eyes. Michelle's hand flew to her mouth as she read the license plate "Chelle".

"Thank you baby, you know you didn't have to do this right?"

"I know," he answered, "that was my biggest reason for doing it."

ANTHONY'S CREW

Jamal followed Willie up the stairs to the small apartment building across from the 5 & 10 store on Kennedy Street.

"Open a window," Jamal said as he waved his hand in front of his nose.

"Sorry, I couldn't hold that."

"You need to go to the doctor, I know you need some tissue to wipe your ass."

"Whatever, Mal."

Willie walked into the small kitchen at the rear of the apartment, pulling a large pot from under the counter. He got into his zone as he repeatedly cooked kilo after kilo of powder, putting just a 16th of baking soda on every ounce.

Jamal started taking each brick, sitting them on the table, turning on three different fans and pointed them to the table.

"Willie," he yelled from the bedroom.

"What's up, Mal?"

"Stretch two and put them in the microwave for me."

Willie whipped up the two kilos, dried them in the microwave and brought them to Jamal who was sitting in front of the scale.

"I'm finished, Mal," Willie said as he pulled the white construction mask from over his mouth. "The other nine are still drying. I'm going to take a nap. Wake me up before you leave so I can do the clean up."

Two hours later Jamal was shaking Willie's body to wake him. "I'm gone."

Willie drifted back to sleep until he heard the front door slam. After mopping the kitchen floor, he poured a half box of carpet fresh throughout the apartment and spent the next hour vacuuming. Willie was wiping the last beads of sweat off his forehead as he walked out the front door.

The entire crew filled the three blue leather sofas in the living room of the Oxon Hill apartment that they have come to call the spot.

"Look!," Ant said as usual to get everyone's attention. "Are you guys trying to hit the Mirage tonight?"

"Hell yeah," Willie yelled, "Ain't tonight Ladies night?"

"Yeah, today is Thursday," Nick answered.

"Not me Champ," Mal said as he stood to leave, "I went to see RE up East Side last night... Fucking with them 501 and Kaper niggas, I still got a hangover. I'll see ya'll tomorrow."

"That's fucked up, ya'll know we too young to get in." Petey spoke for himself and Barry.

"I'll get you in youngin'," Willie assured.

Ant could hear the bass from the club as he circled it, trying to find a parking space. Finally, he decided to park behind the fence of the small lot across from the club. He handed the door man four $100.00 bills and stood to the side as his crew walked in. They went straight to the bar and asked for seven bottles of Moet. The bartender popped the corks and sat the bottles on the bar.

"Damn! Look at shorty in that skirt, come on Barry," Petey pulled him along.

Black tapped Willie on his arm, pointing to the young lady dancing as if she was getting paid to do it.

Willie, who always had the reputation as a pretty boy because of his light complexion, good hair, and light eyes spoke.

"What's happening sexy?" He yelled over the music. She looked to Willie and smiled, still dancing. She couldn't have been any taller than 5'5"and her body went perfectly with her height, 32-24-36. She was stacked.

"You want to drink?"

"Only if he's buying" she pointed to Ant.

DC BLOOD BROTHERS

Ant smiled and patted the stool next to him for her to sit down. Willie shook his head, and then put his arms around Black and Sam's shoulders and the three of them walked off.

Ant fanned his hand at Nick, signaling him that it was OK to leave him unattended.

"What are you drinking, sexy?"

"Um, a hurricane."

Ant raised a finger to get the bartenders attention. "What's your name?"

"Sugar."

"Sugar, what kind of name is that?," He teased. She leaned over towards him and whispered into his ear, "It's because I'm sweet." She stressed the T on the end while picking her glass up off the counter and taking a sip.

"What's your name?"

"I'm Duck."

"Nice to meet you, Duck."

"You got a girlfriend Duck?"

Ant nodded his head.

"Hmmm, a confident nigga. Straight up, that turns me on.

"Oh really?"

"Yes ... really"

Smack. Ant watched as Sugar's body fall off the stool.

"Bitch, what the fuck you think you doing?"

"Get off me! Warren, you don't own me."

Ant put his hand in the center of Warren's chest to separate the two.

"This ain't got shit to do with you, it's none of your business" Warren spoke as the three men with him peered at Ant over his shoulder.

"You made it my business when you interrupted my conversation."

Nick saw the crowd by the bar where Ant was sitting and tapped Willie as he rushed over.

"Sit back down, Sugar," Ant told the young woman.

Warren looked over his shoulder and the man behind him swung a wild right hook at Ant. Ant ducked and landed a left hook that dropped him. Willie hit one of the men over the head with a champagne bottle as Nick swung then dug into his belt buckle. He swung at Warren then the man beside him and stabbed the two in the back and neck. Bouncers rushed into the crowd along with a couple DC police officers and escorted the gangs outside. One officer following both gangs in separate directions to their cars, Sugar followed Ant to the small lot where he disarmed his grey Ranger Rover.

Sam, Black, Barry and Petey piled into Willie's Explorer. Nick got into his jet black twin turbo 300 ZX.

Nick grabbed his Glock 40 off the floor mat and put his duffle bag onto the passenger seat then hit his horn once. After hearing Ant and Willie hit their horns Nick turned on his lights and pulled out of the lot. Making a left, the fleet of three merged into the bumper to bumper traffic.

DC BLOOD BROTHERS

"I'm really sorry about that Duck," Sugar apologized.
"That's alright, shorty. That was some short shit."
"Where you want me to drop you off at?"
"I was hoping we could continue our party somewhere a little more private."

A police cruiser slowly circles the Mirage night club after being called about fights in the club. They were responding to a call to do a drive through because of a reported group altercation just to make sure there was no shooting once the groups were put out of the club.

"Baker, check them out." Two smiles appeared on their lips as they watched the two car loads of women flashing guys in Cadies and Benz's.

"Look at this clown behind them, I mean, what the fuck is he wearing shades for at 2 A.M. in the morning." Baker's eyebrows narrowed as his mind eye raced to find meaning; "Perkins, wasn't the description of the suspect from that 6th St. murder ... slim, and tall with shades."

Perkins nodded, "yeah, why?"

Baker pointed to the Black 300ZX. "Well I'll be damned," Baker said as he noticed the scar on the man's left cheek.

"Get your fucking hands up! Don't move or I'll blow your fucking head off." Perkins dragged Nick's body out of the window as his partner covered him. "I ain't do nothing!" Nick repeatedly screamed as he was laid to the ground and patted down by the officer. After Perkins thoroughly frisked the suspect, he pulled his gun out of his holster. I'll search the car," he said.

After calling for back up, Baker opened the driver's side door and began to search. "Bingo!" He screamed as he picked up the Glock 40 semi automatic hand gun. "Even got the murder weapon, Perkins" he yelled over his shoulder as he ejected the clip and pulled the bullet out of the chamber. He sat the gun on the hood as he continued his search. He pulled out the Wilson's duffle bag. He unzipped the bag finding an AR-15 assault rifle with two loaded clips.

Nick looked up to the officer as the officer began to speak. "Boy, you gonna do ten years up Lorton easy."

chapter 20

NICK

After giving all his information, Nick was placed in a holding cell. The arresting officers appeared at his cell. "I just took a look at your rap sheet Nick, you won't get away with this one. What is he, 24 years old?" Officer Baker asked his partner.

"You will be seventy five years old before you see DC streets again, let alone any firearms."

"You crazy as shit, after I get a lawyer, y'all be lucky if I do five off both guns."

"Guns?" Baker yelled as he repeated Nick. "Who's talking about guns. I'm talking about that boy you killed in N.W."

Nick looked to him without his facial expression changing. "I ain't kill nobody."

"We'll see after the line up and ballistics."

"Whatever, when can I make a phone call?"

"After your line up, you can make as many calls as you can from the jail." Baker walked out laughing, glad he could take another black male off the street.

An hour later..

"Turn to your right," the officer told the six men in the lineup.

"Do you see him in there, Mrs. Daniels?"

"Yes, he's right there."

"Turn to your left, gentlemen."

DC BLOOD BROTHERS

A cold chill shot through Debra Daniels body as Nick appeared to look directly at her through the two way mirror. "It's OK Debra, I assure you that he can't see you," an officer reassured her.

"Is that him?"

She nodded, confirming for the third time that Nicholas Drake was the killer. "Thank you Mrs. Daniels, we're about to charge him with 2nd Degree Murder. You can leave. We'll contact and inform you of when and if we'll need you for trial."

Nick was charged for 2nd degree murder and sent to DC jail to await trial.

The following morning...

Ant woke up, stretched and grabbed his Submarine Rolex watch off the night stand; it was 9:30am. He grabbed his cell phone and called Willie.

"Hello, did you get him out yet?"

"Man, he doesn't even have a bond."

"What you mean he doesn't have a bond, the most he could be charged for is two guns?"

"He's been charged with murder, big homie."

"Meet me at the spot in an hour." Ant ordered.

After checking out of the Embassy Suites Hotel and dropping off Sugar in Clinton M.D., Ant went to the Oxon Hill Apartment where Willie was waiting for him. Ant walked straight to the bar and filled a glass with Remy VSOP.

Taking four large gulps then wiping his mouth with the back of his hand. "Willie, what's the word on Nick?"

"Somebody must have given the police a description of him and they must be willing to testify if they are charging him for murder without the murder weapon."

Ant relaxed a little bit after remembering that Nick got a new G-40 after every move. "Okay," Ant began, "get him the best lawyer we can get him. Put the word out it's $25,000 for whoever can tell me who's snitching on Nick."

SUGAR

Sugar rubbed her eyes, yawned and reached for the phone. "Hello."

"Bitch, where you been all morning? I have been trying to get in contact with you since 9:30am, I sent Ledell for you."

"What you mean you sent Ledell for me? What do you want, Warren?"

"It would be my business if I took that Altima back I brought you, huh?"

"I don't give a shit what you do, Warren. Don't keep harassing me."

"I didn't tell you to sleep with him."

Silence.

"Don't get quiet now and you better call Levell and tell him don't come to

DC BLOOD BROTHERS

my house 'cause I'm calling the police soon as I see his big head ass in my hallway."

"Look Sugar, I just want to know the dude name that stabbed me and Manny."

"Why? Are you going to break into DC jail and get Nick because that's where he's at, he got arrested last night."

"Oh really, now answer my first question, where you been all morning?"

"Since you keep asking, I'm going to give you what you want Warren. I was giving up this pussy that used to be yours. Second, for future reference, anytime you can't catch up to a girl until after 12 noon, she's probably just getting home from the hotel."

Warren almost broke the receiver slamming the phone in the cradle.

"What she say?" Manny asked holding the patch on the back of his neck where he received four stitches from Nick stabbing him.

"Said his name is Nick and he's in DC jail because he got arrested last night."

Warren rubbed his chin with two fingers as he thought. "Manny, your cousin Punch still in DC Jail? Tell him I said, I got $10,000 for him if he can get Nick hit up."

ANTHONY

Ant pulled into the car garage off 14th St. where Ortega was already waiting. "What's up, O?"

"Not much," Ortega answered as he handed Ant the pen.

Ant scribbled the amount he had. O looked to the paper and read 400,000 dollars. Ortega's eyebrows raised then he made a gesture as if he was chopping something in half, asking if Ant wanted half cocaine, half heroin.

Ant nodded yes, so Ortega sent his lieutenant off to fetch the drugs.

"I see things are picking up for you, Ant."

"Yeah," Ant agreed, "but I may have some serious problems coming."

"Like what?" Ortega asked concerned.

"We got into it with Warren last night."

Ant told Ortega everything that happened at the club. Ortega promised to handle the situation himself because of the size of Warren's team.

"Thanks O, I really appreciate it. I'm not trying to start a block war on the blocks I make my money."

"No problem Ant, I haven't forgot the things you've done for me, I consider us family."

Later that day, Ortega met with a 70 year old man named Preacher. Preacher opened his arms to embrace his nephew, kissing him on both sides of his cheeks.

"How are thing going for you these days?" Preacher asked Ortega in a thick Spanish accent.

"Hey Uncle, everything's going alright, I do need a favor though."

"What is it, Ortega?" His uncle asked out of deep concern. His Uncle Preacher was deep in the underworld, even the FBI knew him as Preacher or more properly by his real name, Francis Renaldi.

He had raised Ortega after finding out his little sister was a drug addict.

"Uncle, I need you to set up a meeting with the vets." Preacher's tall thin frame, soft shoed to his desk picking up the receiver and dialing.

ANTHONY

"Hi Baby!" Michelle greeted Ant as he walked in the door, spinning in a slow circle so he could see the Frederick of Hollywood silk short pajama set with matching pink furry skippers she had purchased earlier that day.

"Good morning, Eryka Badu," he teased about the scarf on her head as he kissed her on the forehead.

"Are you trying to be funny about this scarf on my head?" She adjusted it feeling a little self conscious.

"No, it was a compliment, I think Eryka Badu is sexy."

"Boy you smooth, just clean up shit like it ain't nothing."

"How's everything going at hair school?"

"Fine" She replied from the bathroom turning on the shower water for Ant. Anytime he spent a night away from her, she would throw him in the shower saying she didn't know what filth he's been with.

"I only need about sixty more hours to be a certified cosmetologist."

"Good, after that, I want you to take a small business course," he said as he stripped his clothes off.

"You hungry, baby?" She asked heading to the kitchen.

"Yeah, as a matter of fact I am."

"What do you want?"

"Your sexy ass to get up in this shower with me."

Michelle stripped and stepped inside the shower, grabbing her rag, squirting a little bath and body body wash on it. Staring at Ant as she rubbed the rag back and forth between her legs.

"Gimme a minute Baby," she said as she turned toward the shower head and rinsed off. Ant rubbed her butt, while kissing and biting the back of her neck. She spun around and put her left foot up on the side of the tub and whispered, "Breakfast is served".

ORTEGA

Ortega pulled into Haines Point. He saw two old men casually throwing bread to the ground feeding the birds. One short with balding grey hair and a slight runners build. The second was tall with a military style haircut.

The men looked harmless, and it made Ortega smile as he thought of the reputation of the men.

The shorter balding one stood to greet him shaking his hand. "How's the old man doing youngster?"

"Preacher's fine."

He leaned to Ortega's ear and asked "what is that a Glock 380 you got in your right pocket?"

Ortega smiled and nodded, taking a seat to the left of the first man on the bench. He spoke as they continued feeding the birds.

"How many is it?"

"Two." Ortega said.

"That will be $25,000 a piece." Ortega nodded.

"Who are they?"

"Warren and Manuel."

He looked Ortega eye to eye. The man took in a deep breath and exhaled slowly. Ortega looking towards the second man realized he hadn't said a word since he arrived. The old man shook his hand then turned away, sat back on the bench resumed feeding the birds.

Ortega looked around the park as he walked to his car. Pulling his remote control from his left pocket, he pressed a button causing the trunk to pop open. He quickly looked over both his shoulders before pulling fifteen stacks out of one bag and placing them into an empty one. He got the old man's attention before he dropped the bag in the trash can.

ANTHONY

"Where are we going, to City Place to the movies?"

"Nope." Ant answered then stared out the window.

Twenty-five minutes later he pulled in front of a three bedroom, two story house. Michelle followed Ant to the front door, where he rang the doorbell. Five minutes later, still no answer.

Michelle looked around the quiet neighborhood, there were leaves in the yards, very little if any traffic on the street, and kids playing happily nearby.

"Looks quiet around here, huh"? Ant asked breaking her thoughts.

"Yeah, it looks nice and quiet around here; I wouldn't mind living it up in the suburbs. Who are we visiting and why are we still here?"

Ant dug into his pocket and handed her three keys on a ring. She took the keys, staring at them.

"Go ahead and open the door."

Michelle swallowed hard and began unlocking the door. She pushed it open and stared into the empty living room. She followed Ant throughout the rest of the house.

"I just got it, you like it?"

"Like it, I love it Ant."

"Look 'Chelle, I got to step shit up and that means my face needs to be seen less. I brought this house yesterday for us. I don't want anyone to know where we live 'Chelle. Not your Mother. Nobody. You start that business management class next week, I'm already looking around for a space for a salon."

"I love you," she purred as she stood on her tip-toes to kiss him.

"I love you too sexy."

Several months passed, Michelle graduated her business classes and received a certificate. Ant finally found the perfect location for a hair salon. They were calling themselves the Robinson's and were becoming well liked after a few months in their neighborhood.

Ant relaxed more, staying away from all the hot spots. Jamal and Willie were pulling in more money than ever. No one came forward about who was going to testify on Nick, so Ant increased the bounty from $25,000 to $50,000 since Nick's trials was in a couple months.

Millie's cancer had gotten worse and you could evidently see the disease wearing away at her in her face and movements. Ant realized that she may not be alive too much longer and began bringing Michelle to their every other Sunday family gatherings. Three weeks after Ant formally introduced Michelle to the family, he proposed in front of his mother, brother and sister .in-law. There wasn't a woman at the dinner table with a dry eye after Michelle accepted Ant's proposal.

Manny, Warren's right hand man was found on Suitland Parkway slumped over his steering wheel. Warren was gunned down in a drive by. Nick had recently been rushed to DC General Hospital after being stabbed three times in the DC jail.

ANT'S CREW

"Fuck you Barry!" Petey yelled as he threw the joy stick to the Play Station on the sofa. He walked into the kitchen and grabbed a Heineken out of the fridge.

"You want a beer, Barry?"

"Yeah, bring me the one I left in the freezer."

JT, Barry's older cousin picked up the joy stick and restarted the John Madden football game.

Tap! Tap! Tap!

Petey walked to the window seeing the fiend stepping side to side as if he were dancing, or had to pee really bad. Petey opened the window.

"What's up?" The fiend handed him the balled up bills.

"Here we go with the bullshit," he said as he began counting. "What I tell you about tapping on the window? One of us going to be high as shit and pop your ass."

"Can I get a fifty for that?"

Petey thought about it, "yeah, but you got to run across the street for me and get three boxes of White Owls and a pack of Backwoods."

The fiend grabbed the money and returned with the cigars.

Tap! Tap!

JT opened the window taking the bag from the pipe head, then closed the

DC BLOOD BROTHERS

window.

Tap! Tap!

"What!" JT screamed as he opened the window.

"Petey suppose to give me a fifty block."

"Hold on!" He told the fiend closing the window again.

Petey opened the window, handing the man a block of crack cocaine.

"That Motherfucka play too much."

Petey laughed, "what the fuck you complaining for? You ain't going to do shit, we all seen that crack head bitch Sheila slap you up before."

"I let her do that since she my son's Mom. Back in the day, nobody would fuck with me. I was putting that work in."

Petey twisted his lips to the side, " Stop lying."

"Whatever youngin'. I done slumped two niggas before; one out NE around 21st and this dude in front of the 5&10."

Willie pulled out his cell phone and called Ant.

TOYA

Toya circled different court buildings until she finally found a parking space. Chirping her car alarm and waited until traffic broke to cross the street.

After walking past two telephone booths she made a left to walk into the Court Building, she saw Mrs. Daniels standing to the side talking to two men in slacks with badges around their necks. The woman looked at Toya, then quickly turned back to the officers.

Toya stepped into the building and took her place at the back of the line to pay her tickets. She turned her body slightly as she noticed her reflection on the wall and saw the man behind her staring at her butt.

"Hey Toya". She heard a female voice call out. She turned.

"What's up Karen, what you up here paying tickets off too?"

"No girl," she answered while she looked around.

"You ain't heard, somebody offered $50,000 for whoever can tell them who is going to testify against Nick."

Once she got into her car, she thought about who could be snitching. Her head fell to her steering wheel as a revelation came to her.

"Mrs. Daniels, she lives around 6th St., that's who telling on Nick."

ANTHONY

After receiving Willie's call, Ant went straight to Barry and Petey's apartment. Willie looked through the peep hole then opened the door.

"What you say they call him?"

He looked to Barry, Petey and JT. "Bring me that pipe head. What's his name

DC BLOOD BROTHERS

anyway?"

"I don't know, we just call him Bones."

Fifteen minutes later Barry ran in, "we got him out back."

Willie followed Ant outside as he approached the man, "Bones right?"

"Yeah, why what's up?"

"I want you to steal a car for me, dark color and I don't want you to shatter a fucking window. I'll give you a quarter of ready rock."

Bones' eyebrows raised, and his dry crooked lips formed a smile exposing his gums where teeth were missing.

"No prob, gimme fifteen."

He ran off up the hill and disappeared. Ant stood outside with his hand under his chin as if he was in deep thought.

Beep! Beep!

A Honda Accord pulled into the lot and Bones hopped out, waving both arms. Ant circled the car, "what's in the trunk?"

Bones reached in the glove box and hit the trunk button.

"What the fuck is this?" Ant yelled.

Bones quickly stepped to the back of the car hoping it was something he could steal and sell for crack.

"What is it?" He asked as he stuck his head into the trunk. He was completely taken by surprise as his little body was pushed into the trunk.

The three youths looked confused but they were smart enough not to question Ant's actions.

JASON

"Hello Gentlemen!" Agent Stevens of the FBI greeted the room of DC and PG County Detectives. Jason looked around the room nodding to fellow officers.

"Okay men, sitting before you should be a green folder, if you do not have one please raise your hand. Good. Before I begin I would like to introduce Agent Jackson from the ATF, he'll be working with us throughout this investigation."

"Hello Detectives, I'm Agent Jackson, I'll be the quiet guy lurking in the dark, seemingly peeking over your shoulders throughout this joint task force."

With a wave of the hand, Jackson left the center of the room and Agent Stevens reclaimed it.

"Now please open your folders gentlemen. On this first page, the face you see belongs to Cedric Thomson. Now if you turn two pages up you'll see Derrick Price. We were investigating these men almost 9 months before they were murdered on August 14, in separate jurisdictions. These men were heroin dealers with some serious ties to New York and Baltimore. Turn to the following page, the face you see here is Warren Beal. The face on the next page is Manuel Turner, his lieutenant. Both men were murdered about a month ago, once again in two separate places but on the same day.

DC BLOOD BROTHERS

"What I'm about to disclose to you as well as any other meeting is top secret. The FBI and AFT were investigating these four men. In fact, Warren sold to Cedric and his partner. We may have a connection here, maybe not, but I assure you, before this is all over we will have connected all the pieces to this puzzle. We'll meet again tomorrow; I know you all have you own cases. Good luck out there and be safe."

ANTHONY

Later that evening, a Honda Accord pulled slowly into the abandon area with its lights out. Willie and Jamal stood behind Ant as he opened the trunk.

"Get the Fuck Out!" Ant yelled through clenched teeth while grabbing Bones with his left hand and pointing a 357 snub nose with his right. The chilly night wind sent shivers through Bones' body as he was drug out of the trunk. His eyes were taking a few seconds to adjust as they darted over the three men.

"Look, ya'll are making a mistake man."

Ant just stared at Bones as he rambled on.

"I don't even know ya'll. Please, just let me..."

Crack!

Blood gushed from the corner of his right eye as he collapsed, grabbing his head. "Shut the fuck up," Ant whispered as he pointed the gun down at him. "Do you know what you took from me?"

Bones head shook in confusion, as the young face became more familiar. It was one of the two faces that always haunted him in his dreams. Suddenly he was picturing the juice man's body dropping to the ground after the first time he pulled the trigger. He knew he was about pay with his life as he watched tears fall from Ant's eyes.

"We got to hurry up, Dog" Jamal whispered hearing a few cars drive by on Maine St. Ant pulled the hammer back and stepped closer.

"Please don't kill me! I'm sorry man, come on, I..."

The noise echoed as the shot slammed his body to the ground hitting him almost in the middle of his hairline. His skull cracked as the bullet cut through his brains like a hot knife through butter while blowing out the back of his scalp causing it to resemble a peeled potato.

"Come on slim," Willie whispered in Ant's ear as he began pulling him to the car. Ant could barely hear Willie with the deafening constant ring now in his ears. Ant, took a deep breath and looked up toward a few stars, felt an adrenalin rush throughout his tall frame. Everyone remained silent as they drove him back to his car.

Four hours later, the policeman circled the body clicking his camera from all angles. A dark blue Crown Victoria with tinted pulled into the lot.

"What we got here, Ollie?"

Officer Mitch Green asked as he and Jason peered over his shoulder. "One

DC BLOOD BROTHERS

black male, age 35 to 40 years old, single shot to the head."

"Execution style?" Jason asked as he turned to the officer.

"Yep" The officer answered.

"Robbery?" Mitch asked.

"I don't think so, detective."

"Why you say that?"

"Check it out for yourself."

Jason and his partner kneeled to the body bag. Jason pulled the zipper then lifted the bag.

"Oh God!" Mitch said as his arm flew over his nose to block the stench. Jason did a 180 degree turn and threw up, then wiped his mouth.

"Something is definitely wrong with this picture Jenkins, this man is a crack head."

"Look at him. You mean to tell me someone took the risk of prison for life killing him."

"What do you think the motive is, Jenkins?" Officer Ollie asked.

"Maybe he stole something from the wrong person or saw something and somebody wanted to silence him."

"I don't know Jenkins, I'm gonna wait until we identify him and get some background on him before I try and guess."

The smell of the body overwhelmed the scene as the sun rose. Jason wondered when all the killings would stop. It seems as if every year the District of Columbia murders were becoming more senseless than the year before.

TOYA

"What took you so long to answer the door Toya?"

"Girl I just got up." Toya answered as she drug her feet into her kitchen. "You want some coffee?"

"Sure." Lisa yelled back into the kitchen as she sat on the sofa and picked up the Source magazine with Biggie Smalls on the front.

Toya took a deep breath. "I think I know who's going to testify against Nick."

"Who?"

"This lady Mrs. Daniels around 6th St., I saw her down the court building talking to a couple cops."

"Girl, you know you can get $50,000 for that."

"I know"

Toya dropped her head.

"What you feeling like that for Toya, if you don't come forward somebody else is going to get that money. I'll call. I'll get $80,000 out they ass."

Lisa pulled her cell phone from, her Coach bag and began dialing. "Hey Tiffany, what's up this is Lisa. I'm trying to get a message to Willie. Can you gimme Jamal's cell number? Okay, thank you."

She hung up and began to dial.

"Hello. Hey Boo, how you doing?"

"Who dis?"

"It's Lisa boy."

"Oh, what's up fly-girl?"

"About the fifty large for name of who's snitching on Nick. I can tell you who it is but it's going to cost thirty more."

"Yeah!" Jamal, said excitedly. "Meet me out White Corners out SE, I don't want to talk over the phone?"

"I'm on my way, click."

"I'll be back in a couple hours, Toya. Be ready cause we going out by Pentagon Mall for Gucci when I get back."

chapter 22

Nearly a month had passed and Mitch was still frustrated over the Ramsey case. He placed his elbows on his desk and held his face with the palms of his hands.

"What's the problem, Mitch?" Jason asked.

"It's this Benny Ramsey murder. In and out of DC Jail on minor theft charges, spent five years in Occoquan for robbery. I mean, Ramsey grew up and spent most of his life according to his sister on Kennedy St. How the hell did he wind up murdered?"

"I know what you mean Mitch, I've been thinking for the past couple of weeks how over the years, murders are seemingly more senseless. And it's weird that the more senseless the crime the harder it is for it to be solved. At least tomorrow we'll get some justice from the Drake trial, there's no way a jury will hear Mrs. Daniels testimony and give him anything less than twenty."

Ring!

Jason reached for the phone. Robbery-Homicide Detective Jenkins speaking.

"I'm going to my Mother's house for the weekend."

Jason covered the receiver with his hand as he hissed into the phone.

"Shana, why are you doing this?"

"I'm tired of arguing and complaining Jason. You barely acknowledge me and Jr.'s existence. All you do is come in here eat, sleep, shit, shave, and then you're gone again. I understand you're a detective with a demanding job but you should love your family enough to demand some time for us Jason."

Jason could hear Shana getting choked up.

"Let's talk about this when I get home, Shana."

"No Jason, I'm tired of talking. And this house hasn't felt like home in a long time."

Click!

DEBRA DANIEL'S RESIDENCE

The family enjoyed their pizza dinner, showered and retired for the evening. Mrs. Daniels wrapped a pink towel around her body as she stepped out of the shower, grabbed her Victoria Secret Apricot lotion then sat on the edge of her bed.

"You nervous?" Her husband asked. Startled, she jumped, putting her hand to her heart.

"Oh God, you scared me," I thought you were sleep.

"I couldn't get any rest until I knew you were alright with tomorrow."

Her head dropped. "Baby I'm nervous as hell, but I have to do this. Do you think I'm doing the right thing?"

"Yes, I do, but if it's bothering you, or you change your mind, you have my total support."

"Thank you, but I feel I have to follow through. I can't let that boy get away with what he did. Every time I close my eyes I see that boy standing over Chris. Just hold me for a little while."

She lay with her husband, staring at the wall and curtains until her husband began to lightly snore in her ear. She smiled, thinking about how much she loved him.

A little after four in the morning, a black tinted Caprice pulled into a tight parking space in between 7th and 6 St. Black pulled his mask down over his face. JT cocked the 12 gauge in the back seat and pulled his mask down. Ant looked to the driver. "Mal, start the car as soon as you see one of us coming out the building."

The three masked men got out of the car, sprinted to the second building on the right and went in. Going up the stairs and stopping at the first door to their left. Ant looked to JT and shook his head towards the door.

JT kicked the door in after shooting off the locks. Ant and Black ran into the Living Room. Mrs. Daniels clung to her husband as they both woke up after hearing the shot. Their eyes were wide with fright as their bedroom door opened. The masked man walked in.

Ant pointed the Desert Eagle 44 at Mr. Daniels. Blood sprayed over Debra's face as her husband's body flew back to the headboard. Ant looked at the wife, hating what he had to do, but Nick was family and family came first. She never felt a thing as her body fell over the side of the bed.

The two shot gun blasts were heard down the hall. Ant ran into the second bedroom. His mouth fell open as he watched the smoke rise from the two small bloody bodies.

DC BLOOD BROTHERS

"Come on, man we got to go" Black ran into the room and whispered.

The three raced out of the building and jumped in the car. Ant snatched his mask off. "Black, what the fuck were you thinking?"

Black's face turned right as Ant backhanded him.

"What's going on?" Jamal asked, seeing there was a problem.

"This stupid muthafucka just killed two kids." Ant screamed.

"I didn't know, Mal. I swear. When I opened the door, somebody was coming at me and I just panicked."

"It's ah-ight Black and I'm sorry for slapping you." Ant whispered as he realized that under the circumstances, he would've done the same thing. "Look, don't anybody in this car ever discuss this, not even between us. Mal you take care of the guns."

JASON

"Hello. What! I'll be there in twenty minutes."

Reaching for the slacks and shirt he'd warn the previous day, Jason got dressed then brushed his teeth and raced to his car. The sidewalk was packed as he pushed his way through holding his badge in plain view. A forensic team was dusting the glass at the entrance door and stair rails for finger prints.

Jason stepped into the apartment.

"Is it bad, Mitch?"

"The worst... they didn't have to kill those kids."

Mitch's body shook uncontrollably as a female officer consoled him and escorted him outside. Jason walked to the bedroom, seeing Mr. Daniels' face staring at him with a dime sized hole in his forehead.

It was evident that the back of his head was blown out from all the blood on the headboard and wall. He took a few more steps into the room, looking over the side of the bed to see Mrs. Daniels eyes wide open as if they had seen a ghost. Her neck was obviously broken the way it was bent, and by how most of her body's weight was still supported by it. Stepping out of the bedroom, he turned to the right to seeing blood was everywhere. Jason covered his mouth to hold down the bile that was clinging to his throat. Jason was looking from left to right at the two small bodies that lay slumped before him. Their faces were mangled as if they were motorcyclists in a terrible accident. They barely looked human. His left arm reached for wall support as he hurried out of the room, making a silent prayer for the Daniels family, swearing he would bring their killers to justice.

ANTHONY

Ant opened his front door then staggered to the sofa clutching a liter of Hennessey, swallowing so much liquor he was about to throw up. He never regretted shit before but the children Black killed were weighing heavy on his heart.

"Hi Baby" Michelle greeted him as she came down the stairs. Ant stared at the chimney as if she weren't there.

"Do you want to talk about it?"

He shook his head no, and put the bottle up to his lips. Half the liquor was going into his mouth, the rest was spilling on his $300 Iceberg sweater.

Michele got up to get prepared for her day. It was six in the morning and she had a meeting at First National Bank for a small business loan to open her hair shop. By the time she finished showering, grooming, and came downstairs to leave, Ant was passed out on the sofa.

Four hours later, Michelle shook Ant to wake him.

"What's up 'Chelle?"

"We got the loan Baby!" She screamed excited.

He threw up his hands and grabbed his forehead in pain.

"Oh, I'm sorry, I already knew you were going to have a hangover so I brought you coffee from 7-Eleven."

A few hours later, Jamal pulled into the small lot in his brand new Tahoe, all grey, fully loaded. "What's up dog?" He greeted Ant as he opened the door. "Did you talk to Nick's lawyer, Mal?"

"Yeah, they should be letting him go by the end of the week."

Ant looked to the bag Mal brought in with him and told him to start counting. He reclined in the luxury vehicle, trying to put the events of the night before behind him. Suddenly a phone rang and both men reached for their cells.

Jamal answered. "Hello!"

"Hey Mal." The woman's voice was very familiar.

"What's up shorty?"

"Ain't too much, I just.. Shit, I haven't seen you in a long time. I was hoping I could see you later."

"I'll see you later on."

"Who is that Mal?" Ant asked just making conversation after Jamal hung up.

"Huh, oh just some little freak I met a few weeks ago."

Ant looked back to the news trying to see the score of the Wizards and New Jersey game.

"I got $275,000."

"Damn Mal, you stepping your shit up."

"You know." Jamal said as he pulled at his shirt, trying his best to look modest.

"When Nick gets out I want you to give him what you just counted. Explain to him that he got to disappear; the feds are going to be all over him. Tell him I wasn't going to let him go down like that. Tell him don't contact any of us under any circumstance. Get a hundred thou out the safe and pay the lawyer too."

Jamal walked out the bedroom, wondering how his night might turn out.

Chapter 23

"Ladies and Gentlemen please take your seats," Agent Stevens stepped to the center of the room. The room buzzed with conversation until all the officers were seated. Jason sipped his coffee as he dug his case folder from his briefcase.

"Detectives, I'm sure you've all heard of the horrible murders of the Daniels family. Mrs. Debra Daniels was due to testify on a Nicholas Drake. She witnessed him kill a small time drug dealer named Chris Wright, roughly last year. Strangely enough, she, her husband and two sons aged 9 and 10 were gunned down the night before she made it to court. We've already questioned Drake and he's standing firm on his act.

And I'm sad to say that he will be released from DC Jail within the next few hours. We'll have light surveillance on him but we have to keep our distance until we get something on him. There's no doubt that whoever Drake is connected to killed this family to get him off. I assure you that they won't get away with this.

Sorry to have called this emergency meeting today but I need ya'll to knock on a few doors, rough up a few thugs, get in contacts with your informants, whatever you have to do to solve this case, do it. Now get out of here and be safe out there."

"You going to Yums carry out with me for lunch, Mitch?"

"Naw, I got a date with the department psych."

"For what?"

"I guess since I freaked out at the Daniels scene."

"So did I."

"But you didn't have to be escorted off the scene Jason. I usually don't lose it, that's your department Jenkins. But when I saw those kids something just overwhelmed me. I mean every since we became Detectives, all I wanted to do was solve the case and bring in the bad guy. But, Last night, I wish I knew who was so cold and callus that he could do that, just so I could kill him.

Jason squeezed his partner's shoulder.

"You'll be alright Mitch. Honestly, I had the same feeling. Just like when a fellow officer gets killed. You know there's a 9 out of 10 chance the killer will never see a judge."

"That's just it Jenkins, how can police get away with it, but as soon as we lock up some black kid for getting revenge, we throw the book at him."

"Easy Mitch. Just know, we're all hypocrites living in a hypocritical society, we're human."

MICHELLE

Michelle had her biggest smile ever as she cut the giant pink ribbon on the front of her new beauty salon Le-Neuvo. The audience, a few employees and the shops first customers clapped. Ant stood by her side in a black suit.

"Welcome to Le Neuvo she screamed! We have tea and cookies inside, thank you all for coming."

"I can't believe this." She confessed to Ant once they were alone in her office.

"You better believe it after all the money you made me spend to lay this joint out."

She slapped at him playfully, knowing he was right.

The shop was two stories; on the bottom level was a small nursery for customers who had children, the following room was a waiting room, containing three small brown sofas two wide screen televisions, one connected to a play station, there was every magazine from Vogue to Essence, a small pool table and a male and female bathroom. Up the stairs was a hostess with the schedule book or walk in chart, there's a small vestibule and a door to walk through before the actual salon. The salon was in a U-shape, five state of the art chairs with a black sink in between them opposite on each side. Eight dryers at the end in the middle. The wall paint and color scheme for the entire shop was Lavender and white. Michelle took a seat behind the small desk in her office, caressing the wood with her finger tips, smiling ear to ear.

JASON

"Good morning Jenkins!"

"Good morning Mitch, I see you already had your coffee this morning."

"You look a little better yourself lately." Jason just looked at his partner knowing he was referring to Shana coming back home.

"Real funny Mitch".

"No, seriously Jenkins, admit it, you were falling apart without her."

"You're right, Mitch." Jason confessed as he flopped down on his old cushion chair. "Jr.'s getting bigger everyday; he'll be my mom's height soon."

"How's your Mom doing anyway, I haven't seen her since the Policeman's ball last year?"

"She's doing a little bit better, she's just getting older so I'm noticing her slowing down."

Mitch put on his reading glasses and leaned back into his chair opening a folder. "What's that?"

"The Ramsey file."

"God Mitch your obsessed."

"I don't know what it is Jenkins but something won't let me leave this alone."

"I just think we need to concentrate more on the Daniels case."

"Hold up Jenkins, what are you saying, that because Ramsey was a drug addict and a felon, he's not important enough for us to handle his case with priority!" Mitch screamed as his hands slammed against the desk, drawing the room's attention as he stormed out of the office.

ANTHONY

Ant saw Jamal's truck as he parked his new Jaguar. "I'm thinking about taking everybody to Florida."

"Sounds good, I want to..."

"Hold up slim," Ant cut him off. "I need you here to run shit, you can go when we get back."

Jamal thought about it, and liked the idea that he would be running shit. Ant fingered through the brochures 'Chelle gave him from the travel agent.

"Don't tell nobody about the Florida trip. 'Chelle's family is having a little reunion next weekend out South Carolina, after that I'll tell everybody to get ready. We're going to be in Florida for a couple weeks so I want you to calculate how much you'll need then add ten to each, I don't want you running out while I'm gone."

"Ah-ight big-man whatever you say."

"You want to go shopping out Tyson's Corner Mal?"

"Yeah, I got a taste for them Ruby Tuesday's Buffalo wings."

"You got a taste for anything Mal."

One Month later..

After a ten hour ride Ant and 'Chelle finally made it to Columbia South

DC BLOOD BROTHERS

Carolina.

"Michelle!" Her Great Aunt Annie Mae screamed before pushing the screen door open and snatched Michelle off her feet hugging her.

"Child, you done got so big and pretty, and who is this handsome man?"

"Hi, I'm Ant." He said then extended his hand

"Boy you better give me a hug." Annie Mae pulled him into her arms. "Yawl come on in here, where's your suitcases?"

"We're going to stay at a hotel, Auntie."

"Oh Okay, ya'll hungry?"

"Yes," Ant spoke up, "if I taste one more piece of Bojangle's Chicken I'll go nuts."

"I'll fix ya'll something then ya'll come on in and get settled."

The two days they spent before the family reunion was relaxing for Ant. He'd turned off his cell phone and pager since they'd left DC. Everyone was so friendly it was almost sickening to him at first. But the South grew on him quickly..

Michelle picked up the receiver and began dialing.

"Hello, Le Neuvo."

"How's everything at the shop, Candy?"

"Everything is just fine, Michelle."

"Okay, call me if ya'll need me."

"What are you looking at, Ant?"

Ant smiled as Michelle stared at him awaiting his answer.

"Not easy is it?" He asked her.

"What?" She threw her hands in the air, not understanding his question.

"Being the person running something, making the decisions."

"Yeah, it gets a little hectic sometimes, but the fulfillment seems worth it."

"Oh yeah." Ant moaned as he grabbed her and began kissing her face.

"Come on Baby, we have to get ready for my family reunion."

"I can't get a quickie, 'Chelle?"

"Boy, I done spoiled you," she lifted her skirt and shimmied her red thong to her knees and bent over the bed. Ant unzipped and unbuckled his pants, dropping his pants to his ankles. Grabbing his half stiff manhood and rubbed it between Michelle's legs.

"Damn Girl, you already soaking wet."

"You know this pussy stay wet" She said as she looked over her shoulder.

The back of her head jerked to her back as he eased inside of her. She met his thrust wiggling her hips as she began rubbing her clit and contracting her walls to grip him as he slid in and out of her.

"Yeah, throw it back Baby." He grabbed her hair and wrapped it around his fist. She screamed as he smacked her ass. Sweat covered their bodies as their skin loudly smacked together.

"Yes, I'm coming Baby, Oh!" Michelle screamed as her body seemed to transcend from the flesh, wave after wave crashing through her body. Ant started pumping harder as she squeezed him.

DC BLOOD BROTHERS

She jumped off of him and reached back jerking him off hard, making his cum shoot everywhere. "Let me clean this off for you," she whispered as she took him into her mouth, sucking on him softly draining him.

"Girl, you are too fucking good in bed."

"Nigga, you trained me to please you, don't even try it. Ant look," she pointed to the white fluid on her skirt. "Great now I got to change outfits."

Two hours later, Ant and Michelle enjoyed the quiet ride to Dillard, SC to her cousin Glinda's house. Glinda's oldest son Duan was deejaying.

"Ant, these are my cousins, Carlos, David, Boe and Face." Michelle introduced Ant to the men.

"Look at you 'Chelle!" Face screamed. "Those shoes alone $350." He pointed down to her Donna Karen heels.

"How you know," Michelle put her hands on her hips, "you shopping for women shoes these days?"

"My girl wanted me to get her them same shoes but I'll be damned if I'm going to pay that."

Everyone enjoyed themselves over the grilled foods, cold salads, and ice cold beer. "I'll be right back Baby, that's my cousin Genevive that does hair. She is moving to DC."

Ant nodded as Michelle excused herself to talk to the rest of her family.

"Ant, walk with us, we just going to see a few friends around the corner. I like that sweat suit you got on too Ant." Michelle's cousin Boe complimented.

"Who's that by?" Boe asked.

"It's Coogi."

Ant while silently in the background as they went three houses down. Two brand new Cadillac DeVille's on Vogue's sat in front of the house.

"Yo!" Carlos screamed. A few seconds later the screen door squeaked as it opened. A pretty dark skinned woman with the thickest prettiest legs Ant ever saw opened the door. Sucking her teeth then rolling her eyes as she twisted her neck, finally she crossed her arms. "What do ya'll fools want?"

"Where Punch at?"

"He ain't here."

"Stop lying Tosha, I just saw him drive up the street."

"Who is that, Tosha?" They heard a man yell from the house before a 6'4" frame darkened the doorway. "Come on in y'all follow me out back." They followed Punch to the back of the house.

"What's up, Niggas?" Punch greeted his guest as they stepped out on to his patio.

"Punch, why you ain't come up to my Momma's house to the family reunion?"

"Man, I'm still waiting on my connect to call, you know what I'm talking about?"

Ant looked around. Punch was obviously a hustler, not doing too bad for himself either. Ant had already pegged Carlos and Boe for hustlers too.

DC BLOOD BROTHERS

"Who dat?" Punch asked nodding his head in Ant's direction.

"Oh, this here is my cousin 'Chelle fiancé. Ant, he from D.C."

"The District, I got an Uncle out there, he says it's crazy."

Ant nodded.

"So you ain't ready for me yet?"

"No Carlos," Punch answered. "But as soon as my folks get at me, I'll holler."

"Just hold on to that twenty-eight hundred and I'll look out, know what I'm talking about."

They began walking back to Glinda's house.

"Carlos!"

"What's up, Ant?"

"Let me holla at you for a minute."

They walked to Ant's Lexus SC. Carlos smirking as he rubbed the leather through the open window. "This nice Dawg, I'm trying to get one of these by next summer."

"What kind of work you do anyway?"

Ant looked to him. "Look Los, I ain't trying to get in your business but it's evident you a hustler. Even if you was trying to be discreet, that dude up the street put your business out there."

Carlos nodded. "Yeah, I get my grind on."

"If you don't mind me asking Los, what were you going to cop from him?"

"Two ounces."

"What! Ha Ha," Ant bent over the steering wheel from laughing so hard. "Look slim, I got a proposition for you. I'll sell you ounces for seven hundred a piece."

"No bulllshit dawg!"

"I ain't finished Los, I know this is kind of far from DC so I'll have somebody meet you half way when you need to re-up.

"Thanks Dawg, Carlos shook Ant's hand."

"I'm telling you now Los, don't ever discuss me with nobody, no family, best friend, no one. I don't give a fuck if it's a Catholic Priest at your confession. If I find out you mentioned me to anyone out here, I'll kill you."

JASON

Mitch ducked under the yellow tape and stepped behind Jason. Putting his hand on Jason's shoulder. "I heard over the radio, Jenkins I know it's my off day but I had to check it out."

There was a shooting; two teenagers were killed, one innocent bystander, and one nine year old girl who was jumping rope when the shots went off, she was shot in the chest. They rushed her to Children's Hospital.

"Any witnesses Jenkins?"

"Those kids on the front of that building say some teenager came up the parking lot, began shooting towards the teenagers he killed, then ran back towards 14th St.

DC BLOOD BROTHERS

They say he's a black male, light skinned, had waves in his hair, looked 13 to 16, wearing a black jogging suit and a pair of grey New Balance tennis shoes."

Two ambulances turned on their sirens to get through the busy 14th St. traffic, rushing the injured victims to a nearby hospital.

"Any word on the little girl?" Jenkins asked an officer.

"Sorry sir, she didn't make it."

"Come on, Jenkins. Let's circle some blocks and see if we can catch this bastard."

Every corner the Crown Victoria turned, drug dealers stared at the car wondering if they should run.

"Look Mitch, up there." Jason pointed seeing a young man with a black hoodie over his head who also had on grey sneakers.

Mitch stomped on the gas, as Jason drew his 9mm. Jason jumped out of the car, gun drawn. A snickers candy bar dropped from the young man's left hand as he saw the gun while his right hand pulled a small child behind him to protect the little boy.

"Sorry, sorry." Jason apologized getting back into the unmarked car.

It all happened so fast, the hoodie, the candy bar, then Jason noticed the man had on acid washed jeans and was walking a child. He put his gun back in his holster and his face in his hands. Ahhhh! He screamed, feeling as if the walls were closing in on him.

"Jenkins, calm down, we'll get him."

"I can't believe it Mitch, I mean, it's like these murders are getting crazy. Now we're looking for some teenager who just threw his whole life away."

Ring!

Jason answered his phone. "Okay, thank you." Click.

"Turn around Mitch, we got a girl who says she knew the two boys and a couple of people who would definitely want to do them harm. I guess we'll get the bad guy after all."

Ten minutes later, Jason's hand was cramping on him from scribbling in his little pad. "Okay Timeka, let me repeat this stuff to see if I have it all correct. You were Joey's girlfriend?"

"Yes," she whispered as she wiped tears from her eyes.

"Joey and Lamor were both selling drugs?" She nodded yes.

"And they had got into a fight with a boy named Wayne from 13th and Fairmont. And you heard them talk about robbing some guy named Bobby from Spring Rd.?"

The seventeen year old girl nodded again.

"Can we finish this some other time, can't you see my daughter's distraught?" Timeka's mother asked the detectives.

"Yes Ma'am, well, here's my card. Please call if you can think of anything else."

They began walking to their car.

"Oh! One more thing Timeka," Jason jogged back to the building.

"Is Bobby or Wayne light skinned with waves in his hair?"
"Yes, Wayne is the light skinned one with the waves."

JAMAL

"Slow down Willie, you know the feds be playing down here real tough."
"Chill out Mal, I got this."
"Thank you Willie, that comedy show was the shit."
"You welcome Dana".
Jamal rubbed the woman's thighs sitting beside him. "How you like the show Tammy?"
"It was the bomb Boo, Tommy Davidson was crazy and funny as ever."
"You don't look like you enjoyed yourself."
"I'm sorry Jamal, I just feel down. I think I'm fighting a cold or something."
"Willie, take me to my truck. And can you drop off Tammy for me, I got to go get this money?"
"No problem, Mal." Damn I hate when this nigga act like I'm his flunky. I bring in twice as much as this nigga. Ant, never treated me like this, Willie thought as he felt Dana's hand slowly rubbing his crotch.
Willie smiled, looking in his rearview mirror, there was no traffic behind him, and Jamal was looking out the window in deep thought. Tammy's eyes were locked on the rearview mirror looking at Willie. Fifteen minutes later, Willie pulled beside Jamal's new Infinity truck.

LISA

Lisa leaned up to see who was pulling up behind her. That ain't Mal's truck, she thought until she saw his 310 pound frame stepping out of the truck. She got out of her car.
"When did you get this new truck?"
"Earlier today, I saw some bamma uptown with a tahoe that looked exactly like mine."
"You are terrible Mal." She laughed and followed him up the stairs to his townhouse. "Where you been anyway, dressed to kill?"
"I had a little business to take care of."
"Um hummm, tell me anything."
After eating they sipped on Malibu and Orange Juice, smoked a joint of weed as they sat on the sofa waiting for BET Uncut to come on. Lisa looked towards Jamal every few seconds in thought. Damn I hope this nigga don't trip on me, I never asked him for more than a Grand. Shit, he buying Infinity trucks and shit. I can get six and seven hundred a week from one of them young hustlaz.

DC BLOOD BROTHERS

Ring!

Jamal felt around the sofa for his phone. Once he found it, Ant was on the other end letting him know he was on his way back in town. Jamal told Ant that the money was counted and ready to be picked up.

"You look tired Baby, let's go upstairs". Lisa suggested.

She helped Jamal take off all his clothes then excused herself.

The hot water relaxed Lisa as she washed her every crease and crevasse with Victoria Secret body wash. Looking down inspecting her body as she rinsed off the soap. She stepped out, patted herself dry and lotion her body. Making a mental note to get a bikini wax. Then walked back to the bedroom, opening the door and grabbed her overnight bag. Which she always keeps in her trunk. It had a new pair of thongs, a box of Lifestyle and Magnum condoms, toothbrush, toothpaste, lotion, deodorant, and just in case she needed, a small container of mace. But tonight she put what she liked to refer to as one of her costumes in it.

After putting on her cherry flavored lip gloss, she stepped into the bottom of her outfit, pulled her breast through the openings and tied the leather strings behind her neck. Jamal took a long pull of his joint, exhaled and closed his eyes. Still smelling the faint smell of Lisa's perfume in the air. The bathroom door swung open and his mouth fell to the floor.

"Oh my God" He quietly mumbled as she stood before him in an all leather sexy outfit, made like a bikini but there was a zipper at her crotch, her breast stood firm through two openings, and her belly chain shimmered as light hit it.

"You like it?" She whispered as she did a 360 degree turn revealing the thong and open back. She walked to the side of the bed and began to climb on top of Jamal and began kissing him. Jamal broke out in a light sweat and panted as he squeezed her large firm backside. She sucked from his ears to his neck, licked down his three rolled stomach and began sucking his manhood. "I want you to fuck me, Mal," she got up and straddled him, rode him slowly at first, and then rocking back and forth. "Whose pussy is this, Mal?"

He whispered "Lisa's."

"No baby, this is your pussy, Mal."

"Tell me Mal, whose pussy is this?"

"This my pussy."

She hopped off of him, snatched off the condom then straddled him. "Oh shit! Jamal moaned as the hot, moist walls of Lisa's vagina clamped down on him. "Yes!" She screamed as she rode him harder. Jamal felt his balls tighten. Their bodies slapped together loudly then silence. Jamal's head fell back on his pillow with a slight smirk. Lisa looked to him, got him, she thought.

Chapter 24

Weeks later, Michelle was out preparing for her trip to Miami. She decided she should call Ant to find out how long they would be gone so she didn't spend too much.

"Two weeks."

"Okay, I'll see you at home later. My cousin Carlos asked me for your number, can he have it?"

"Yeah, I've been waiting for him to call."

Ant took an inventory of his surroundings on the busy Georgetown Streets then walked to the parking lot and got in his cherry red Acura NSX with black interior and red piped seats.

An hour later, after switching cars, now in his Jag he pulled into the small parking lot of the apartment in Oxon Hill. Getting out he looked down the hill and saw two Prince George's County Police cars go into Riverview Terrace. Two more police cars now drove slowly up the narrow hill. Probably on the way to Colonial Village he thought, stepping into the building. Noticing the scrapes around the locks, he knocked.

Tap! Tap!

"What's up dawg?" Petey greeted as he opened the door.

"Looks like somebody tried to break in" Willie said before Ant got a chance to inquire. "Not surprised, I mean, we drive expensive cars, dress good, the dudes in the neighborhood know we don't spend the night, they think it's a stash house."

DC BLOOD BROTHERS

"What you want to do about it big-man?" Jamal asked, then shoved most of a slice of meat lovers' pizza into his mouth.

"Just make sure ain't nothing over fifty G's in here."

Ant looked around the room, "who wants to go with me to Miami?"

Everyone raised their hands. Jamal burst out laughing. "You motherfuckaz look like ya'll in a classroom some fucking where."

Ant flipped open his cellular, called his travel agent and ordered seven more first class tickets. Noticing the time, he told his boys to get there shit together for the trip. He left the apartment and drove across town to meet with Ortega.

"I can watch your car and make sure nothing happens to it."

Ant felt the money in his pocket and handed the hundred dollar bill to the boy.

"Thanks Yo, I got you."

"Better not let anything happen to my shit either."

There was a fairly long line waiting to get into Bennigan's. Ant grabbed his phone off his waist.

"What name is your table under"

"Simmons, I told them I was waiting for one more guest."

After making his way through the crowd, the host showed him to the table. Ortega stood to greet him, "what's up Ant?"

"Hey, who are your friends though?"

Ortega began introducing his company clockwise, "This is Shicola, Yaneek, Trace, Lacrecia, and Terri."

"Hi" The women greeted with welcoming smiles, they were beautiful.

"So, you finally taking my advice and going to Florida huh?"

"Yeah, I think I can use a break."

Ortega began scrolling through his cell phone then writing on a tablet and handed it across the table.

"What's this?"

"The top number is this Haitian dude Marky. If you need anything, mention my name and he'll take care of you. I already told him to look out for you. And the second number is Shawn, she's this sexy chocolate sister I met my last visit. She's worth every penny and she got plenty of buddies."

Ant nodded and stuck the numbers in his pocket.

"Let me see your pen" Ant began scribbling.

Ortega took the paper, read it and looked at Ant. His order was almost 3 million dollars worth of product. He smiled, shaking his head as if saying no and raised his glass of Chianti.. "Here's to a wonderful life."

JASON

"Be seated Gentlemen." Agent Stevens looked as if he were going more bald every day. The short white man paced the floor as he waited for the room to quiet down.

"Good afternoon gentlemen, I hope all of you are still working diligently. I know we haven't been able to solve any of the cases yet, but we can't give up. Does anyone have any new leads concerning any of these cases?"

Everyone looked around the room.

"Okay, ah, you all know Nicolas Drake was released from DC Jail. Unfortunately, we lost surveillance within the first hour of his release. We expected for someone to pick him up. We never expected him to catch a bus then use the subway; we lost him in Metro Center. We just missed him at his baby's mama's house in SE. We haven't been able to locate him since."

Ring! Ring!

All the detectives felt for their cell phones. "Detective Jenkins Jason answered. "Alright, I'm on my way."

Jason was the first to walk into the small interrogation room.

"Wayne Hamilton?"

This skinny boy looked up. "Yes," and tears began filling his eyes.

"You did it didn't you?" The boy just stared, his face tightening as he fought to stop crying and regain some pride.

"Why did you do it?"

"I didn't do it."

"You don't want to admit to it fine, but I want you to know I'm about to take a picture of you to everybody on Fairmont St. As soon as I get a positive ID on you, I'm booking you for murder with no bond so have it your way."

Jason walked to the door and opened it.

"Officer Wright, come here. Put my little friend here in a holding cell."

"Did he confess?"

"Nope, he denies it, in fact and I hope he's telling the truth because if he killed that little girl. As young and pretty as he is, Lorton will tear him apart.

Two hours later

After knocking on neighbors doors and asking witnesses if they recognized Wayne, it was a resounding yes. He was charged with one count of first degree murder, one count of second degree murder and assault with a deadly weapon then sent to DC Jail.

"He still wouldn't talk. Can you believe that little boy just killed four people?"

Mitch looked up to Jason. "Jenkins nothing surprises me with this job anymore."

VACATION

The roar of the plane's engines made a slight hum as the passengers were instructed to put on their seat belts.

After downing at least nine double shots of vodka, Ant leaned his seat back and passed out. Michelle looked to him; he was so quiet, so innocent. She smiled, knowing he was doggish just like most men. There were plenty of nights he didn't come home and called with his famous line, "I'm about to get into something". But, she loved him for the way he looked at her and how he treated her like a queen. She leaned her chair back and closed her eyes.

A few hours later a female voice came over the loud speaker and announced that the plane would be landing at Miami International Airport in five minutes. Ant lifted his chair then wiped the cold out of his eyes. Looking at the Presidential Rolex on his left wrist he saw that the time was 1:50pm.

"You okay, Baby?"

"Yeah 'Chelle," he lied, swallowing hard as he looked out of the window seeing that the plane appeared to be dropping out of the clouds. Before he realized it, the 747 was on the ground and braking.

The plane parked in the terminal, 10 minutes later they were exiting. The buzz of conversation was getting louder as they stepped into the airport. The party of nine walked to baggage claim. Ant put both hands into his tan linen slacks as he surveyed the airport, wondering how many people were smuggling things or who looked like they were major players. It was hard to distinguish because everyone had that I'm somebody style.

Michelle grabbed her two Louis Vuitton trunks and was looking for the Samsonite bag. She spotted it and struggled to pull it off of the carousel.

"Excuse me Miss," a man said.

Ant turned to Michelle and his world began moving in slow motion. His anger rose as he watched the two men in suits step behind her. She reached for the Samsonite, which they had spent a better part of the morning shoving $300,000 into. The man grabbed her wrist. The noisy airport seemed to grow silent as Ant charged the man, pushing him into the second one. People in the vicinity noticed and began stepping away.

"Baby, what are you doing?" Michelle screamed. "He was just helping me pull the bag off, he'd seen me struggling."

"What's your problem buddy?"

The man who was helping her asked as he pulled out a wallet, showing his airport security badge. He swallowed his words as the seven tight faced men who appeared behind the couple, looking like pit bulls ready to attack.

"Sorry sir, but this is my brother and he's very protective" Michelle explained.

"Okay, I'm going to let you slide for that, enjoy you stay in Miami." The two men walked off.

The afternoon sun momentarily blinded them as they stepped out of Miami International Airport.

"Champ, what we going to catch cabs?"

"Yeah" Ant answered Willie, there up here.

They walked past people shoving their luggage into cars, trucks, and some into cabs. Couples embraced and kissed. They walked by two men in black suits holding up signs that read "Montgomery" in front of two white stretch limousines.

Ant stepped towards them, "I'm Mr. Montgomery." Michelle's mouth fell open as she smiled.

"This is me and 'Chelle's. Ya'll take the other one."

The chauffeur opened the doors and the cool air from the limo hit Michelle in the face as she stepped into the limo. She began looking from left to right, clapping and bouncing in her seat like a little child.

"Baby, this is nice."

"You like it 'Chelle?"

"Do I? Look." She pointed to a panel of buttons, pressing one causing the track lights to come on. Hitting another button, the partition came down and they could see the driver.

"Thank you for rescuing me back there Mr. Montgomery," she teased.

"Real funny 'Chelle, but you know I wouldn't let nothing happen to you."

She kissed his lips, then leaned back into the seat.

"You know, I always had a secret fantasy of making love in one of these."

"Oh yeah," Ant moaned as he climbed on top of her. Twenty five minutes later, the limo's made a right and came to an abrupt stop. Both of them raced to put their clothes on after they felt the car was no longer moving. Oh! She screamed covering her breast as the driver opened the door. He apologized, quickly closed the door.

"Oh my God! Ant that was too funny."

Ant spoke to the drivers, tipped them and the cars pulled off.

"Look" Ant began speaking, "We're out here to have fun. The first one of you niggas starts some shit or get in trouble, you going home. And, if your ass gets locked up, don't have your folks call me. Now, Willie, Black, Sam, East, and Tony, ya'll can get any car you want. Barry and Petey, ya'll can't get any sports cars. "

They walked through the A1A showroom floor like children in Toys "R" Us. East walked to the red V-12 Mercedes and opened the door yelling "this is me!"

Tony pointed out a black and chrome H1 Hummer. Barry and Petey chose a grey and gold SL600 Benz. Black chose a Porsche 911 turbo in electric blue. Sam decided on a convertible S430 Mercedes in black with 19" rims. Willie picked a white Bentley Azure. Ant and Michelle were torn between both a red Ferrari and a yellow Lamborghini but decided on the latter.

The convoy of eight followed each other down Highway A1A into South Beach. Michelle loved the powerful engine as every head turned when she drove by.

"What hotel are we going to Baby?"

"Just drive until you see the tallest one."

"Oh my God" Michelle said as she pointed.

"I know you ain't talking about that hotel."

"Yep, that's it Boo."

"That hotel got to be thirty stories high, Ant."

"See that's where you're wrong, its forty stories high. What's the name of it?"

"The Mint."

After giving their cars to the valet, they checked in at the front desk and were given their key cards. Doormen in burgundy and gold uniforms escorted them to their suites.

Michelle and Ant stood in amazement as the double doors opened showing the massive elegant living room with Cathedral ceiling. The suite must have taken up the entire 36th floor. For the first time ever, Michelle looked to Ant and her eyes narrowed as she wondered just how paid he was. He must have spent $75,000 - $100,000 already and the vacation didn't even started yet.

"What are you thinking about 'Chelle?"

"Nothing" She answered while walking to the balcony.

"The view was absolutely breath taking."

"I'm going to lie down."

"Not me, I'm ready to hit the Malls."

"Take Willie with you. "

MILLIE

Millie walked through her townhouse trying to detect where the slight buzzing noise was coming from. Finally, she narrowed it down to the refrigerator. Walking back into the living room, smiling after realizing that her eyes were always drawn to Franklin's picture. Oh Franklin, she thought as she flopped down in his favorite chair. The 10th anniversary of his death was coming up. "I miss you more and more every year Franklin. I'm mad as hell that you left me here alone."

The phone rang and she reached for her antique style phone receiver.

"Hello."

"Hi Ma, what you doing?"

"If I told you Shana you'd probably think I was crazy. I was talking to Franklin." She answered, and then laughed.

"What's wrong Shana?"

"Millie, you really need to stop trying to read me."

"Are you saying nothing's wrong?"

"No."

They both laughed.

"I try Ma; I really do try to cope with Jason's job. I think I'm a good wife."

"And you are." Millie agreed.

"Then why does Jason do his best to make me feel guilty like I'm being selfish concerning our time. Do you think I'm being selfish?"

"Shana you know me better than to ask me to judge you or my son. No matter what I say, you're going to have reservations if it doesn't agree with how you feel. I know you love my son. And I know the past few years have been rough, but that's life Shana. Even Franklin and I had disagreements; we were just lucky they were never serious. And you know I raised my boys; I know they can be hard headed. If you feel that his ignoring your request is slowly killing your marriage, then I suggest the next time you two are alone, tell him the severity of the situation. I wish ya'll the best."

"Thanks Ma, I'll see you soon. Bye!"

LISA

Lisa looked out her blinds, and then reached for her black and white Be Be hand bag that matched her outfit. Jamal rolled down the tinted window of his black Suburban XL, watching Lisa's jingling body bounce down the steps.

"Hey Mal" she greeted as she struggled, climbing into the big truck.

"Damn you looking good girl!"

She smiled. "You like it, I wore it just for you."

Jamal pulled off; turning up the volume to the Marvin Gaye CD he was listening to.

"Where we going to eat, out Cheffields?"

"No, Maybe Hogates or Phillips."

"Mmm, I love Phillips; we threw a party for Toya up there last year."

Twenty five minutes later they were pulling into the parking garage. They walked down the walkway to the front door where they saw at least twenty people waiting to be seated.

"You can go sit down Mal; I'll wait for the table."

Jamal walked into the small lounge area and leaned back on the plush sofa. The waiter escorted them to their table and took their orders.

"Why you keep staring at me girl?"

"I was just wondering, do you still deal with Ant?"

Jamal's head turned to the side. "Why?"

"Please don't get mad Mal, it's just that I'm really starting to feel you and I'd feel a little uncomfortable because of me and Ant's past."

Jamal sipped his Bacardi Lemon, then answered. "We severed ties a while back."

"Good," she smiled and began fork feeding Jamal after their food came, doing her best not to make him mad. She kicked off her heels, leaned back in her chair and began rubbing her foot up and down between Jamal's legs.

Ring!

Lisa dug in her bag for her phone. She covered the mouthpiece and leaned towards Jamal. "Do you mind if I tell Toya to come up here?"

Jamal shook his head no.

"Toya come up Phillips, we sitting on the patio in the middle."

Ten minutes later the waiter was escorting Toya to the table. Jamal looked Toya up and down, she was built like a brick shit house. Short, a hand full of breast, but a behind you could sit a glass of Remy on. The women hugged and sat down.

After three rounds of drinks, a few jokes and flirtatious stares, Lisa excused herself to go to the ladies room.

She stood. "You ain't coming with me Toya?"

"I had just gone before I sat down girl, go head."

Lisa smiled, and then walked off light headed from the drinks.

"Soooo!" Toya slurred to Jamal. "Why you keep staring at a bitch? You know you couldn't do anything with all this ass."

"Shit!" Mal answered.

"Write down your number for me and maybe I'll let you play in Niagara Falls later on ."

Jamal wrote down his cellular phone number and passed it to Toya.

"Damn!" Lisa slurred. "I can't even go to the bathroom without you scandalous motherfuckaz exchanging numbers."

"Girl sit your drunk ass down, Jamal just gave me his man's number." Toya lied.

JASON

Two days later, Mitch looked across the desk to his partner seeing him smile from ear to ear.

"What's up?" Mitch asked, curious about what made his partner so happy.

"Wayne Hamilton confessed to a psychologist about the shooting."

Jason put his elbows on his desk and held his forehead. "It's a shame that little girl didn't make it."

"Yeah I know," Mitch agreed.

"I disagree Mitch, and I been religious all my life, but what kind of God allows a little girl to be randomly shot and die. She wasn't even old enough to do anything wrong."

"Hey, look at it like this Jenkins. What my Grandmother used to say is that children who die young are the lucky ones because they don't have to go through the test and suffering everybody else did and they get to go to heaven because of their innocence."

"Sounds good to me, Mitch but this whole world is going to hell if you ask me. We got to go get the psychologist's sworn statement; I knew the kid would break down."

Ring!

"Robbery Homo.."

"I know the routine," Shana cut him off playfully.

"How are you doing Baby?"

"My day has been going well so far but it's too early to call it."

"Well, I just want you to keep me updated because I was hoping we could go eat some soul food from TNT out Oxon Hill."

"Sounds good, and Jr. loves their iced tea."

"I'll call you before I leave."

"OK I don't want to hold you up Mr. Detective."

"No problem, thank you for the brief reprieve."

"Love you."

"Love you too." Click!

Jason stood, grabbed his sports jacket off his chair and put his left arm into the sleeve. "Come on Mitch, let's hurry up and get his statement."

Chapter 25

The following week was very busy; Millie was surprised by a phone call from Shana telling her that she was pregnant. Jason was happier than he's been in a while but the Wayne Hamilton trial had started and it weighed heavily on him.

After Wayne had confessed to the murders, and attempted to hang himself in his cell, he was put on suicide watch. Wayne was now given medication, and lately he just sat in a zombie state through the preliminaries while his life balanced itself in the hands of others. His Mother, Liz Hamilton, who was arrested numerous times for crack paraphernalia, stunk up the courtroom every morning with her foul body odor. It amazed Jason and his partner how even a crack head Mother who probably ran the streets all night getting high still showed up for court every morning to support a son she knew was going to do a lot of time.

JAMAL

Jamal was stepping on the heroin two times more than normal. Adding an extra two grams of milk sugar to every ounce he cooked up. Not even a week since Ant left and he'd already pocketed over seventy five thousand, not including his cut of the profits. Getting bored with Lisa and her I'm the shit attitude, he'd been seeing Toya and a few other women lately. He'd just dropped off his Infinity truck to Epps' detailing shop on central Ave. He had a gold package put on; a new marble wood dash, console and steering wheel; and he had five televisions put in. He'd never felt so powerful in his life. He was in control of everything and didn't have to answer to anyone. He fantasized about it remaining this way. Ant was his best friend, but who wouldn't envy the big man he thought to justify his mutinous cognitions.

ANTHONY

Ant was enjoying his time in Miami, he was very relaxed. Partially because he was away from the business, secondly because he was in a place where he could blow as much money as he wanted and not stand out because everyone was doing it. He'd phoned Ortega and begged him to join him. Ortega declined but promised they would go to an Island together soon. Ant thanked Ortega for the contacts even though he hadn't used them yet. He called Millie and was given the good news about another niece or nephew. He was more at peace now knowing his Father's murderer was dead. He'd let the crew run around and do pretty much whatever they wanted.

Michelle was having the time of her life; it was a nonstop rush for her. Everyday it's been something; shopping, clubbing, dinner boats, snorkeling. The biggest rush was the boat trip to the Dominican Republic, Haiti and Jamaica. The islands were beautiful and she joked about how the water got bluer as they ventured further away from the U.S. Everything was going well for Michelle at their hair salon. It looks like she will reach her goal of having the shop pay for itself within six months. Ant could care less but she learned to have goals like that in business school.

JASON

The typewriter sang as Jason typed at record speed of thirty-five words per minute.

There was actually no rush, since the follow up reports for the back files should have been completed months ago. He had a lot on his mind however, Wayne Hamilton was held in contempt of court first thing this morning after he hurled his public defender's water glass at the judge. He was sent back to a holding cell. Throughout the morning's confusion, officers somehow missed the suicide warning on Hamilton's paperwork, He was left unattended from 9:30am to 11:00am after which he was found dead in his cell. He'd hung himself with his blue jumpsuit off of the bars of the cell. His eyes were bulging out of his head as if he were surprised. Dried blood was caked up around his mouth from his biting the insides of his lips and tongue. Behind him on the wall read "sorry" written in his own blood.

To make matters worse, Shana's chemical imbalance from the pregnancy has been driving Jason crazy. He'd never seen or heard a woman cry so much for seemingly no reason. He stopped typing and looked around his office. It was 2 a.m. now so the office was almost empty. Jason looked over his shoulder as Mitch walked up behind him.

"Jay, can you come with me to the conference room? I need to show you something."

Without saying a word Jason followed his partner down the hallway and into the room Agent Stevens usually holds their task force meetings.

"What's up Mitch?"

"Remember when I told you how something kept bothering me about the Benny Ramsey case."

Jason shook his head up and down.

"And?"

"Well, this is what I ... your..." Mitch couldn't say the words so he just placed the two folders he held under his arm in front of Jason.

Jason opened the top one, before reading the name and began to have a shortness of breath as he read the two names in front of him. The files read Detective Anthony Brown, and Franklin Jenkins. He looked to Mitch in confusion.

"Just read Jenkins," Mitch urged on.

Tears formed in the wells of Jason's eyes and dropped down his cheeks as he read the horrific details of his Father's murder. The report read that there were several witnesses, all giving the same description of the killer. Dark skinned, petite man, with noticeable scars on the left and right side of his face.

After reading the file, he placed it under the second one. This time, Jason decided to read the name on the file before he opened it, Benny Ramsey. Suddenly, it all came together as he read the report. Ramsey grew up on 5th and Kennedy street and stayed there most of his adult life. His juvenile report was about twice the thickness of his adult report. He started out with petty crimes like shoplifting and ended up with more serious crimes like armed robbery and assault.

Chills ran through Jason's body as he turned to the page that had a juvenile mug shot of Ramsey. He fit the description of his father's murderer so much so that Jason went back over both reports wondering how the detectives missed it. Five minutes later he had found his answer. Ramsey was arrested for attempted robbery on an elderly couple two days after his Father's murder.

Mitch put his hands on Jason's shoulders and whispered. "I'm sorry Jenkins."

Jason just stared at the folders, filled with hatred as he stared at Ramsey's picture, then his mood changed to content. Live by the gun, die by the gun, he thought.

ANTHONY AND MICHELLE

Michelle stretched, blocking the sunlight with her right arm. She smiled as Ant started moving. Anytime she got up, he was soon to follow. She kissed him.

"Good morning sexy."

"What's up 'Chelle?"

Ain't nothing Daddy, I want to go to Disney World."

" Go ahead."

"You're not going to come with ?"

"Chelle you already know I don't like theme parks. I spent three thousand in Kings Dominion Amusement Park and I don't even get on rides."

"OK but when we have kids you better come with us."

She got up and walked to the bathroom while he stared at her nude body glowing from the sunlight. After ordering a huge breakfast, Michelle prepared for Disney World. Ant asked who wanted to go; Black and Sam seemed more excited than Michelle. She kissed Ant and walked to the door grabbing her suit case.

"Baby you sure you can survive without me for two days?"

"I think so, if not I'll just have Sam or Black bring you back."

She rolled her eyes and stepped onto the elevator, blowing a kiss as the doors closed.

ORTEGA

"Ortega! Telephone!" Maria the maid yelled to the top of the stairs.

"Got it Maria, thank you. Hello."

"Ortega, how are you doing?"

"I'm fine Uncle what's up? Is everything alright?"

"Yes, but I would like to speak with you later, face to face if your schedule allows."

"Preacher, you need to stop. My father is probably laughing in his grave at that one" Ortega teased.

Preacher laughed. "You're right, I don't give people options, but I learned that from your Father."

"And I learned it from you" Ortega shot back.

Then noticed his Uncle had grown quiet on the line.

"I'm sorry for bringing up Poppa, Uncle."

"It's okay Ortega. He was just a good man, he was so respected and dependable, and throughout life he'd had very few enemies. He was just so wonderful, it's people like your Father who people never stop missing and mourning for after their gone. I'll see you later! Click!"

Ortega hated when his uncle hung up on him. But he knew the topic was emotional. Ortega never really knew his Father; D.E.A. Agents had killed him in a raid when he was 9 years old. The D.E.A. vowed to get Preacher every since the Agent who killed his brother disappeared from the face of this earth. So Preacher was the only father Ortega could remember, Preacher was always there spoiling him rotten. He was the only child at Shaw Jr. High driving at 13 years old. Preacher never missed a game or a graduation. It seemed that there was nothing the old man couldn't do, or make a phone call and have taken care of.

A few hours later, upstairs in his uncle's office, Ortega nodded to two of Preacher's oldest body guards Tony and Felix. Every time Ortega came into the house it reminded him of his childhood.

Tap! Tap!

"Who is it?

"Me," Ortega answered pushing the door open. Preacher opened his arms and embraced him.

"How's my favorite nephew doing?"

"Fine Preacher but curious, what's got you wanting to see me in person."

"Let me ask you this Ortega. Who out of everyone that you deal with do you trust?"

Ortega pondered the question for a minute. "No disrespect Preacher, but I don't trust anyone."

"Smart boy, but if you had to choose between all of the snakes and rats in the street, humor me and tell me who would be the most reliable."

Ortega briefly looked toward the window, hearing the rain drops crashing into the pane. "I'd have to say Ant, but why?"

"Calm down Ortega, although I'm in my early 70's my doctors assured me I'm in the best of health."

Preacher raised his slender wrinkled index finger. "Out of the six doctors that I have, I've been their only patient for the past 12 years. I swear Ortega, all they do is sit around plotting and planning on how I can live forever, he laughed. Ortega's head leaned to the side and Preacher knew he was tired of waiting for his answer.

"Sit down. See, although I'm in good health, I just like to prepare for things. Nobody's promised tomorrow, heaven forbid I go out like your Father. He would be so proud of you Ortega, just as I am. Everyone in the higher ups knows you'll be running things at the event of my demise. And, you'll need someone you can trust Ortega. I trust Felix and Tony. I could easily leave orders for them to be at your aid. But when you're this high up on the food chain you need to be comfortable."

Ortega smiled. It wasn't often that Preacher tooted his own horn.

"But that's about it. I apologize for any inconvenience that I may have caused with you driving out here."

"You know it's no problem Preacher." Ortega hugged him tightly. "I'll talk to you tomorrow, Preacher."

Ortega was given an umbrella by Tony as he walked towards the front door. Ricky, one of Ortega's top escorts and enforcers, stepped out of the passenger side door of the Black 850 BMW as soon as he saw Ortega exiting the house.

Ortega pressed a button unlocking the doors and starting the ignition to his Lexus truck, the inside lit up from the five televisions he had installed. He jumped in and turned the heated seats to dry his now wet clothes.

A BMW backed out of the driveway waiting for Ortega to back out, and then

DE BLOOD BROTHERS

followed him. His windshield wipers automatically came on. The rain was now dropping heavier than before so he slowed down to 60 miles per hour. He turned down his system, "Call Kira" he ordered his phone and the line began ringing.

"Hi Ortega!" A woman's voice sang.

"What's up Baby?"

"Not much, I just left the hospital, the ER stayed packed today."

"Sounds like you need to unwind."

"Does that mean you're paying me a visit?"

"Sure does, I'll be there in a half."

Ring! Ring!

Ortega reached for his phone and dropped it. He reached down towards the right feeling the floor until he grabbed his phone... When he rose up...

His foot automatically slammed on the brakes as he saw the vehicle in front of him spin out of control. The truck hit a puddle and hydroplaned out of the fast lane and spun out into a series of 360 degree turns. The driver in the Dodge Ram pickup never saw it coming. Ortega saw the lights right before the Ram pickup crashed into the driver's side door at 80 miles an hour. The impact sent glass and metal flying everywhere. The collision caused the Lexus truck to continue spinning until it stopped in the middle lane. The horn wailed as Ortega lay slumped over the wheel.

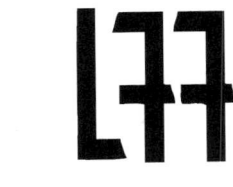

LISA

Lisa grabbed Jamal's black and grey North face jacket out of his hall closet and threw the hood over her head. Ran to her BMW and drove to Toya's new apartment on V Street.

"Damn I hope I didn't get my hair wet."

"I got a blow dryer waiting for you in the bathroom."

Lisa turned it on high and dried where her braids got wet. Toya stepped to the door and crossed her arms.

"Damn bitch, what you grilling me for?"

"Because you keep faking like you ain't feeling Jamal when all you been doing is clocking this nigga for the past couple months."

"Toya, you tripping, please, I got bookoo niggas with that" She gestured rubbing her fingers together implying money.

"So, if I told you Melody fucked him last week.."

"Melody what!"

Lisa's neck rolled as she stormed out of the bathroom. Toya followed her to the living room, watching Lisa dig her cellular out her Coach bag.

"What's that bitch number Toya, I ain't never like that hoe no way."

"I was just playing Lisa I swear, calm down. See what I mean. I thought we were girls; you got to keep it realer than this."

"Okay! Okay!"

DC BLOOD BROTHERS

Lisa plopped down on the old leather sofa.

"I have gotten attached to the fat bastard, how I don't know. He got this little ass dick but girl his mouth be on some other shit. That nigga can eat some pussy, lick some ass and suck some toes, you just don't know."

Yes I do, Toya thought. "So you admit it, so what, do you love the nigga?"

"Honestly Toya, I can barely get to sleep unless I'm with him."

"Awww Lisa," Toya hugged her best friend. "I'll get two spoons and the ice cream, you find something to watch."

"It's five in the morning ain't nothing on television Toya."

Lisa grabbed the remote off the coffee table and began surfing the channels.

"Toya!" Lisa screamed to the kitchen after seeing the picture of the mangled truck.

"Who do we know out Maryland with a Lexus truck?"

"Why?" Toya asked returning with the ice cream and spoons. Lisa pointed to the TV

"This is Channel 9 eyewitness news, I'm Jim Vance, and I'm Andrea Roan. Good morning, today we start off with a fatal accident on Branch Avenue between Allentown and Auth Roads. We're going to Morene Bunion who is live on the scene... Morene."

"Thanks Andrea, what you see behind me is the beginning of a six car pileup. Local authorities say the man in the Lexus truck swerved to avoid another vehicle and hydroplaned to the third lane where he was hit by the driver of a Dodge Ram pickup. So far we have one fatality. The driver of the Lexus truck was killed instantly on impact. The driver of the pickup was flown to P.G. County Hospital and is in critical condition. The authorities say they haven't confirmed the identity of the driver of the Lexus truck, but F.B.I. Agents have just arrived on the scene so I believe they...Hold on. Andrea, I was just given the name of the driver, Ortega Renaldi."

"Oh my fucking God, Toya."

Lisa's hand flew to her mouth as a photo of Ortega took up the screen. She grabbed for Toya's phone.

"Who you calling this early?"

"Jamal."

"Why, he was dealing with O?"

"Come on now Toya, half the niggas Uptown to NE deal with O, if they don't the niggas they cop from do, he had shit locked."

"Where the fuck you at?" Lisa asked.

"I'm at home, Lisa. What's up?"

"I think you better get up and turn the news on."

"Why?"

"Ortega's dead, he was in a car accident early this morning."

Jamal wiped the cold from his eyes and pressed the power button then 09 on his remote. His mouth fell open seeing Ortega's face on the screen. He grabbed his cell phone and dialed Ant's number. The answering machine picked up. Jamal tried three more times then he tried Willie's number. Once he told Willie about the accident, Willie rushed to Ant's room and banged on the suite door with his forearm. Nobody answered, but a nearby elevator door opened and Ant stepped off. Upon hearing the news, Ant immediately called up Jamal.

"I'll be back home tomorrow."

"Dawg, you might as well stay, there's really nothing you can do."

"Oh Yeah Mal, so my man gets killed and I'm supposed to go on like nothing happened? Would you want me dancing on you grave?"

"You right Dawg sorry…"

Ant hung up on him and told Willie to round up everyone. After calling Michelle, by 6pm they were all packed and ready to head for the airport.

"Look, I'm sorry we've got to cut this short," Ant addressed the room, "but some serious shit just came up. Once we get home, I'll have Mal hit ya'll off, don't give out no deals cause things gonna be tight."

After boarding the plane, Michelle whispered "I'm sorry Baby," as she put her arm around Ant's neck.

"If it ain't one thing it's another 'Chelle. Ortega had everything, and just lost his life in some fluke accident."

Chapter 27

The following morning, Agent Stevens heels clicked as he paced in a small circle as officers filled the room. Jason sipped his coffee after taking a seat.

"Gentlemen, please quiet down. I apologize for our hiatus with these meetings, I just got finished with an undercover operation. I called this meeting because we have a serious upcoming situation. Hit the lights please."

After the lights were turned off, a projector came on

"I don't know how many of you heard of Ortega Renaldi, but he was a major figure in the narcotics game. He probably supplied at some level, most of NW and NE Washington along with Palmer Park and Landover, MD. I'm sure most of you saw the news and saw the mangled Lexus truck he died in. The DEA as well as the ATF, FBI and rumored CIA were all investigating Mr. Renaldi. Mostly because of this man."

With a push of the thumb, the picture changed to a frail looking old man.

"This is Fredro Renaldi, also known as Old Man, better known as Preacher.

This harmless looking old man has been targeted since the late 70's when his brother Alfredo Renaldi was killed by an FBI Agent in a raid. As soon as the Agent's name was put in the paper, he hasn't been heard from since. No witnesses, no body."

"Damn! Like Hoffa" One of the officers outburst.

"Yes, very much so. But the reason we're here is because now Ortega's out of the picture. There's a lot of money to be made. A lot of power to be taking. I assure you men that we'll have fifteen bodies in two weeks if not more."

DC BLOOD BROTHERS

Agent Stevens began digging in his pockets pulling out his wallet, then all the cash in it. He counted it, then held it up.

"I have eleven hundred dollars here. I bet anyone we'll have fifteen bodies within two weeks. And if we don't, I'll be the first of the third week 'cause my wife will kill me once she finds out I wasted money."

"Seriously though, Renaldi's funeral will be this Sunday. The place will be flooded with all types of felons and local government officers. Check my list on your way out." He clapped his hands. "Meet me here, Sunday morning 0800 hours in black suits, bright eyed and bushy tailed. Be safe.

"Well, Jenkins" Mitch put his hand on his shoulder. "Looks like we'll be busy."

"I hate to say it, Mitch but it's good because Shana is literally driving me crazy."

"Have you told your mom yet?"

"No, I'm waiting for my little brother then I'll tell them both. Thanks again. I know we'll all need the closure. Finally, I think my father can rest in peace."

They took the elevator down to the garage.

"Hey Jenkins, I just thought about it, ain't Ortega Renaldi from your neck of the woods?"

"Yeah, Ortega and I never got along. I'm sorry to know he's dead though."

ANTHONY

Ant pulled into the small parking lot of the Oxon Hill Apartments seeing Jamal's Infinity truck with a new paint job and rims.

Tap! Tap!

Jamal opened the door, then sat his 357 snub nose on the coffee table after Ant closed the door.

"You straight Mal?"

"Of course, but shit running low."

Ant scratched his head in thought. "Plug up the money machine so we can get the count out of the way. We'll figure out something after that."

Four hours later the two sat back on the sofa exhausted sipping bottled water.

"4.2 million," Jamal sat back proud of himself while Ant thought of Ortega.

"Mal, I want you to call everybody and tell them I don't want them attending Ortega's wake or funeral." Ant knew the Feds would be all over both events.

"I'm going to miss Ortega, he was a good dude, real good dude."

Ant got up and walked to the bar. He brought back a liter of VSOP Remy, pulled the cork out and guzzled until he was about to gag.

"So Mal, you and that chick getting tight, got her all up your crib answering the phone and everything."

"Yeah," Jamal laughed. I can't believe that bitch answered my phone, he thought.

DC BLOOD BROTHERS

"Since ya'll so tight, I got to meet her. I like what you did with your truck too. I'm thinking about getting something new. But enough small talk," Ant put the bottle to his lips again and guzzled, then wiped his mouth.

"You know anybody big enough we can cop from? You ain't got no connects that was fucking with O?"

"Hell naw Mal, you knew O didn't play that everybody knew everybody, shit."

"Well, I have been hearing a lot about these New York dudes, they own a car lot up Silver Hill Rd."

"Okay, see what's up with them niggas."

"Spend a couple hundred thousand, see how their shit move and we'll go from there. Oh, and tell everybody I said stay strapped 'cause now O gone, it's gonna be a lot of niggas out to make a name. Tell them I got money for their lawyers and bonds, shoot first."

"Ah-ight Big Dawg, I'm out, I'll holler at you later."

Ant picked up the newspaper and read the article on Ortega. "Damn O."

JAMAL

The brisk wind was a nice compliment with the heat blowing in Jamal's Lincoln Mark 8 as he put his left blinker on at Branch Avenue and Silver Hill Road. The light turned green and he followed the flow of traffic then moved to the middle lane. Soon, he was putting on his right blinker and pulling into the parking lot.

He stepped out of the car and was approached by a smiling, short, stocky, dark skinned man.

"How are you doing this afternoon?" Jamal looked the man from head to toe. He had manicured nails, wore a Movado watch and a white gold cuban link chain with a New York Yankee medallion. He also had a bulge on his right hip which was barely noticeable until he extended his arm to shake hands.

"I'm doing alright," Jamal replied.

"Okay, how can I help you today?"

"You're a big man so you probably want to check out the Acura's."

Jamal agreed and twenty minutes later they were stepping into the office trailer where Jamal would begin paper work for the car. Occasionally looking up, taking inventory of the room. There were three men in the room with him. Fingers was the name that the men in the office called the guy who sold him the car.

One man sat over by the far right wall at a desk talking on the phone. The other two men were closer to the office door which Fingers kept going in and out of. They were probably guarding whoever was in that office.

Anyone with street smarts could have peeped it was a front. It was a damn good front though. Fingers came out of the office. "Ah-ight Big Money, you fill out that paper work yet?"

"All but these last two, I was just thinking, is the owner here?" Jamal felt every eye in the room on him because of his slightly intrusive question.

A split second later, he heard footsteps coming behind him, Fingers stepped to the blinds peeping outside, one of the two men by the office stepped into the office, and the second pulled out a 9mm and approached Jamal.

"What's going on?"

"Yo! Shut the fuck up" the man screamed putting the tip of the barrel between his eyes.

The man behind him began patting him down, pulling his 357 snub nose off his waist and three stacks of hundred dollar bills out the pockets of his Eddie Bauer coat.

The office door opened and a thin dark skinned man with wavy hair stepped out.

"Come in here"

Jamal stepped into the office.

"Sit down, the man ordered him."

"What the fuck are you a cop or something? What you want?"

"I'm gonna just come straight out with it since my subtle approach didn't work." Jamal leaned towards the desk. "My connect died last week, I can't just get what I need from anybody."

"How did you hear about this?" The man cut him off.

"I know all the rollers. This is my city, you feel me?"

The man nodded.

"Besides, if I would have heard about you through some weak niggas I wouldn't have come."

"My names V," the man's hand came over the desk. "Pablo, go get his shit."

"Gun too, boss?"

V just looked at him. A few seconds later Jamal's gun, money, pager and cellular were in front of him. "So, how much you trying to spend at first?"

"A hundred thousand in white, two hundred thousand in blow." Jamal stood to leave; "I'll be back later with whoever I'll have coming on the regular."

"Big man, you forgetting your change."

Jamal looked back, "That's for the car."

"How much is it?"

"Thirty thousand" Jamal answered.

"But the car is only eighteen."

"I'll send this chick Lisa for it, keep the change."

MILLIE'S HOUSE

The next day.

"Coming!" Millie yelled after hearing her door bell. She opened the door, "Come here, handsome."

She squeezed Ant as if she hadn't seen him in years. "You come here too

DC BLOOD BROTHERS

Michelle, I heard your shop is doing well, I'm so proud of you."

"Where's Jay?"

"He should be here in a minute, you two hungry?"

"No ma'am we just ate."

Ding Dong!

"I'll get it," Ant opened the door for Jason, Shana and his nephew Jr who looked more like his uncle every day.

"What's up, Bro?"

Ant slapped Jay on the back, then dug in his pocket handing Jr. a $20 bill, "Here you go little man."

"Thanks, Uncle Anthony."

They all stepped into the small living room and sat down with the exception of Jason.

"I'm sure you all are wondering why I couldn't wait till Sunday to tell you this." He looked to his Mother's face. Jason took a long breath then began.

"We found out who killed daddy."

"Oh my God, praise the Lord!" Millie yelled. "Who, I mean how, is he locked up?"

"No Ma, he's dead, my partner wouldn't let up off our case because it didn't make since to him that no one had any idea it was a link but he put the pieces together."

"Are you sure?" Ant asked.

"Yeah bro, it's him."

"Good, he got what he deserved." Ant walked out of the living room to the kitchen. Millie stood with her hands covering her mouth and tears rolling down her face. Shana got up and put her arm around Millie.

"I've waited so long for this day, Shana" she whispered as tears fell freely from her eyes. "Franklin can finally rest in peace."

"I'm going to talk to Ant. He took this a little hard."

Jason found Ant out back. "Mind if I join you little bro?"

"Sure."

"Are you alright?"

"Yeah, I'm just glad that's one less question in the back of our minds - who killed Dad?"

"Yeah, they found his body in SW a while ago, he was a crack head, and the case is still unsolved."

"If you don't mind Jay, I rather not discuss this."

"So you're cool? Why you seem so distanced then?"

"Oh it ain't this" Ant smiled. "A good friend of mine passed last week."

"Do I know him, it wasn't Jamal was it?"

"You don't know him, he's a guy I got close to at work," he lied.

"Speaking of work, Shana tells me Michelle's shop is doing very well."

"Yeah, it is."

"You don't have any issues with that do you?"

"Why should I, Jay?"

"I don't know, some men just go on a ego trip when their women are more successful or simply bringing in more money."

"I love it, how are things at home with you and Shana?"

"She's crazier than when she was pregnant with Jr. I'm telling you Ant, when you get a woman pregnant that chemical imbalance is terrible."

"How about work?"

"Being a homicide detective is a lose/lose situation because two lives or more are always lost. And the killers are getting younger and younger. I think these gang related movies and rappers are a terrible influence."

"You can't say that, white people done killed more than any other people. Their music is crazier than ours and they celebrated killing with their Clint Eastwood and Charles Bronson movies, as well as the very way they obtained this country. But every time a white man commits a crime you don't hear them blaming music or movies."

"You may have a point, Ant."

"I know I got a point. No matter how successful a black man becomes in this country, they try to use one fuck up to down the entire race."

JAMAL

"Damn Lisa, why the fuck you gotta act like I just fucked up your day by calling?"

"Mal, you been missing in action for the past couple weeks, how am I supposed to act, I thought we were becoming something."

"I need you to go up to Maryland Motors and pick up a midnight blue Acura. Ask for Fingers and tell him I sent you."

"What do you want me to do with the car, Jamal?" Asked Lisa slightly disappointed because he called given her an assignment instead of asking how she's doing it.

"It's yours."

"Excuse me."

"I said the car is yours. I brought it for you this morning."

"That is so sweet, thank you Baby."

"Am I going to see you later?"

"Yeah, I'll call you."

Jamal finished counting up the $300,000 and told Petey to put it in his truck.

chapter 28

ORTEGA'S FUNERAL

JASON

The loud buzz of a few hundred hushed conversation filled and echoed off the wall of the large church in College Park. Every type of street legal foreign car sat parked outside. Many of them had out of state tags.

Ortega's casket sat open, pearl white with gold trimming. He looked as if he were merely taking a nap. He was looking dapper as usual in a white suit. Jason put his finger to his ear as he stepped out of his car.

"Team two are you in position?"

"Not yet he answered back, while scanning the crowd as he and Mitch stepped into the church. It was a mad house. Channel 9,7, and 4 along with Fox 5 news cameras set up across the street from the church."

"Damn, Mitch! You would have thought there was a celebrity in here."

"It is Jenkins, look at the cars we passed, Mercedes, a few limo's, Rolls Royce's, the dude was big."

"Jason and his partner were among seven other people in team two that sat in the church along with another seven from team three."

A priest stepped to the podium and without uttering a sound the church quieted.

DC BLOOD BROTHERS

"Excuse me!" Lisa whispered as her and Toya squeezed into a pew.

"Girl, this shit is larger than life, you see all them news camera's out there?"

"Hell yeah Lisa, but forget that, I'm trying to find out who got them Ferraris and Rolls Royces outside."

"Look!" Lisa tapped her arm. "There go Fats and them Trinidad niggas from N.E , there go Dave from Langston Lane. Bootsy came from down bottom, "Damn, it's some money up in here."

"Didn't Ant used to fuck with Ortega though?"

Lisa's top lip curled up, "Bitch, you can fuck up a wet dream."

"Is Jamal coming?"

"Naw, he said it'll probably be feds everywhere."

"I still can't believe he just brought you that big Acura.," Toya said trying to conceal her jealously.

"I know, I told you I got that Nigga whipped."

The funeral service was more regal than any of the attendants would probably ever see again in life. Preacher did Ortega's eulogy, breaking down into tears half way through it, and was escorted back to his seat.

What shocked everyone most was when a woman, probably in her late thirties or early forties, interrupted the service asking if she could say a few words.

"Hello," she said. "My name is Kira Thomas."

"I met Ortega at a Children's Hospital fund-raiser to raise money for sick children about a year ago. He was one of the smartest, most caring and..." she giggled as she wiped a tear, "sexiest men I have met in a long time. The night of this terrible accident, I had just gotten off of the phone with him. He was coming to see me in fact." Kira's voice softened and quivered slightly as she began to show signs of the hurt that she was obviously feeling. Fist clenched together at her heart she looked to the sky and took a deep breath.

"I fell in love with this man over six months ago without even truly knowing who he was. He'd told me he owned a construction business." The crowd chuckled. "Well, you see, I'm a Doctor, a specialist, at Children's Hospital. I guess he felt the need to have a business other than the one that I am hearing about now. I've heard a lot of terrible, horrific stories about him, but I knew an entirely different side of this man. I just wanted to tell him goodbye and that I'll always love and miss him. Thank you."

She stepped off the stage, walked to the casket, and kissed Ortega on the cheek. Then she dropped a necklace that she had bought for him as a surprise, but never had the chance to give him, along the side of his casket.

Soon the service was over and everyone stood and began milling around the casket. There were people in attendance who loved Ortega and cherished their bond, as well as people who inwardly celebrated his demise and were glad that he was out of the way. His body was loaded into the back of a Cadillac stretch limo and the procession was lead off by Ortega's usual escorts and enforcers in the Black tinted 850 BMW. Everyone turned on their car lights and slowly drove through the streets of PG County as they made their way to his final resting place,

DC BLOOD BROTHERS

Harmony Hills Cemetery.

MICHELLE

Michelle pulled in front of her Silver Spring home seeing Ant's Range Rover and gold Maxima parked in the driveway. Exhausted from a hectic morning at the shop, she was glad she decided to leave early. She was even happier to see that Ant was home so that he could massage her aching feet. She put her key in the door and pulled off her heels the second she stepped in.

She was surprised that Ant wasn't watching ESPN and lounging across the living room sofa. Walking into the kitchen, she grabbed a bottle of water from the fridge, then made her way up the stairs.

"Baby!" She yelled.

When she opened the bedroom door her eyebrows narrowed because there was no evidence that Ant had returned since morning. She checked both guest rooms.

"Where is this boy at?"

She walked downstairs opened the basement door and yelled, "Baby are you down there?"

She lowered her head to look into the basement. After checking the back yard she decided to give up. He probably took one of the cars out of the garage. She went back up to her bedroom and started the hot water for a bath.

Afterward, she put her favorite salts and mixture of oils into the tub, lit her sandalwood scented candles, and then dimmed the lighting. Stepping in front of her full length mirror she took off all her clothes.

"Damn, I put on a couple of pounds." Turning her back to the mirror and looking over her shoulder. Still got it, she smiled after tooting her own horn about her beautiful behind. She cupped her breast and tilted them noticing they didn't stand as firm as they used to. She squeezed them softly and pinched her nipples until they became erect. Then she began rubbing her breast in small circles, checking for any lumps or soreness.

Her eyes stretched in surprise after hearing a noise. "Ant!" She yelled out without getting an answer.

Running to the bedroom door, then locked it. She rambled through her night stand draw and pulled out the 380 Ant had bought her when they moved in. Her heart pounded so hard in her chest it felt as if it would jump out her skin. Her slender fingers fumbled with the gun as she began the steps Ant taught her.

Pressing a button on the left side ejecting the clip, then pushing it back in. She cocked the gun and took the safety off. She put on her robe, cocking the gun again, scared she didn't do something correct, a single brass bullet fell to the floor. She opened the bedroom door slowly and began searching every room for her intruder. Remembering Ant told her, always keep your back to the wall, and step close to the wall because the middle of the floor creeks and shoot first, ask questions later.

DC BLOOD BROTHERS

JASON

Jason sat in the passenger seat of his unmarked car, holding binoculars to his eyes and listening to the traffic over his ear piece.

They hadn't been in the Harmony Hills cemetery a half hour and plain clothes officers had already arrested several wanted men. Some for homicides, one for jumping bail, and two for armed robbery along with their girlfriends.

"Mitch, I'm going to walk around."

LISA

"Toya, I wonder who that old man is up there killing them softly in the Faragomo loafers."

"I don't know, but he must be related to Ortega."

"And he must be big time, did you see how all those guys had his back when he told the police, next time they interrupt in anyway their going to need back up."

"That's fucked up how they locked up Tootsy and Man Man.," Toya commented.

JASON

Jason stood in awe as he watched beautiful woman after beautiful woman pass out crying for Ortega. Once the preacher said his final words and the crane began lowering Ortega's casket into the ground a few women even tried to jump in with it.

Jason tried to understand the love, or more likely the fear and respect everyone had for Ortega here. There were hundreds of people. So many people that he'd been there an hour and the last car of the procession that left the church, pulled in twenty minutes ago. Jason watched the different news stations, stopping mourners asking them about the great Ortega Renaldi rumored to be connected to the Mafia. He looked around seeing fellow officers blend in with the crowd.

Over his ear piece he's heard countless wanted men were pointed out, but they were under direct order from Agent Stevens to stand down. The old man who threatened them obviously meant business. A light rain began to fall. How predictable for a funeral, Jason laughed then silently prayed that Jr. or his unborn child would never get caught up in the glamorous lure of the street life.

"Rest in peace O."

DC BLOOD BROTHERS

ANTHONY

Ant pulled up behind 'Chelle's SC 400 Lexus, grabbing a bottle of Hennessey and putting the bottle to his lips. Half was burning his throat, the other half was spilling down his face onto his sweater and Gortex jacket.

He staggered out of the car, slamming the door. Fighting gravity as he stepped wide left to right, Ant tried to stay on his feet long enough to make it to the door. He stopped and guzzled more of the cognac. He thought about how fucked up he felt that one of his closest friends had died and he couldn't even say goodbye and pay his proper respects.

He fumbled with his keys, dropping them to the ground. He put his left hand on the door to balance himself as he bent over to pick the keys up. After five minutes he finally had the door open.

"Chelle!" He yelled, sounding a lot like Sylvester Stallone in Rocky. He turned back around, seeing her other car was also parked. He shut the door and locked it, hearing footsteps he began walking to the kitchen.

"Oh no! I'll give you anything. Please, just don't hurt her." He begged the two masked men who stepped out of the kitchen. One was pointing the handgun he'd bought 'Chelle to her right temple. The left side of her face was swollen and her lip was busted.

"Tie his ass up!" The gunman told his partner. The voice sounded familiar but muffled from under the mask.

Tears fell from Michelle's eyes down to the silk robe she had on. Ant felt the duck tape go around his wrist numerous times. The same was done to his ankles, then the man started to put duck tape over his mouth.

"Please!," He screamed. "I'll give you twenty five million, just let her go, please!"

Ant heart filled with rage as he saw Michelle wince as the gunman began grabbing her breast and digging his gloved hands between her legs.

"Please!"

The gunman began pulling his mask off.

"No!" Ant blinked and shook his head.

"Yeah, it's me Big Dawg, I'm tired of being your flunky."

"Jamal, how can you do this? I'll give you anything!"

"Yeah, as long as you can run me around like your gofer. Nigga, we were best friends. I should never had to touch shit."

Ant realized two things in this instant; He should have listened to Smiley when he told him never trust a nigga, and that he and Michelle were dead now that Jamal pulled the mask off.

"Duck tape that nigga's mouth." Ant didn't protest as the tape went over his mouth.

"Make sure that nigga don't move!," Jamal ordered the second man as he threw Michelle's body onto the sofa.

"No! Stop Mal!"

"Shut the fuck up, bitch!" Smack!

He'd slapped Michelle so hard blood flew from her mouth. Ant felt his worst nightmare was about to come true as Jamal began unfastening his belt. "Yeah Michelle, thought you was always too good for this fat nigga, huh?"

She didn't respond as he pressed the gun to her head and penetrated her. She yelped as he violated her, she looked down to Ant then closed her eyes as tight as she could.

"No!" Ant mumbled under the duck tape, as he tore the flesh on his wrist and ankles fighting to break free. Tears filled his eyes as he watched Jamal's fat ass begin to sweat as he pounded between Michelle's legs.

"Oh, bitch, you ain't gonna make no noise like you don't feel nothing?"

He grabbed her by her head, dragging her behind the sofa and bending her over it.

"Yeah, bitch, that's what I'm talking about!"

Jamal slammed himself into her anus over and over again until he came.

"You want some of this ass, nigga?" He asked the second man who shook his head no. "Fuck it, your loss, she was good." He grabbed her by the hair and dragged her over to Ant. "Are you watching, Ant? Bitch made my head ache with all that screaming and shit. I am going to give her back, but first..." Jamal place his gun against the back of her head and pulled the trigger. Michelle's body jerked and collapsed as her brain splattered against the floor.

"Now that's how you give a bitch head! Well, your turn, Big Dawg."

"Ant! Ant!" Michelle screamed loud as she violently shook Ant.

"Chelle!" Fully awoke, he pulled her face to his and kissed her as tears rolled down his cheeks.

"Man, you scared the shit out of me." He jumped and looked around after seeing the 380 in her hand. "It's OK. Nobody's in the house. What were you dreaming about?"

"I can't remember," he lied, wondering why he would have such a fucked up dream about his best friend.

JASON

Two weeks later, officers filled the conference room as Agent Stevens sat on a desk in the front center. "Hurry up, ladies and gentlemen, I have other engagements this morning."

After everyone settled, he jumped off the desk and waved his arms side to side. "Sad to say, people, I was just off by seven days with the bodies. Hit the lights".. The projector came on. "Since Ortega Renaldi's funeral, we've got twelve murders from 7th St. N.W. to Jay Street in N.E., and eight from Oxford knolls in Suitland, MD to Strafford Woods in Landover."

DC BLOOD BROTHERS

"They're getting re-established at all cost, people."

"This is why most people wonder how come the feds lock up say, Mikey who was selling three kilos a week, but left his supplier Tido who sells about a 100 kilos to thirty different people."

He clapped his hands. "It's really easy see; it's the same way with building or restarting or transforming a company. You start from the ground up."

"The more top dealers we snatch off the street without making sure because one of our informants or someone close to our informants, is ready to pick up slack quickly, will only create more bloodshed."

"I know that only half of you are narcotics, but this especially goes for you. Find out who are becoming the heavy hitters out there. Robbery Homicide, if we don't catch these killers soon, they'll put a couple new notches under their belts. Even if they killed on accident the first time, it's still easier to do it again. Go out there, be safe and bring in the bad guys. I'll see you all at our next meeting."

"Why your face so tight ‚Jenkins?"

Jason pointed to the conference room they'd just walked out of.

"That was bullshit, Mitch, and you know it!"

He told him louder than intended.

"Calm down, Jay, what are you talking about?"

"Stevens just basically told those narcotics officers to target low level drug dealers and ignore the bigger ones."

"Well, it's not like they won't get to them eventually Jay."

"Yeah, after they saved enough money to beat their trial with a good lawyer, or at least live like a king in prison. I'm going outside I need some air."

chapter 29

ANTHONY

"This is nice, Willie, when you get this?"

"Last week. Every time a new CLK comes out, I upgrade."

Ant smiled at his #1 money maker as they flowed with the busy F St. traffic downtown.

"Mal says he had no complaints with the New York boys shit. How about you?"

"Naw, it moved good and my niggas so picky and complain so much, I think they smoke and sniff."

"Good then, we going big this time."

"Cool," Willie answered then wiggled his fingers to the lady staring at him in the next car.

"Anything you want to bring up Willie, how we can tighten shit up, anything?"

"Well, this is more personal than business but..."

"Go ahead and speak your mind, Slim, we family."

"I'm just sick of Jamal's pompous attitude. I was down with you out the gate, from the jump. Now I bring in the most because I'm popular. And you give me my space, I like that. But Jamal be ordering me around and making little comments like I work for him. I do it just to keep the peace, but my patience is running low for real."

"Okay. I'll get Jamal straight…"

"Willie, you remember when I couldn't buy 'Chelle shit?"

Willie smiled and nodded, "You turned her out, Champ. Sis is well worth it. If I found somebody like her, only darker with a bigger ass, I might lay it down."

"Whatever nigga. I don't want you getting caught up in this block war shit going on. Get you a few good dudes, lay back, monitor them niggas, but lay back, I got you slim."

JAMAL

Jamal followed Black as his Honda Accord wagon took the Silver Hill Rd. exit off Suitland Parkway.

"Call B." Jamal ordered his phone.

"Hello."

"Don't forget what I told you, and if anything looks funny, get out of there with the money."

"Ah-ight."

Jamal's Tahoe cruised by the Accord as he put on his left signal to U-turn into the car lot. Black pulled into the lot and parked, stepping out as the short stocky man approached him. The man's eyebrows narrowed as he inspected the car then the driver.

"Welcome to Maryland Motors." Fingers extended his hand,

"How can I help you?"

"I'm looking for a good deal."

"Okay. Let me show you some 300 ZX's."

Black smiled to himself as he followed the man, thinking how he felt like a mason with all this secret lingo.

"What color you like?"

"Gimme that black one right there with the classics."

"Alright, let's go fill out the paper work. You are trading in the Accord right?"

"Yeah."

Black took another look at the Accord, thinking how much money could be in the two big duffle bags in the back.

Following Fingers into the trailer, he toyed with the fantasy of just jumping in the car and hitting the highway, knowing there was enough cash to be set for life. Then the reality hit him that Ant, Jamal and Willie knew where his Mother and Grandmother lived. He shook his head to erase the thought.

Twenty minutes later after filling out the paper work he was given the keys, which he then handed over the Accord. He didn't like these dudes, these niggas are too fucking quiet. Stepping outside, he pulled his cell phone out of his Northface Parka and dialed Mal's number.

Two days later, Sgt. Robert Shaffer from Narcotics 2nd District called Jason.

DC BLOOD BROTHERS

"Oh hey Shaffer, how's the two left feet going?"

"Here we go, I can't live down my wife cursing me out at the policeman's ball three years ago for stepping on her favorite shoes."

"What can I do for you?"

"Actually it maybe something I can do for you. I've been getting letters from some kid you guys got at the jail for murder."

"Letters about what?"

"About some dealer he knows down 7th St., but here's why I called. Remember the Daniels case?"

Jason's body involuntarily froze as the corpses came to memory. "Yeah, how can I forget?"

"Well, this kid claims whoever this drug dealer is, was involved with the guy that walked; Nicolas Drake."

Jason picked up the pen on his cluttered desk.

"What's the kid's name?"

"Tyrone Skinner."

Not even thirty minutes later, Jason and his partner sat in a small room waiting for a correctional officer to bring in Tyrone Skinner. The kid was only seventeen, charged as an adult for the kidnap and murder of Steve Davis, a well known PCP dealer from the Hechinger Mall area.

The door opened and the 6 foot 230 pound Tyrone Skinner, cuffed and shackled, shuffled in his blue jumpsuit until he reached the plastic chair on the opposite side of the officers.

"How you doing Tye?"

He looked to Mitch. "What do you care?" Jason put up his hand to stop his partner from antagonizing the kid. Jason and Mitch always agreed that the good cop, bad cop roles were corny but Mitch always initiated.

"Tyrone, excuse my partner we're here because we received a call from a Narcotics Officer Sgt. Shaffer, saying you may have some information about the Daniel's case."

"What ya'll gonna do for me? Ya'll gonna give me immunity?"

"We can't do that, Tyrone, because your co-defendants already turned on you."

Tyrone's body slid down in his chair as if he had nothing to lose or gain by staying silent. Jason racked his brain for awhile. "OK Tyrone, here's the deal, you tell us what you know and if we can work with it, I promise to do my best to have the judge sentence you as a juvenile."

"Try! Try!" The kid repeated for the second time, looking as if the words left a nasty taste in his mouth.

"Look Tyrone!" Jason's hands slammed onto the desk, and his nostrils flared. "What, do you want me to lie to you like any officer in my shoes would do? I'm giving you my honest to God word, even if he doesn't sentence you as a juvenile, I can almost guarantee you he'll do something."

Tyrone looked at the wall as if weighing his options.

DC BLOOD BROTHERS

"Ah-ight, I'll tell you."

"We're going to record this, just in case we need this for the grand jury..."

Mitch pressed the record button, "Go ahead, Tye."

"Well, I know about this dude Barry who be around my way, he about my age."

"He sell everything, coke, weed, dope. Well, four years ago before that family got killed, he used to always hang with them older dudes down 7th St."

"Do you know their names?" Jason asked.

"One of them was the dude Nick."

"Are you referring to Nicolas Drake?" Jason cut him off..

"Yeah him, the dude used to wear the shades all the time."

"Who were the other men?"

"The only other one I knew was Willie."

"He was the one who had little Barry hustling."

"Are you sure this man Willie and this kid Barry were directly involved with Nick?"

"Yeah, one day these dudes tried to rob Barry around M St. and Willie brought Nick around there, Nick put a Glock 40 in one of their mouths and made him suck it."

"Is that it?"

"Yes."

"Why are you telling us this?"

Tyrone's face became tight and he didn't utter another word. Jason pushed the stop button on the small tape recorder... "Look Tyrone, I need you to be straight up with me, why are you telling us this?"

"Ah-ight man, that nigga Barry fucking my baby Mother Iesha. Nigga even had the nerve to answer my call a couple weeks ago."

"OK Tyrone, I just wanted to know, I'm going to look into this and I'll be sure to ask Judge Harper to charge you as a juvenile."

After returning to his office, Jason set up a meeting with Sgt. Shaffer. Both agreed there wasn't enough credible testimony for Robbery Homicide to investigate. Shaffer had promised to run it by his captain and send in an undercover cop on the pretence of a drug investigation.

ANTHONY AND MICHELLE

"... Baby, you look good enough to eat." Michelle whispered.

"Remember that when we're in the car."

Both their heads turning towards the back of Rev. Gibson's Church as the organ began playing the brides marching music. Everybody in attendance cheered for the bride as she made her way to the groom. Rev. Gibson had the warm deep smile many had come to love on his face as he admired the couple.

DC BLOOD BROTHERS

"We are gathered here today.." Ant's mind wondered, too much shit was going on. Ortega died, the hair shop still has a few loose ends, and these fucked up dreams about Jamal. It's true he thought of the verse in the Bible that said; "Money was the root of all evil..."

"I do." He heard the groom say.

"I now pronounce you man and wife; you may now kiss the bride."

"I'll be right back baby, hold the camcorder." Michelle said as she moved to the front.

Ant watched the man-crazed women leap and dive to catch the bride's bouquet. He smiled as Michelle, held the bouquet toward his direction then flashed her engagement ring. Twenty minutes later, they were at Michelle's BMW Wagon.

Ant loosened his tie. "Where you trying to go, Pier 7, Wilson's, or the Hard Rock café?"

"I want to go to the reception, Baby." Michelle whined.

"You didn't say anything about any reception, Chelle."

"Please, Baby? Look, no more than a hour." She crossed her heart. "I swear..."

Ant sipped his second glass of Moet as he and Michelle watched the newlyweds dance. Everyone clapped as the music; "I Only Have Eyes for You" came to an end.

Ant and Michelle walked straight towards them from the dance floor. Michelle hugged her friend. "Congratulations girl, I am so happy for you."

"Thank you for coming, 'Chelle."

"Baby," the bride addressed her husband, pointing to Michelle.

"This is Michelle, I told you about her, that's her shop Le Neuvo on H St."

"Oh yeah nice to meet you 'Chelle, my Mother loves your shop."

"And this is her fiancé James."

The men shook hands, "Nice to meet you, James, I'm Mike."

"Nice to meet you, Mike. Congratulations."

Ant felt someone looking at him so he looked over Mike's shoulder and noticed an old man. Now that he thought about it, he'd noticed the old man staring at him in the church. Suddenly the old man and two other older men approached.

Putting his arms around the bride and groom, kissing the bride on the cheek, "Congratulations you two, I really hope you like your presents."

The old man looked to Michelle, then to Ant, winked his eye then put up an OK sign with his fingers.

"Let me introduce you," Mike began. The old man put up his hand cutting him off then extended his right hand to Ant, "It's good to finally meet you face to face."

For a old man, Ant felt he had a strong grip, but what puzzled him was why this old man now seemed vaguely familiar, "Let's go for a walk." The old man suggested.

"You know him, baby?" Michelle asked.

"I'm not sure, I'll call your cell phone when I'm finished."

Ant caught up to the old man, who was followed by the same two men. The old man looked up to his right, smiled at Ant, and placed his right hand on the back of Ant's left shoulder.

"I have a suite upstairs, I deem will be more suitable for us to speak."

After the elevator ride upstairs, the old man instructed the two others to wait in the hall. Ant followed him in.

"You want to drink Anthony?"

Ant's eyebrows narrowed.

"Please, don't be alarmed, please sit."

Ant sat back in his chair.

The old man dug in his suit pocket, pulling out a wallet and tossed it to Ant, "check those out."

Ant opened the wallet, first seeing a picture of a white baby, the next picture obviously a few years later. The third picture almost brought tears to his eyes. The picture was the same boy around age 10 or 12 years old, but he could clearly see it was Ortega.

"I'm his uncle, Preacher or roughly Old Man is what everybody calls me. Not Mike though, he's a young lawyer, he knows none of the business."

Ant nodded, understanding that statement. Preacher sipped his drink, then sat the glass down. "Ahhh, that's good brandy."

"I'm not going to hold you up. I just remember Ortega telling me you didn't like your name used.. James. Ah James, very original."

They both laughed.

"I just know you were more than just business to my nephew. As a matter of fact...." Preacher paused to wipe a tear.. "Excuse me, but I sometimes blame myself for his death. See, he was leaving my house the night of that terrible accident. I asked him who he trusted, first he said, no-one."

Ant smiled.

"But then I asked him, if he had to choose who it would be, he told me you. You were like family to Ortega, I know about that boy Nick and that family, and that snake Warren. What I just want you to know is, any family of Ortega's is my family as well. If you ever need anything, anything...." Preacher repeated as he leaned closer putting a hand on Ant's knee, "please let me know, business or personal."

Ant nodded.

"I'm going to miss Ortega," Preacher said as he wrote a number down and handed it to Ant. "God bless you."

Chapter 30

Five months after Ant met with Preacher, he decided to have a meeting with Jamal with hopes of a glimpse of reason behind the terrible dreams. Not being able to relinquish the horrid thoughts, he picked up the phone and dialed.

"Hello." A woman's voice answered the phone.

"Can I speak to Jamal?"

"Hold on please."

Lisa shook Jamal's arm, first his snoring stopped then his eyes opened. She laughed, "Boy, you is too much, huh take the phone."

She kissed him on the cheek then got out of the king sized bed.

"Hello."

"Oh yeah, I want to meet her."

"What's up, Big Dawg?"

"I want everybody at the spot later on. And I want to go check out the new ESPN Zone in Baltimore next weekend so bring your shorty".

"Ah-ight, let me get up so I can call everybody.

"Willie already knows, so you ain't got to call him. Tell your girl, since ya'll so tight, she can get her hair done for free up the shop."

Lisa walked into the room wearing Jamal's 4X Madness T-shirt, "Do you want bacon or sausage with your eggs?"

Jamal reached for his cell phone, which was vibrating all over his night stand.

"Hello, hold on."

"I want bacon, and put some cheese in the eggs."
"Hello."
"What's up big cuz."
"Who dis? It's little Mel; Your cousin nigga."
"Oh, what's up?"
"My man, Jive, doing it big now and I got something you might be interested in."
"Ah-ight, cuzo, swing through in about an hour."

Little Mel was Jamal's older cousin, he was heavy into robbery but kept good connects. Every time Mel got some new guns he called Jamal for the guaranteed sale. After breakfast, Jamal showered and got dressed then waited on his cousin's arrival.

"Baby, which lip gloss do you think I should wear, pink or red?"
"Red." Jamal answered without even looking. Lisa put her arms around his neck and kissed him, she loved his tongue. "Damn nigga, I will kill you if you eat another bitch; you hear me?"

She waved a finger.

"Get your ass out of here." Jamal laughed then smacked her hard on her butt following her to the door.

"Mal, somebody's pulling up out front."

Jamal stuck his head out the door and saw his cousin's bubbled tinted caprice. "Oh, that's my cousin."

"I almost forgot, Jamal, can I get $500?"

Jamal pulled a huge knot out of his sweat pants.

"Thank you." She walked to her car switching that butt of hers like crazy, got into her Acura then pulled off.

Mel got out of the car, jogging up the walk way to Jamal's front door.

"What's up cousin?"

Mel grabbed his hand and half hugged him.

Pointing his finger back to the street he asked, "Wasn't that the light skinned chick ,Lisa."

"Yeah, come on in."

Mel walked in sitting the duffle bag on the floor. "Man, Lisa is mad as a motherfucker." He laughed, "Aye cuz, you look just like my man City, digging in his pockets kicking that bread out to her. He told me the other day, that head worth a G, easy."

"What?"

Mel noticed his cousin's attitude. "Aw, don't tell me you bunned up with that bitch ,cousin."

"When the last time your man said he saw her?"

"Shit, I just saw her leaving his house three nights ago. She left Toya, Nicky, and Barbie in her Acura, came in, sucked him off, got five hundred and bounced."

DC BLOOD BROTHERS

WILLIE

Willie leaned back on his new Kelly Green 600 Mercedes with his arms crossed, talking to Suave, one of his runners on 7th N.T. "I'm telling you, Suave... the Bullets should have kept their name. The racist Motherfuckas gonna name them the Wizards. Only Wizards this country ever had was the Ku Klux Klan's Grand Wizard."

"You right as usual, Willie."

"I know, look though, when you gonna finish that half brick I gave you?"

"Gimme like, to next week. Damn, look at shorty." Suave pointed across the street to the bus stop.

Willie surveyed, "Yeah she is nice."

The woman stood about 5 feet, dark skinned, pretty face and thick. Just how I like em, he thought.

"Ah-ight slim." He shook Suave's hand, "I got to go make shorty's day."

Willie waited for a break in traffic then walked across the street. The woman looked from left to right as if she was looking for someone.

"How you doing, pretty?"

She looked over her shoulder then turned to face Willie. "I'm fine, do I know you?"

"No sweetheart, I look forward to getting to know you though."

She smiled, "Oh you do?"

He shook his head up and down as he pulled a pen out of his Avirex leather jacket.

"You got a piece of paper?"

She felt in her pockets, finding a receipt, "Here."

He handed her the pen instead of taking the paper. She shook her head and smiled, crossing her arms.

"Go ahead and write down your number, girl."

"How you know I want you to have my number?"

Willie smiled, always up for the challenge. "Look sweetheart, it's like this. From the moment I initiated conversation I knew I could get your number. See, I ain't one of these young dumb dudes. I got two sisters, so trust me I know women. The only way I wouldn't get your number is if I somehow turned you off in conversation."

"See, I should leave you alone right now, for pulling every woman's card like that, you know too much. How you know if I don't have a husband or boyfriend? Or do you care?"

"Whoa, ease up sister, of course I care, I'm very picky. As intelligent as you seem I doubt you're the type of woman that would have given so much conversation to me, if you were involved."

"Very well spoken."

"My names Willie, what's yours?"

"I'm Nique."

"Um, can I give you a ride somewhere?" She looked at him as if he were crazy.

"What, do you want to see my license first?"

"Yeah, I don't know you, boy."

He laughed. "Where you from?"

"Why, you hear an accent? I'm originally from Charlotte, NC."

"Oh yeah, I've never met a country girl."

"What ever, pretty boy. You probably got women all over DC!"

"I..."

She put up a finger, "Don't ruin our moment by dignifying my statement with a remark, I thought you knew women."

"I do."

"Well, you should know when we make insecure comments like the one I made, it's not a challenge to men to see if you can say the right thing. It's a challenge for you to prove us wrong. Now, let me see your license, your name probably ain't even Willie."

"Come with me across the street. It's in my car."

She followed him to the corner, mouth dropping open as he disarmed the alarm on the Benz.

"Tell me this isn't your car."

"Yes, it is."

"How old are you? Where do you work?"

"I'm twenty seven. Nique, I ain't hard to figure out. I'm out here in a $700 leather, $400 sweater, $200 jeans, and $380 boots. I could wrap this Benz around a tree and pull up in a new 600 tomorrow afternoon."

"I don't know..."

"Look..." he cut her off. "My car is clean, and my papers are legit. Let me give you a ride home."

Without answering she stepped closer to the passenger door. Willie started the ignition and turned down the televisions.

"This is really nice.," she complimented.

"Where were you going?"

"Home, I have an apartment in Maryland's Andrews Manor."

Willie pulled off into traffic, making a right on Florida Avenue heading towards 3rd St. tunnel.

"You in a rush to get home?"

"Not really why?"

"Let's go down to Georgetown's Bar and sip a little Remy, eat some buffalo wings."

"Oh my God, I am addicted to those things. Do they come with celery like at Outback Steak House?"

"If you want."

Willie stole a glance at Nique while navigating through traffic. She was dark and beautiful and had the prettiest teeth and smile. A little green far as street wise, but that was part of the attraction too.

"Call Duck," He ordered his phone. Ring.

"Hello."

"Hey Champ, I'll be there later. I maybe a little late but I'll be there."

"Everything ah-ight?" Ant asked concerned.

"Ah, Yeah, I'm just taking a new lady friend of mine to the bar down G-town to get acquainted."

"Well honestly, Willie, you ain't got to come."

"Yeah, Mal would have a fucking fit."

"You're probably right but he'll manage. I won't give him a choice."

"Aw-ight, Big Dawg."

Nique looked to Willie after he hung up. He felt her eyes staring at him.

"What's up?"

"Can you play that last song, Him or Me again, that was some deep shit."

Willie pressed the rewind button and turned up the volume.

ANTHONY

A brisk wind gently rattled the window as Ant laid across his suede sofa in deep thought. The product the N.Y. boys have is good but he couldn't shake this feeling about them jokers. Ant reached for his phone. "Call Jamal." He commanded, and waited for his friend to answer.

"Hello!"

"Aye, Mal, I changed my mind about meeting later so call everybody, tell them my bad."

"You alright ,Big-Dawg?"

"Yeah, I just want to go over a few plans."

"Talk to you later."

Ant picked up the piece of paper he'd been looking at off and on for the past few days. It was Preachers number.

An hour later Ant was parking his Jaguar coupe. The front door opened as he reached for the door bell.

"Come on in, Ant, follow me to my study."

Ant sat down on the rich dark leather sofa admiring all the animal heads around the wall, also the gun and knife collections that were encased in a lovely display.

"What would you like to drink, Ant?"

"Remy."

After handing Ant his drink, Preacher sat and asked Ant to speak his mind.

"Well here's what has been happening. Since we lost Ortega, I have been dealing with these New York dudes but only a few hundred at a time. Which makes me have to re-up more and I don't like large amounts moving three times a month."

Preacher nodded sympathizing with the young dealer.

"What I want to ask is if I can get packages from you, I want to cut those dudes off."

Preacher put up his hand to interrupt, "Say no more, just tell me how much you have and take what you need."

"Thanks Preacher."

"Let me ask you something, Ant, do you have a getaway plan?"

"What do you mean?" Ant asked puzzled.

"I mean like fake identification, credit cards maybe even a passport. Give me two weeks, Ant, and I'll have ID and a credit card with at least ten grand on it for you."

Preacher paused for a minute and continued. "I must tell you Ant, if you ever have to run, do it alone."

"Alright, Preacher, I'll call you later once I have the paper together and we can meet.

LISA

"Lisa, are you alright in there what does it say?"

"Toya, I'm pregnant, it just turned pink."

"Well, are you coming out of the bathroom?"

Lisa stormed out of the bathroom holding her head as if she caught an instant migraine. Toya hugged her best friend, "So what are you going to do, Lisa?"

"I don't know. I don't know if I'm ready for a child, but you know I do not like the thought of an abortion so I just have to tell Jamal, plus that fat bastard caked up, he can support us well."

"Well now is a better time than any." Toya remarked handing Lisa her telephone.

Lisa contemplated on what she was going to say to Jamal as she nervously dialed the phone.

"Hello."

"Hi Jamal I.."

"What do you want, Lisa?" Jamal barked, cutting her off.

"Why you talking to me like that, Jamal?"

"Cause my big cousin gave me the 411 on your freak ass. You up in here acting like you feeling me and running around town sucking dick and shit!"

"Jamal, you are tripping..."

"So you don't know a dude name City, huh?"

"Well yeah, he's an old friend."

"Well, your old friend bragging about how good your head is and my cousin told me he just saw you leave dude house about 4 nights ago. So, Bitch, lose my MothaFuckin number!"

The phone went dead and Lisa's hand flew to her mouth in shock.

"What's wrong, Lisa? Why didn't you tell him? Who was he asking about?"

"City. His cousin saw me at his house the other night and told Jamal that City was bragging on how I give head."

"Damn, Lisa, I'm sorry to hear that, with you being pregnant you sure don't need this extra bullshit. Come on girl let's go shopping and we'll figure this out later."

JASON

"Shana, can you bring me a glass of wine?"
"Sure Baby let me answer the phone first."
"Hello."
"Hello, Daughter, how are you and my son on this beautiful morning?"
"Hi, Ma, we've been up for a while going over the bills and trying to get this paper work straight so we can build our dream home."
"Oh, I'm sorry to disturb you."
"It's no problem, Ma, just give me a second... here Jay." Shana handed him the glass of wine. "It's Ma."
"Hello, Ma? Hello?"
"Yes, I'm here, Shana." Millie responded extremely low.
"You alright, Ma."
"Yeah it's just my breathing is becoming so shallow..." Shana heard a loud crashing sound.
"Ma! Ma, are you there? Ma!"
"Oh my God, Ma said her breathing was becoming shallow then I just heard a loud noise and now she's not responding. I still hear her television in the background."
Jason leaped out of bed and grabbed the receiver.
"Hello Ma..."
He hung up and dialed 911.
After giving the operator Millie's address Jason grabbed Jr. and they rushed to her house with sirens wailing.
An hour later at Prince George's Hospital Ant, Jason and Shana paced the floor awaiting news from the doctor. Paramedics said she just had a major coronary attack. They couldn't stabilize her before she was rushed to the hospital. It didn't look good for Millie.
Six hours later, Ant was the first to notice the Doctor approaching so he leaped out of the uncomfortable plastic chair.
"So how is she, Doc?"
Ant asked with tears already brewing in the wells of his eyes.
"I'm sorry, son, we did everything we could."
"No, Jay!" Shana screamed pounding both fist into Jason's shoulder.
"It's gonna be alright, Shana."
"One more thing, I don't know how relevant it is but in all my years of being a doctor, I've never seen this. After we performed the bypass she was stable, then the nurse nudged my arm and pointed to your mother and she had a genuine smile

on her face. Next second later we lost her.

Jason smiled and reached to shake the doctor's hand.

"Thank you, sir, and don't take what happened to heart, we know you all did your best. When it's our time, I guess that's it."

A solitary tear fell from Ant's eye and slowly descended to the floor as if in slow motion. "I can't believe she is gone, Jay."

Jason embraced his brother in a way he hadn't since before their father was killed.

"Don't you get it, Ant? The doctor said Ma smiled right before she went under. She let go, Ant. I think she really wanted to be back with dad. So don't be selfish and take this personal. She's back now with the person she's been missing for all these years."

"You right, Jay."

"Like I was saying..." Jason stopped mid-sentence and pointed towards the nurses' station.

"Isn't that, Michelle?"

"Yeah, let me go talk to her. I don't want her to have rushed all the way up here to hear the bad news while she's still out of breath."

The next few months were up and down for the Jenkins's family. Jason took a couple days off to make funeral arrangements. Ant threw himself more into the street. He made the right decision to cut off the N.Y. boys. Preacher was selling dirt cheap like he brought it from Columbia and Africa himself.

Millie's funeral was quaint. Just close family members and friends. Everyone had decided to keep it small.

Chapter 31

Willie and Nique has been spending every spare moment with each other, things are getting serious fast.

"Baby you know what I was thinking? I've been hearing about this restaurant in Georgetown named Sequoia's have you been there?"

"No, not yet but I've heard some good things about the place. This girl I was talking to in CVS told me she had been there and how nice it was."

"Give me a kiss and I'll think about it."

Nique leaned over to Willie, first gently rubbing her lips across his then parting her mouth to taste him. "So, have you thought about it now?"

"Yeah I think we can work something out. Look I got some shit to take care of tonight. I may be late getting back. I'm about to go get my hair cut."

"Hair cut!" Nique yelled. "You just got your hair cut four days ago."

Willie laughed, "I always get my hair cut every four days. By the time a dude wait a week, his shape up lines are gone."

"Whatever, pretty boy. Just take me to Sequoia's.

"I got you, Boo. I meant to tell you I got tickets to the Redskin game, you trying to go?"

"Yeah just let me know in advance. I'll be back, Willie. I need to brush my teeth that pizza we ate from Eddie Leonard's was good but I'm not trying to be a walking advertisement."

Willie surveyed Nique's apartment, one love seat and a little television on a stand that looked like it would collapse any moment. I got to get my boo's shit together, he thought to himself.

Reaching into his pocket pulling out three large wads of cash wrapped in rubber bands, he began counting. "Boy, why do you have all that money on you?"

"Girl, this ain't any money."

"Oh yeah well how much is it?"

"About ten thousand."

Nique stared at the money.

"Take the money, Nique."

"I don't know, Willie, that's a lot of money."

"Look Nique, I understand how you feel about me hustling so I do my best to keep the streets away from you. I want you to know it's refreshing to meet a chick I have to bend her arm just to spend a few hundred on. I'm feeling you like shit, Nique. I ain't saying I love you but I know I'm falling for you. There are no strings attached to this money."

"No strings?"

"Nope, well there is one. I want you to spend at least half of this on a new TV and living room set."

"Willie, I'm going to take this money and do as you asked but I have a string attached."

"And what's that Nique?"

"Well since I don't make very much, I haven't been able to treat you how I would like. So, since you're giving me, well forcing me to take this money, I want to do something nice for you. Willie, I know you're a good looking, well groomed man at that and I know chicks be on you. Please don't break my heart. If you meet someone else and want to be with her, let me down easy. Don't have no chicks causing drama for me and don't bring anything in my house you didn't bring when you first came, promise."

"I promise, Nique."

JAMAL

"Damn look at that ass. Aye, Shorty, come here." Jamal yelled out the window of his Lexus 400.

"You called me?"

"Hell yeah, Shorty, what's your name?"

"Tia, what's yours?"

"Jamal, but let's skip the small talk, how old are you?"

"I'm 19 but I'll be 20 next week."

"Yeah? Why don't you hop in and let me show your sexy ass off for the day."

Tia walked to the passenger side and got in. An Acura cut Jamal off so close it almost hit him. Lisa stormed out of the car holding her stomach, she was already showing.

"Who the fuck is that little bitch, Jamal? You are robbing the cradle now, motherfucka?"

"Lisa, get away from me with that bullshit."

"Bitch, get the fuck out the car."

"Don't move, Shorty, you alright."

"She ain't alright and if the bitch doesn't get the fuck out the car now, Imma cut her face up."

Tia opened the door and ran away from the car. Jamal put the car in reverse and began slowly backing up since Lisa was in front of the car.

"Jamal, this is your baby. How can you treat me like this?"

"You freak ass bitch, I don't know who's baby it is, you running around town fucking for money. Bitch, matter of fact..."

Jamal reached into his lap then extended his arm out the window brandishing a Desert Eagle 44 magnum. Lisa jumped away from the car as Jamal sped off.

"That's how it is, Jamal ... You want to kill me and our baby?"

ANTHONY

Barry brought Ant a beer then playfully slapped Petey behind the head.

"Stop playing, Barry."

"Man, ya'll youngins pipe the fuck down before I put my foot in both your asses."

"Damn, Tony, it's like that?"

Tony just looked at the youths and they sat down.

"Pay attention." Ant began. "Now I got all of you here, somebody tell me what the fuck is going on."

"Them niggas from down the barber shop shot at Petey's car."

"I just got that Benz wagon too."

"Shut the fuck up and let me finish, Petey." Barry demanded "I was driving the Benz so they must have thought I was him because as soon as I bent the corner, the niggas was gunning'. Why would they want your head, Petey?"

"I slapped that nigga nephew that supplies them dudes down there for claiming he gated my dice and he reached for him after I made my point."

Ant laughed in astonishment, not humor, then asked, "So three niggas dead behind a crap game?"

"It's the principle..."

"Fuck the principle, don't I take good care of you little niggas? I need ya'll to take care of me too and you can't do that dead or locked up. So don't be so quick to blow your cool over money, if a nigga owe you I'll double it; Just let him go and come to me square business, you hear me? That's my cue to leave, I got to meet Willie up 'Chelle's shop anyway."

chapter 32

LISA

A light drizzle tantalized the pavement as the sun's brilliance cascaded the day.

"Toya, come on let's go in Nordstroms again, I think I'm going to get that sweater."

"Lisa you crazy if you're going to pay $175.00, on a plain pink sweater."

"Bitch! This is Yves Saint Laurent!"

"Boo, it's not about that if nobody knows."

"They are not suppose to if you're on some top-flight shit. I just love the confidence of knowing the best rags are wrapped around this beautiful body of mine."

"You conceded bitch, and don't forget you pregnant, so that beautiful body of yours needs to be in maturity right now."

"Stop hating, Toya. I'm going in the dressing room."

Bzzz

Lisa looked down at her cell phone screen seeing Patrice's number. Patrice was an old neighborhood friend, among the ranks of the most top-flight chicks in the city.

Lisa answered, "Hello, Patrice . . .What's up?"

"Ain't nothing girl, I just..."

"Hello! Patrice are you there?" Lisa looked at her phone and saw the battery had completely died. Shit!

DC BLOOD BROTHERS

She stepped out of the dressing room. "Toya, I think I want to try a size down. Oh! Let me see your phone, mine just went dead talking to Patrice."

"What that slut want?"

"Boe and Jay around 103rd supposed to be throwing the biggest cook out next week, so she's giving me directions. It's going to be at a beach house in Ocean City."

"Didn't they throw that party on the Spirit of Washington last year?"

"Yep, that's them, but enough with the thousand questions. Bitch, this ain't Jeopardy give me the phone."

"You evil ass bitch, and I want you to know your big ass is not going to fit into that sweater!"

"Fuck you, Toya!" Lisa walked back to the dressing room, and admired herself in the mirror after trying on the sweater. "Let me call Patrice back."

Since Patrice was a mutual friend, Lisa knew her number would be programmed in Toya's phone. She scrolled down from the A's heading down to the P's. Lisa eye's almost bulged out of their sockets seeing Jamal's cell number.

What the fuck?

She pushed contact info, and along with the cell numbers, she also had his home number and pager as well.

"This sneaky bitch," she mumbled under her breath after suddenly recalling when they were all at Hogates, she returned to the table seeing Toya and Jamal exchange numbers.

"That nigga changed his cell phone number three times and ducks me, I'm pregnant by him, but Toya has both his new numbers and house number."

Hoping her instincts were wrong, but knowing all too well they weren't, Lisa pressed talk to call Jamal.

"Hey, what's up sexy?" Jamal asked before hearing the caller's voice.

"Sexy! Sexy!"

The familiar voice turned Jamal's stomach sour as it registered. "So, you have been fucking my best friend Jamal?"

"Lisa..."

"Lisa, shit!" She cut him off. "You are beefing with me, because I did dirt, and you doing it too." Lisa wiped her eyes as tears fell. "Jamal, how could you do this to me? I love you."

"What? You love me? Lisa, your ass doesn't love anything but money."

"Jamal this is your baby, and you are the only person I slept with without a condom. Why, is it so hard to believe this is yours?"

"I ain't saying the baby can't be mine. I just didn't appreciate hearing your business."

"How you think I feel right now, Jamal? I just found out you're fucking my best friend. We're even now, Jamal, so can we please sit down and talk, baby? I'm not even gonna whip Toya's ass as bad as I want to, but I'm gonna cut this bitch off after I bomb her conniving ass out. So, can I come talk to you please?"

"Okay." Click!

DC BLOOD BROTHERS

Lisa yanked the tight sweater off and stormed out of the dressing room to confront Toya. She was smiling as Lisa approached.

"That sweater was too tight huh, Bitch!"

"You the bitch, Toya! What the fuck is this?" Lisa screamed drawing attention from everyone within earshot, as she held Toya's phone.

"Lisa, I'm sorry"

"I'm sorry shit, Toya! You been fucking this nigga, and even after I confessed I was starting to feel something for him." Lisa started to cry.

"Lisa, calm down you're pregnant."

"How can I calm down, Toya, huh!" Lisa yelled as she threw Toya's cell phone toward a clothes rack. Storming away, Lisa looked over her shoulder, "...and don't call me you scandalous bitch!"

30 minutes later, Lisa parked her new Acura coupe in front of Jamal's house. The front door slowly opened as Lisa approached. Jamal's face was so tight he could have been a statute.

"I'm sorry Jamal baby; I swear. I know how bitches be on you cause you a fly ass nigga. I was just fucking around, so I wouldn't get caught up in my feelings too much. Please forgive me? I swear if you give me another chance I'll never let you down, but you have to promise me you won't fuck Toya anymore."

"Lisa, I don't know..." Jamal started. "Jamal please, I'll take a paternity test as soon as the baby is born. It's yours, please Jamal! What you saying, you don't miss me Jamal?"

"I'm not saying that but..."

The tension was broken as Jamal's phone interrupted his train of thought.

"Hello, what's up, Big Dawg?"

"I need you to pick up the kids later. Barry is taking care of something else for me."

"No, problem I'll take care of it."

Click.

"Lisa, I have to talk to you later."

"No, problem Jamal. I don't want to pressure you. I just want you to know we're here for you."

As Lisa began walking to her car, Jamal's phone started ringing again. This time it was Toya.

"What was Lisa doing with your phone?"

"Her's went dead, so she asked to use mine. I know I never speak on you and Lisa's business, but Jamal I was there when she calculated the date back to her getting pregnant. I know I'm not with her 24 hours a day, but from all I've seen, that baby is yours." Jamal held his phone in silence as a wave of guilt washed over him. "Jamal I don't mean any harm, but we can't see each other anymore. Lisa's my best friend, and I can't tell you how bad I'm feeling right now."

Jamal hung up then pulled his 357 magnum from under his pillow, tucked it in the front of his jeans then began pressing the combination on his safe. He counted out $50,000, stuffed it in a book bag and walked out to his Mercedes to meet Preacher's delivery man.

DC BLOOD BROTHERS

WILLIE

"What's up Suave'? How you living?"

"Hey Willie, you know when I grow up I want to be just like you.," Suave joked as he shook Willie's hand.

A police car pulled in front of them. Officers started getting out with guns drawn. "Put your hands on the car!"

"Come on man, we ain't doing shit.," Suave' blurted in disgust.

"You clean?" Willie whispered. "Fuck it then, you ain't got any warrants do you?"

"I don't know, Willie. These hot ass niggas around here; you never know."

The officers patted the men down, after seeing they were clean they called in their ID's to run a warrant check. Two minutes later one of the officers, known as Officer Savage who worked Uptown DC, walked behind Suave' pulling his arm's behind him, and reached for his cuffs.

He looked to Willie; "You can go. Mr. Watson here has child support warrants in P.G. County."

Willie watched as the officer ushered Suave' to the patrol car.

"Tell my girl to come get me." Suave' yelled out the back window as the patrol car pulled off.

Willie grabbed for his phone just as it started to ring.

"Hey Willie, I got off early today, so I'm about to see if I can get my hair done."

"My sister got a shop, and they'll do it for free."

" Well, can you give her a call to see if she can fit me in, and give me the address, so I can catch the bus over there."

"Nique, let me buy you a car?"

"No, Willie you just gave me ten grand. No, I got enough if I want to buy a used car."

"Used! Fine Nique, but I don't have to call to see if she can fit you in, and I'm getting off the strip anyway, so I'll pick you up. Police just jumped out on my man and me."

"Really? Are you alright?"

"Yea, where are you?"

"Downtown by the International Shops."

"Cool, gimme about 10 minutes."

MICHELLE

"Hi, Shana, come here, and give me a hug. I didn't know you were coming. Why didn't you call?"

"Girl, I was just driving by, so I decided to stop in and say hi."

Michelle looked over Shana's head then around her shop to see who was close to finishing an appointment.

"Why, are you looking at me like that, 'Chelle?"

"Girl, you might have stopped by just to say hi, but you could use a touch up. Now, it's okay walking into my shop like that, but I cannot let you walk out of my shop with your hair looking like this; people will think that's our finish product."

"Oh, stop it, 'Chelle!," Shana playfully gave her the finger.

Ring!

"Hello, Le Nuevo... How may I help you?"

"Hey, Sis! I'm parking out front, and I have my girl with me; she needs her hair done."

"Just bring her in, Willie; Shana already popped up on me, so the more the merrier."

Nique was surprised as Michelle walked up to Willie with her arms opened to hug him.

"Are you sure this is your sister, Willie?"

Michelle extended her hand answering, "Yes, I'm Michelle and what's your name?"

"I'm Nique."

Michelle softly elbowed Willie. "She's cute; ya'll would make some pretty babies."

Willie put both his index fingers up to form a cross as if he were warding off some hex of evil.

"Come on, Nique, since Willie brought you in I'll do your hair myself. Willie, there's a bottle of champagne in my safe. You know the combo just use a glass please."

Willie popped open the bottle of Moet, poured a glass and made his way downstairs to the entertainment room. Grabbing the play station controller, and resumed the John Madden football game someone abandoned.

"So, Nique, what kind of work do you do?"

"I'm a teacher's aide part-time and a full-time student."

"What age range? Or grade, excuse me?"

"Fourth grade, I don't ever want to teach above that grade, kids are too grown these days."

"I know what you mean, Nique."

"So, how long you had this shop, Michelle? You did a beautiful job decorating."

"No, a friend of mine. I just paid her, but I've had this shop a few years now."

"That's good, looks like you doing well."

"I guess we're doing all right. No matter what business you're in it has it's pros and cons."

"So, are you married?"

"No, I'm engaged though," Michelle showed her five carat princess cut diamond."

"Oh, girl! Somebody loves you! So what's his name?"

"Sam." Michelle lied.

"All right, Nique, let's get you under the dryer, so this hair can set." Michelle gathered a few magazines for Nique then left her under the dryer.

"'Chelle! 'Chelle!"

Michelle turned around seeing Shana smile from ear to ear. "You're right! Tricie is good," walking two circles around Shana nodding in admiration of Tricie's work.

"Thank you Tricie; remind me to pay you out of pocket for the favor."

Shana looked around the shop before opening her purse, pulling out her checkbook and pen. Michelle's hands fell to her hips. "And, what you pull that out for?"

"I'm gonna pay you."

"Your money is no good here; get out Shana."

"Okay," Shana said as she grabbed Michelle's arm. "Tell Dana I said, Hello."

"I'll tell her, but which one is Dana?"

"The short lady under the dryer."

"Oh, you mean Nique."

"No, her name is Dana. We met a couple of years ago at the DC Policemen's Ball."

Willie is not going to like the idea that his girl used to date a cop, Michelle thought.

"So she was dating a cop?"

"No" Shana laughed. "She's a police officer. Well, come to think of it I remember Jason saying she made detective."

"Well, 'Chelle let me get out of here. I have to get back to work."

"All right, Shana, tell Jay and Jr. I said, "What's up."

Oh, my God! Ant's not gonna like this.

Chapter 33

Ant was starting to get frustrated with the amount of time it was taking for them to finish the count. Barry realized the money machine wasn't reading a stack.

"What the fuck!" Barry blurted.

Ant and Petey turned to Barry. "What's wrong?" Ant asked?.

"This stack didn't count; I think it's broke."

"The stack wasn't able to be counted because this shit is counterfeit. From now on, everybody count the money they bring in separately. This is the little shit that can get our asses caught up."

Just then, his phone rang.

"Yeah, what's up 'Chelle?"

"Baby, I need to talk to you ASAP."

"I'm on my way."

"No...No! Don't come to the shop."

"Why? What's going on?"

"I'll tell you when we're face to face. Meet me at the Giant Food on Blair Road."

Thirty minutes later, Ant parked his Range Rover beside Michelle's 850 BMW after circling the parking lot. Her head was down in her hands. Ant got out of his car and opened her passenger side door.

"Oh shit!" Michelle's hands went to her heart in fear.

"What's wrong?"

"Baby, oh shit where should I start?"

DC BLOOD BROTHERS

"Just take your time and calm down."

"Okay, first Shana popped up at the shop, next thing Willie calls me telling me he's out front, and his girl needs her hair done. I did her hair, and we conversed, you know nothing odd to be in the hair shop, but she was asking, how long you had the shop, you married, what's your man's name, general shit you know.

Shana was about to leave, and on the way out the door she asked me to tell Dana she said, "hi," referring to Willie's girl, but Willie's girl told me her name was Nique. The fucked up thing is when I asked her where she knew her from since there was a conflict with the names. She said she met her at a Policemen's Ball."

"Ha! Ha! Ha!" Ant exploded in laughter. "Willie's girl used to date a cop?"

"I thought the same shit, but no!" Ant's smiled disappeared, and was replaced with concern.

"Don't tell me"

"Yes, baby. She's a cop; Well detective."

"Shit!" Ant screamed as he slammed both hands to the dashboard.

"Baby, I know Willie has no idea."

"Yeah, I know, but if she's his girl, that means he may have gotten a little comfortable around her."

"You think she's an undercover cop or something?"

Ant shook his head up and down.

"So, what are we going to do?"

"Don't worry 'Chelle, I'll take care of it. Let me get out of here, so I can brain storm."

Ant had never been so confused on what to do. He called Preacher. Ant's heart felt like it was going to beat out his chest as he explained the situation to the old man. Even after he explained to Preacher that she was cop, Preacher's facial expression never changed.

"So what should I do Preacher?"

"First, Ant, don't panic. It's like playing poker down to the last person, and knowing what they have in their hand. After you've put all your money into the pot chasing everybody off, the last thing you want to do is fold. Have you met this woman face to face?"

"No."

"And you still never use your name with your men correct?" "Right, but Willie took her to Michelle's shop."

"Honestly Ant, I don't know how close or expendable your people are, but I would down them both. See, if the cops had enough Intel you'd be locked up already, so they're digging. I would do them both only to make sure I didn't put the other 300 people and their families at risk."

"That works for me."

"So you make both plates as my grandmother used to say. You might not like either dish, but you can't starve. Something has to be done, and before you leave I guess now is a good time as any to give you this ID, and credit card ~ Robert Smith… original huh Ant?"

DC BLOOD BROTHERS

Ant laughed. "Not really Preacher. I guess it will do though."

"Oh, I also had a passport made for you. I have a 20 acre compound in Italy, and the 35 acre compound in Cuba. You could never leave either property and live like a king. I'm in good standing with both governments. The only thing we would have to worry about is if they want you so bad they'd send Special Forces to kidnap you from countries you can't be extradited from."

"So, do what you have to do, but now you have options."

"All right Preacher. Thanks for everything."

Ring!

"Hey, what's up Big Dawg?"

"Willie, you still with your girl?"

"Yeah why, what's up? You sound a little serious?"

"Drop her off then meet me at the spot ASAP"

One hour later, Ant stood with his arms crossed as Willie pulled up.

"What's up Champ?"

"First, go in and change clothes. Take off everything; watch, ring and chain."

Willie returned a few minutes later. "We about to go put in that work huh Homie?"

"Naw, Willie somebody's putting that work in on us. Willie, your girl is 5-0. Yeah, my brother's wife recognized her from a Policeman's Ball a couple years ago. She is a detective."

"Shit! Homie you know I didn't know. And, before you ask; I kept her out my business. But shit, I bought her to the shop."

"I know Willie; the reason we're here is to figure out what to do."

"Anything you say Homie."

"We gonna play dumb until I figure this thing all the way out.

LISA

"Hello... you've reached Lisa, but unfortunately I'm unable to take your call, leave your name, number, and a brief message, and I'll...." Toya hung up and redialed.

She knew Lisa was home, because she was parked directly across the street from Lisa's townhouse.

"Hello! Toya, what the fuck do you want?"

"Lisa, I miss you, and I'm so sorry for what I did. I'm sitting across the street from your house. Please at least come to the door and talk to me, so I can explain myself."

"Okay, Toya, I'm coming to the door now."

Toya stepped out the car heading to the door. Lisa opened the door and stepped out, face red with anger. She crossed her arms over her swollen stomach.

"Lisa, I'm so sorry. My guilt has been killing me. I spoke with my mom about this, and a lot of issues reached surface. Lisa I know I was wrong. I really didn't even like Jamal."

"Then why you fuck him, bitch!"

"Because he was yours. I envy you Lisa. You're smart, beautiful, fly as shit, and have always been that way." Toya's eyes filled with tears as she continued. "You don't know how hard it is for us to go out, and every guy that approaches us wants you. You don't know how many men I've slept with that moaned out your name. I don't even know why you wanted me as a friend. I was a nothing ass bitch until you made me somebody. I just wanted to be you, walk a mile in your shoes. See the world through your eyes. I never wanted to hurt you. I swear."

Tears now began forming in Lisa's eyes as Toya continued. "You think I don't know how you flirt and seduce guys I talk to."

"But you didn't like them, Toya."

"So what! Everybody has shoes. Some shoes we like more than others, but that doesn't mean our friends can go in our closet, put on a pair, leave with them then bring them back when they feel like it."

"Okay, Toya, I'm sorry too but that doesn't ease the fact you carried an ongoing relationship with Jamal."

"Lisa, I spoke to Jamal 5 minutes that day just to say, "No more," which he agreed also. I also told him your baby is his."

"Well, first, Toya, I know you haven't spoken to Jamal, and just so you know we're back together, and he is claiming his baby now. He even gave me this ring." Lisa turned the back of her left hand to Toya.

"What! You're engaged now... congratulations!"

"Thank you. So, how do I know I can trust you to be around Jamal?"

"I swear Lisa; I love you like a sister, and I promise you can trust me. Lisa we been through entirely too much bullshit for us to just go our separate ways."

Lisa opened her arms to her best friend, and they embraced as the sobbed in each other's arms.

"I've missed you too, Toya. Just don't hurt me again."

"I swear I'll die first."

Ring! Ring!

Toya followed Lisa in the house. After Lisa talked briefly to Patrice, Toya notice her friend was upset again.

"What's wrong, Lisa?"

"Toya, remember when I told you I thought Jamal was no longer dealing with Ant."

"Yeah, why?"

"I've been dealing with Jamal all these years, and I never heard him mention Ant's name once, but Patrice told me she saw them together in B-more. I'm not gonna mention it though. Jamal and I have enough to deal with."

The thought of Ant churned Lisa's stomach like fresh butter. At the same time she swore to herself that she would never mention this to Jamal.

JAMAL

Jamal ordered a double shot of Louis XIII as he waited on the young model he'd just met at the club.

Ring! Ring!

DC BLOOD BROTHERS

Jamal looked down seeing Lisa's number, and decided not to call her back until they got outside.

"Okay, let's go big sexy!"

Jamal put his arm around her waist escorting her out of the club. After squeezing through the parked nightclub they made their way to Jamal's Acura NSX.

"Damn, this is yours?"

Jamal just smiled and pressed this remote to open the wing doors of the coupe sports car.

"What's your name again baby?"

"It's Molina."

"Well, Molina I need you to be quiet for a minute, so I can call my girl."

"Anything you say Big Daddy."

Jamal started the ignition and dialed Lisa's house number. Ring!

"Hello; hi baby, I was getting worried. Are you on your way?"

"Naw, I got to meet my man. We're going to Virginia to look at some property to invest in."

"At 3am in the morning Jamal?"

"No, the meeting is at 7am with the builders doing the construction."

"Okay, well be safe."

Molina unzipped Jamal's slacks pulling at this manhood; then dropped her face in his lap swallowing him whole.

"Ah! Whew!"

"Jamal, what are you doing?"

"Putting my stuff in the truck."

"Then why are you moaning in my ear?"

"I'm fat, Lisa. That's what fat people do; we breathe hard."

"Whatever Jamal." Click.

Jamal closed his cell phone then grabbed the back of Molina's head, pushing it down harder, forcing himself deeper, and faster into Molina's wet mouth. He yelled in satisfaction, feeding her his sweet release, then dropped his head back into his seat. Molina licked her lips, smiling, then wiped her mouth with the back of her hand. "Damn Boo, you was a little backed up, you almost drowned my ass. You have a napkin or something in here I can wipe my hands with?"

Ring!

"What's up, Mal? This City, you trying to shoot some dice?"

"Where at?"

"Me and my man leaving the club now, we got about 15 dudes. Stevie gonna open up his store, so we can shoot in there. Make sure you bring at least $50,000 we rolling a grand a shot."

"You ain't saying shit, City! I'm on the way nigga."

Chapter 35

JASON

Jason sat in the C&P telephone van along with his partners. Mitch listening to the conversation their informant who is wearing a wire is having a drug dealer attempting to buy 3 kilos of heroin, they were also discussing the possible murder of rival heroin dealer. The informant Joe Wyans and the drug dealer Rodney Meeks were long time friends. What Rodney didn't know is two months ago Joe was pulled over by a Park Police Officer for doing 40 mph in a 25 mph zone. After smelling marijuana smoke in the car, the officer called for backup and summoned a K-9 Unit to justify the search of the vehicle.

Later discovering half kilo of heroin and a fully loaded 9 mm handgun along with an extended clip, Joe was arrested and charged with Intent to Distribute and Possession of a firearm while being a felon.

Joe was already on five years probation for felony possession of narcotics. He quickly began snitching knowing he could get sentenced to 20 years easily. He told the officers of this long time friend and supplier Rodney Meeks who was involved in an open street war with is competition that's already resulted in two murders.

"So what's up with them S.E. niggas, Rodney? I heard they shot up your girl's car. Man, Joe, I ain't even playing with them niggas no more. I'm putting in $20,000 hit on C.J., his right hand man, and his freak ass baby mother, you know how I get down nigga; Eye for an eye."

"That's right, Rodney, handle your motherfuckin' business."

DC BLOOD BROTHERS

"Enough about them bitch ass niggas. What you working with?"

"I got $210,000, but I want to buy three can you front me one?"

"Yeah, I can do that for you little Homie. Go get your money and meet me back here in 2 hours."

"Aight Homie, see you in a minute."

Jason stopped the recording after he saw Joe come out of Rodney's apartment.

"Mitch, pass me a donut please?"

"Here you go Jay, you better slow down; It's your third one this morning."

"I know; Shana already hinted about my weight the other day, saying she was gonna buy a treadmill and some free weights."

"Oh yeah, guess who Shana ran into at the hair salon the other day?"

"Who?"

"Nique."

"She didn't blow her cover did she?"

"No, Shana said she seemed to be by herself anyway. Mitch, go ahead and call downtown so we can get the bust warrant on Rodney Meeks. I'll call the U.S. Marshal Service, so they can put Joe into Protective Custody. Trial should be over in 6 months. They'll send him out Idaho somewhere. And by the way, I'm inviting you to my brother Anthony's wedding."

"I'll be there Jenkins. I don't have a problem going to anybody's wedding as long as I'm not the one with my hand on the chopping block."

ANTHONY

"Come on 'Chelle and help me with this money."

"Baby, you don't even have the safe opened yet."

Ant unlocked the commercial size safe that was so full, money fell out in ten thousand stacks as the door opened.

"Baby, how much you got in there?"

"Probably a couple million."

"I believe you to, how much are we taking to Vegas with us?"

"How much you got in the bank, 'Chelle?"

"Last time I checked the balance it was almost hundred thousand."

"Then help me count out six hundred thousand."

Ant began breaking down the figures that they'd need. $500 a day for the limo, $10,000 to rent the private jet for a week (fuel not included), $25,000 a night for their hotel suite, and $20,000 for VIP seats for shows, one at the Beluga, and the other at the Mirage. That's roughly $180,000 he thought.

An hour later, Michelle looked out the window after hearing the limo blow it's horn. "Baby! The limo is out front!"

"Aight 'Chelle, tell him to come get the suitcases out of the foyer."

The limo driver got out and did as Michele instructed. She was very impressed with his mannerism, it wasn't often a man could talk to her without his eyes roaming the contour of her body.

The ride to the airport was enjoyable with the champagne, fresh fruit, and jazz playing in the background. They didn't feel one speed bump or pothole. They didn't even feel the limo stop for a red light. So lost in the conversation they didn't even know they were at the airport until the limo driver opened their door.

The inside of the private jet was decked out in creams and gold. The plane's name was Phantom I was embroidered in the center of the Egyptian carpet, and also initialed in every headrest. The bathroom was full sized and fully functioned, robes, towels and wash cloths, which also had the emblem and name. The plane's staff included the pilot, copilot, two stewardesses, a masseuse, chef, manicurist, and hair stylist.

"Baby thank you, this is so nice. Oh my God! I can't wait till I tell the girls at the shop about this. Where is my camera?" Michelle said aloud digging through her small bag.

Ant stretched out in the overwhelming seat and folded his fingers behind his head. "Yeah, this is living 'Chelle, I've been thinking. Don't you have a couple of the girls at the shop trained good enough to run it in your absence?"

"Yeah, why?"

"I think I want to move to another state. Preacher introduced me to a banker."

"Preacher is the old man you walked off with at my friend's wedding right?"

"Yeah, that's him, but the banker said, "Any money I gave him, he'd clean up for eight cents on the dollar."

"So you want to move?"

Ant leaned in close to Michelle and began to whisper. "'Chelle, I got about thirty million not including assets or even the money we bought with us; I'm talking cash."

Michelle's hand went to her heart. "Are you serious?" She whispered back as if someone would know what they were discussing.

"What's the point of having all this money if we can't do what we want with it?"

"Well, I guess your right baby, but when do you want to move?"

"I was thinking about a month after we get married. I want to move to Florida or California. I want us to drive Bentley's and shit. I want to buy you a mansion baby, so you can live like the queen you are.

"How does that sound to you?"

Michelle's smile was from ear to ear. "It's whatever you want Daddy, it's been like that from the beginning, and it will be that way to the day I die! And honestly I can't begin to tell you how nervous I am about us getting married, I tell the girls in the shop every day I even caught myself biting my nails."

Ant burst into laughter. "Well, sexy lady, we're getting married in a month, so get yourself together."

"Oh, don't get me wrong, I hired the best wedding planner for our wedding ceremony as well as a large reception hall."

"Well 'Chelle, since we have a couple of hours; why don't we shower, get manicures, and top it off with a massage."

WILLIE

Knock! Knock! Knock! Willie took a deep breath as he waited for Nique to answer her door.

"Hey Baby, come in and give momma a big hug. So what are we doing today?"

Willie looked into Nique's eyes, wondering why he didn't notice anything odd. She never asked intrusive questions; they had sex, everything in a typical relationship.

"Willie! Willie!" Nique yelled breaking his train of thought. "Baby, I asked what we are doing today."

"Oh, I'm kind of tired, so I want to chill."

"What's on your mind that has you not hearing me?"

"Nothing, I just need to relax. I got some bad news yesterday. The guy I copped from got killed." He lied.

"Really, Baby sorry to hear that were you close?"

"Yeah, but I don't want to talk about it. Can you make me a drink, Hennessey and coke please?"

"Okay, I'll be right back."

Willie's eyes glanced over the new living room set, looking for any sign that she was a cop. " Here's your drink baby. The remote control is on top of the TV. Since you want to chill, I'm gonna go to the grocery store. Is there anything in particular you have a taste for?"

"I can't think of anything."

"Okay, I'll be right back."

No sooner than Willie heard the car ignition start, he was on his way upstairs. "I didn't feel a gun when I just hugged her, so it has to be here somewhere."

Not that he didn't believe Ant, it's just his feelings were involved with Nique, so he needed something, some proof that Nique was a cop. Rumbling through her drawers, nothing. So he looked under the mattress, closets, bathroom, even checked inside the toilet, nothing.

Having worked up a good sweat, he felt hungry and suddenly had the urge for cereal. Opening the fridge, he shook the carton of milk making sure it was enough for a least two bowls. Reaching for the box of Captain Crunch, Willie accidentally knocked the box of Cocoa Puffs off the counter.

Thump!

"What the...?"

Willie reached down and picked the box up. It was heavy, so he jammed his arm in the box, digging around, finally feeling the compact semi-automatic handgun in the box. He pulled it out, then dug into the box again, feeling Nique's badge, he put the gun back into the box and placed it back as he found it.

Lying Bitch! He thought, no longer feeling anything for the woman, but anger. How could I be so stupid?

JAMAL

Jamal sat in his Jaguar waiting on Roy to purchase two kilos of cocaine from him. Periodically looking up whenever someone drove or walked by. Lisa just went to the doctor yesterday for her second test and the doctor told her the sex of the child. It was a boy. Jamal always wanted a son, and was now looking forward to becoming a father. He reached for his cell phone, and began dialing.

Ring!

"Where you at, slim? You know I don't play this waiting around shit, and you asking me for a favor. I'm on the way, gimme two minutes. Click!

Jamal hung up on Roy. Five minutes later Roy's Suburban pulled into the Pentagon Mall's parking garage. Jamal got out of his Jag and climbed into the back of Roy's truck.

"Jamal, I'm sorry about the time, I got stuck in traffic coming across the bridge."

"No prob Roy let me count this money, so I can get outta here. Did you put it in thousand stacks like I asked you?"

"Yeah, it's all there. I really appreciate you fronting me the other two ki's."

"Just make sure you have my half; my 30 G's by next week."

After counting the forty thousand, Jamal placed the two-footlocker bags in the passenger seat of the truck. "Aight Roy drop me back off at my car."

DC BLOOD BROTHERS

Roy pulled up in front of Jamal's Jaguar. "Aight Mal, I got you next week."

Jamal stepped out of the truck, noticing Roy looking in his rearview mirror; he looked over his shoulder to see what Roy was looking at. Four men were talking in front of a Yukon Denali. All had on hoodies and boots.

Jamal looked back to Roy as he shut the door; then began pulling his keys out his pocket. Roy sped off. The four men who were now walking fast in his direction.

As he stuck the key in the lock, the men began running. Jamal reached under his t-shirt for his gun. "Don't be stupid nigga!" One of them yelled pointing his gun.

Jamal shot in the men's direction; then scrambled to get in the car, starting the ignition and putting the car in drive. The men commenced firing on the car. Jamal shot back through the front windshield. Panicking, he hit this car parked to the left of him as he sped out of the parking space. Slivers of glass cut Jamal on the back of his neck and top of his head as the bullets shattered the back window. Ears ringing and adrenalin pumping, Jamal's life quickly flashed before his eyes.

A round entered his lower back; slamming Jamal's body against the steering wheel. "Shit!" He yelled, fighting to regain control of the car as he watched his blood spray on the dashboard.

Finally making his way out of the parking garage, he looked in the rearview making sure he wasn't being followed. Digging for his cell phone. Call Willie! He ordered the phone knowing Ant and Michelle were still in Vegas.

"Aye Willie, niggas just tried to rob me. I'm hit."

"What? Can you make it to a hospital?"

Yeah, I think so, but I'm losing a lot of blood."

"Where are you?"

"Coming across the bridge from Pentagon Mall, but I'm scared to keep driving this car. I just threw my gun out the window, but I got forty thousand in here and ten ki's in my truck."

"Park your car on some back street. I'm coming across South Capital Street now."

Ten minutes later, Willie with Barry in the car pulled up to Jamal's bullet riddled Jaguar. Rushing to his car, they saw he had passed out. " Jamal! Jamal!" Barry yelled slapping Jamal's face. They dragged him out the Jag, laid him across the back seat and rushed him to D.C. General Hospital. When Jamal recovered a little, two police officers came into his room. After bombarding him with several questions, the detectives knew that there would be a retaliation. The Officer who as writing down Jamal's answers on the pad, looked to this partner. "We're not gonna get anything out of him; let's go."

Jamal watched the Officers walk out and began contemplating what he was going to do to Roy. It was an obvious set up. He's dead!

"Did any of them look familiar?" Asked Willie.

"Naw, but when I catch up to Roy I'm gonna make him tell me who them niggas was."

"When you getting out of here, so we can handle this?" Tony asked in his raspy voice.

"I should be released tomorrow."

"Roy knows I ain't dead, so his bitch ass probably in hiding, but I remember hearing him say his kids go to that Catholic School, in N.E. behind H Street. Bet snatching they asses draw him out of hiding." East suggested. "Yeah, either way he's dead."

"I already called Big Homie, Mal; they on their way back." Willie said.

Three days later, Jamal, Willie, Tony, and East peered up and down the street through the dark tinted windows outside of St. John's Catholic Academy Elementary School.

"Ain't that his truck parking back there, Mal?"

"Yeah, that's it."

"Pull around the corner and let us out Willie."

Willie pulled around to H Street, N.E., and Tony and East got out of the car. They walked around the corner; Roy had pulled into a tight parking space and had his windows down. Roy looked in his rearview, seeing the two men approaching; then began looking through his CD's for the MDK CD he'd just purchased."

"What the fuck."

"Shut up you bitch ass nigga, drive!"

Tony ordered, now in the back seat with his 9 mm pressed hard into Roy's ribs. Willie followed Roy's Suburban on 95 South into VA finally parking in a small trailer park in Dumfries, Virginia. They quickly escorted Roy into the trailer, and tied him up. Roy was surprised seeing Jamal's large frame walking into the trailer.

"Take the duck tape off his mouth, Tony."

Tony snatched it off; laughing after he saw that some of Roy's mustache hair came off on the tape.

"Jamal, what's this all about, Homie?"

Jamal slapped him across the lips with his gun, blood splattering on East's sweat shirt, and the trailer wall.

"You set me up bitch ass nigga."

"No I didn't Mal, I swear to God!"

Jamal noticed a place of broken metal pipe outside the trailer, so he went to get it then began severely beating Roy with the metal.

"Put the tape on this niggas mouth, and turn the stereo on!"

"Okay! Okay! I'll tell you Mal just don't kill me, please!"

"Start talking nigga."

"The dudes around my way said, "They would kill me if I didn't set you up."

"What dudes?"

"The main one is Greg. He drives a Navigator; it's the only gold one on the block."

"Who are the other niggas?"

"I swear I don't know them." He pleaded with Mal as he was hit repeatedly with the bat.

DE BLOOD BROTHERS

Willie, East, and Tony watched in amazement as Jamal beat Roy with the bat until his arms were so sore he couldn't lift the bat anymore. Roy had already been dead at least a half hour before Jamal stopped beating him.

Chapter 37

Ant was walking with Michelle to cop the latest Blackberry. "The 8820 has built in Wi-Fi" he explained as they waited for the associate to finish a transaction. The salesman pulled out the phone and began explaining all its features.

"I'm gonna buy it." Ant said digging into his pocket for his money, looking to the left, he happened to see Jamal pushing a shopping cart through a baby store across the mall. "Here's your change and phone sir, enjoy your day."

Ant quickly grabbed his bag and rushed to catch his best friend. Jamal turned seeing Ant, and thought.... Oh shit!

"Who you buying baby clothes for?"

Jamal quickly ran over his options of lying. He's gonna see me with the baby someday. "My girl's pregnant; we're having a boy."

"Yeah, congratulations man! When am I gonna meet her?"

"It'll be soon; the due date is a couple of months away."

"Yeah, I'm surprised I didn't bump into her at the hospital when you got shot."

"Well, I told her don't come. I didn't want her to be freaking out being pregnant, you know."

"Yeah, well, holla at me later. I know 'Chelle is probably looking for me.

JASON

Ring!

DC BLOOD BROTHERS

Jason hung up and started putting his jacket on. "Come on Mitch, we got a floater at Haines Point."

Fifteen minutes later they were making their way through news reporters. "How long he been in?" Jason asked the officer in charge.

"Probably a couple weeks Jenkins, maybe three. Someone beat him to death, no ID, but cash was found in his pocket, so looks like someone just wanted him dead."

"Well, I'm going to take a look at the body after you get him downtown and run his prints; call me. I want to close this ASAP. It's gonna be pressure on this with all these news reporters down here."

A few hours later... John Doe was now known as Roy Saunders. "Jenkins, this guy has to have the longest rap sheet I've ever seen in my life. Robbery, drugs, guns and assaults. Man, what is this guy even doing on the streets."

Jason looked over his partners shoulder. "You're not lying Mitch, come on, let's knock on some doors and get this case closed."

ANTHONY

Ant shopped alone walking the streets of Georgetown, going into his favorite shops. Deciding he was tired of walking and his bags were heavy; he started making his way to his Range Rover. Walking pass an exclusive Boutique, he changed his mind. Seeing baby Gucci sneakers, Coogi sweat suits, and linen outfits. He spent $1500 on Jamal's future son.

Ant put on his right signal to turn onto Jamal's street. Driving down he saw a BMW parked in front of Jamal's house seeing the top of a female's head getting out. Good, I'll finally get to meet her, Ant thought. He couldn't believe that he was seeing Lisa's pregnant frame waddle to Jamal's door with her keys out as if she was about to unlock the door. He sped up trying not to be seen.

I don't believe this nigga fucking with this Bitch! ...Behind my back, couldn't even come to me like a real nigga... Lying to me. I'm too deep in the game to have nigga on my team I can't trust. Can't just cut him off. As much as Ant hated the thought, he knew what had to be done. Shit Jamal!

Ant pulled over to think. Thinking how he didn't want anybody in the crew to know he dropped the hammer on Mal. But he needed to talk to somebody. Even though Willie and Jamal never saw eye to eye, he found no pleasure in knowing he was a walking dead man.

"Willie, one more thing. With all this bullshit going down, I'm starting to feel leery. So it's time to clean up all loose ends; that includes the cop."

Willie swallowed hard and nodded in agreement.

"Do you think you can do it or you want me to bring in somebody from outside?"

"Honestly, I don't think I can pull the trigger."

"Then lay low for a week, go outta town. I'll make a phone call and by the time you get back all this will be over."

NIQUE

Nique pulled the covers over her face to block the sunlight. Rolled over then turned off her alarm clock, 10:45am. She picked up her phone.

This was the 4th day in a row she hadn't heard from Willie. Honestly, she was worrying to the point her stomach hurt. And this scared her because she knew her feelings has gotten involved. She dialed again, but left a message.

"Willie, this is Nique. Baby, I haven't heard from you all week, and I'm really starting to worry. Please call me just to let me know you're alright."

She picked up the phone again.

"Ring!"

"Third District; can I help you?"

"Paula Hi, this is Dana."

"Hey girl, where you been? I haven't seen you in a minute."

"Working, girl, but I'm calling because I need a favor, and I want it kept quiet; I'm undercover, and I haven't heard from my guy in four days. Can you check the hospital and local jails for me please?"

After Nique hung up she decided to take a shower. Turning on the water then lighting her scented candles. She put on her favorite CD by Jodeci, and stepped into the shower. The hot water was relaxing, but still couldn't ease the tension from thinking about Willie,

JAMAL

"So do you like this Mal?"

"$4,432,000. Jamal looked up once again from the pile of money he was counting to look at yet another baby outfit Lisa had purchased. "Yeah Lisa that's nice. Look Boo, I really need to count up this money.   I'm not even half way finished yet."

"Alright, I won't bug you anymore."

Bzzz! Bzzz! He picked up the phone; it was Ant.

"What's up fat boy?"

"Hey, what's up Big Homie?"

Lisa looked to Jamal knowing it was Ant. Lately, she started picking up on the Big Homie thing, along with the fact whenever Jamal said that, his conversations were longer, he did less talking, and more listening.

"Mal, I'm supposed to meet with these dudes tonight, but I can't make it, write this address down." Jamal grabbed a pen and paper and began writing. "Don't be late, I got a lot of paper riding on this."

DC BLOOD BROTHERS

ANTHONY

Ant popped open the bottle of XO Remy Martin and guzzled until he choked, then reached for the top paper and began rolling a joint. It was a rare occasion Ant smoked marijuana, but he felt he'd need all the help he could get to make it through today. He took a long drag of the joint and held in the smoke until he choked. Remembering his childhood, he started laughing about the time he and Jamal fought the older boy, because he had hit Jamal. Taking another toke of the joint, he wondered when exactly Jamal got so envious that he started fucking Lisa.

"Niggas." He mumbled out loud recalling when he had the dream about Jamal raping and shooting Michelle. Ant felt guilty, but rationalized that Jamal sowed his own fate planting the seed of deceit. Ant's thoughts switched to thinking about Nique, the undercover cop.

He became intoxicated from the power he came to hold, and fearful at the same time. Knowing that if his phone were to ring only once, it would mean that their lives had been brought to an end... simply because he wished it so. He didn't want to do it but the game had rules and both Nique and Jamal knew the risk. Though, he was going to have Willie murdered for being involved with Nique, he changed his mind and decided to give him a pass. At least the nigga Willie's honest.

Ant guzzled more of the liquor then wiped his mouth with the back of his hand.

Ring! He reached for the phone, but it stopped ringing. It was done.

Chapter 38

JASON

"Mitch, I'm telling you Redskins are going to the Super Bowl this year."

"Jenkins you're crazy. I got $50 saying they won't beat my Cowboys next week.'

"I can't believe you're a Cowboy fan, if I would have known that when I first met you, we wouldn't be partners."

"It's like that?"

Ring! Ring!

"Robbery Homicide, Green speaking."

"Wait!" Jason looked to his partner after hearing him screaming.

"Oh no, we're on the way. They just found Dana's body in Laurel, MD."

Forty five minutes later, There were at least one hundred officers, a mixture of P.G. County, MD State Troopers, DC and FBI agents all mourning their fellow Officer.

"What happened?" Jason asked Agent Stevens.

"A jogger noticed this was the second day in a row Dana's car was here, along with her in it, so he stopped to ask if she was okay. After banging on the window for 10 minutes he called the police."

"But how did she die?"

"We have to wait until we get her downtown to discover that. There's no visible bruise, so that's a mystery."

DE BLOOD BROTHERS

Ring! Ring!

"Mitch, this is not our day. Don't tell me."

"Yeah, we got another body."

"What we got, Jones?" Jason asked as he and his partner crossed under the yellow tape. "Black male, single shot to the back of the head."

"Professional?" Mitch asked.

"Got to be, Mitch. Street thugs are never this clean."

"Any ID on him?"

"Yeah, his name is Jamal Watson."

Jason wrote down the name then unzipped the body bag. The victims face had swollen, but for some reason looked familiar.

"Oh yeah, we found a 9 mm on him too; He never saw this coming."

"Alright Jones, fax me a copy of your report. We're heading back to the station. Today is gonna be hell."

Ring!

"Jenkins this is Agent Stevens; I just wanted to call you before the press got a hold of this. They found heroin in Dana's body."

"That's bullshit and you know it, Stevens."

"I know, but it's obvious it was murder. There was enough dope in her blood to kill ten people. They also found skin under her nails, so that proves there was a struggle."

"We're snatching Willie Wright off the streets though. Somehow he made her; we just pulled his prints off her gun. I'll call you back once we have him in custody."

"Thanks Agent Stevens."

Jason flopped down in his chair, and grabbed his head with both hands. Then prayed to God to put an end to this madness.

LISA

Toya contemplated if she should tell Lisa she saw Ant on 9th Street in Gibson Plaza yesterday when she went to visit her mother. "I know you may not care about this, but I saw Ant yesterday on the 5th floor in Gibson Plaza."

"He probably is fucking one of them money hungry bitches."

"I don't know Lisa, my cousin tells me she sees him all the time going in and out of an apartment, but he's always alone."

"Well, you were right Toya, I don't care, fuck Ant."

"You still haven't heard from Jamal?"

"Nope, and it's been three days. I hope his fat ass didn't get locked up. I want him there when our baby is delivered."

Ring! Ring! Lisa looked at her cell phone seeing Patrice's name. She pressed the ignore button.

Ring! Ring! Ring!

"Lisa they just found Jamal's body." Lisa dropped the phone and began crying. Toya picked up the phone.

"Patrice what did you say?"

"They just found Jamal's body, Toya!"

Toya hugged her friend. "I'm so sorry Lisa." Toya held onto Lisa until she cried herself to sleep.

ANTHONY

Ant and Willie walked into the Florida Avenue Grill together. Got a table, ordered and began talking.

"So, what's up Big Homie?"

"After me and 'Chelle get married; I'm disappearing. I got what I need. And this shit that went down with Jamal got my head swimming."

"Ah-ight, but what you want me to do? I already talked to Ortega's folks about you going into business directly with them."

Willie nodded.

"Thanks for staying loyal, Willie. I can't even eat, I'm about to roll, just make sure you watch your people since your girl's body was found they may gun for you."

"I know, but they ain't got shit. If they snatch me up I'll just stay quiet, and ride it out."

LISA

"Toya I'm telling you, Ant probably killed him. I just got that feeling."

"How you know it wasn't behind them dudes who tried to rob him a few months ago?"

"Toya, I got to go." Click!

Lisa stared at the phone, extremely emotional from being pregnant and feeling vengeful towards Ant. She thought about what Toya suggested for a moment, but ruled it out. Somehow Ant found out her relationship with Jamal and had him killed. If losing the father of her unborn child wasn't bad enough, deep inside she knew it was all because of her. She began dialing 911. "Hello, hi, um this isn't an emergency…"

"Then you need to call (202) 555-6000.," the operator cut her off.

Lisa dialed the number the woman gave her. "Can you give me the number to the Homicide Detective who's in charge of the Jamal Watson investigation?"

Lisa jotted down the numbers, hung up, then dialed back out.

"Robbery Homicide Detective, Jenkins speaking." Lisa made the connection with the last name, and remembered Jason, Ant's older brother was a cop.

Lisa fought to get her words out over tears.

DE BLOOD BROTHERS

"I just wanted to let you know. The person who killed Jamal Watson is the same person who murdered the Daniels family."

"What? Who is this?"

Click.

Jason stared into the receiver, the Daniel's family murder now piled onto his thoughts with Dana's murder. Lisa grabbed her car keys and rushed out of her house wiping tears from her eyes. She started the ignition and sped off. Twenty minutes later she found herself parked directly across the street from Gibson Plaza High-rise. Grabbing her phone, she pressed *67, and called Jason's number again.

Ring!

"This is the lady who called before. The same person who killed Jamal and the Daniel's family also killed Cedric…, and Nate…"

"Who is…?" Lisa hung up again. Seeing a Range Rover park in front of Gibson Plaza, Lisa ducked down in her seat and leered over the door. Ant's tall frame step out of the Range Rover. Her body instantly felt like she was on fire.

She dialed Jason back with Toya's words echoing in her head, 5th floor. "He's here."

"He's there with you now?"

"No, I know where he is."

"Well, tell me so I can get this monster off the streets. I don't know what apartment he's going in, but it's on the 5th floor in Gibson Plaza on the 7th…"

"I know where it is. I'm on the way."

JASON

Jason jumped out of his chair suddenly realizing if the man, the anonymous woman was speaking of, murdered the Daniel's family, that Nicolas Drake was connected to Willie Wright, this guy was also behind Dana's murder.

"Gentlemen!" Jason yelled "I need every available officer to apprehend a murderer and possible cop at 1301 7th Street, 5th floor, not sure of the apartment number, but I just had a call that ties this man to at least seven murders, including the murder of Detective Dana Robinson."

The detectives and officers grabbed their jackets and rushed to their cars. Jason had dispatch send every available officer in the vicinity of 7th St., NW to the 5th floor. With order to hold anyone attempting to leave the 5th floor. Jason called Agent Stevens to arrange the largest search and seizure warrant for one apartment building ever. Jason pulled behind the high-rise and waiting for the okay to go door to door. He was not worried about the killer getting away, because there were already four uniform officers, and two plain-clothes officers in front of both stairwells and elevators.

"It's a go; move in!" Jason jumped out his car, and waved toward the building to the other 20 officers.

DC BLOOD BROTHERS

ANTHONY

"Hey 'Chelle, what's up? I was just calling to see how you're doing?"
"I know Jamal's death has been hard on you."
"Yeah, it is, but I need to finish what I'm doing."
"Okay, I love you, and I can't wait to marry you."
"I love you too, baby."
Click!

Ant looked at the ten boxes he'd just stuffed full of cash. He laughed to himself, because he had one more safe to empty. He had done it. He was going to leave the game on top. He imagined how peaceful his life with Michelle would be, No more guns. No more violence. Ant pressed the keys to unlock the safe. After emptying the safe, he taped up the last box and grabbed his jacket.

Knock! Knock! Police!

He looks through the peep hole and saw two officers at the door across the hall. He rushed to the window and saw that the building was completely surrounded.

"What the fuck....." Two officers turned to his door.

Knock! Knock! Knock! "Police! Open it up" Ant heard an officer say then heard the lock turning on the door. One officer stood at the door while the other officer looked through the apartment. Ant pulled out his gun and stepped around the corner. As the officer walked past, Ant shot him behind the his left ear.

The rookie officer at door saw blood splatter against the wall. He jumped then ducked behind a sofa. Jason rushed up the stairs when he heard the gunshot. He drew his gun as he entered into the apartment. The rookie officer rose from behind the sofa, glad that Jason was there to back him up. "DC Police! Step out her and put the fucking gun down!" Jason raised his weapon as a figure slowly walked around the corner. He couldn't believe what he was seeing, his eyes nearly jumped out of their sockets as Ant emerged with his weapon pointed at the Rookie.

"Ant! What's going on? You, you killed all these people" Tears filled in the wells of Jason's eyes. "Put the gun down Ant; it's over! We don't have to do this."

"I ain't putting down shit! I ain't spending the rest of my life in prison! Tell your boy here, I'm playing."

"Put the gun down!" The rookie officer yelled.

"You put your fucking gun down!" Ant yelled back as he took two steps toward the officer.

"Fuck this! I'm taking him down." The rookie yelled to Jason.

"Nooooooo!" Jason screamed as he jumped between his brother and the rookie cop.

Both men fired their weapons, trying to defend themselves while aiming at the other. Time seemed to stop as Ant watched most of the bullets meant for him strike his older brother. The rookie paused as Jason fell backward into Ant's arms. He could not believe what just happened.

"Can't say I wasn't there for you." Jason whispered. He cracked a smile. "I love you, Ant. You have to make it out of here so you can take care of my family."

For a moment, a quiet peacefulness filled the room. The rookie lowered his Glock as he watched Ant kiss his brother on the forehead and lay him on the floor. But the silence would not last long.

"Drop the weapon! He's dead! It's over!" The rookie yelled as his backup entered the room.

"Not yet" Ant calmly replied with his eyes filled with controlled rage.

He raised his weapon and managed to fire one shot before a barrage of hot lead tore through his flesh.. The bullet made small hole the size of a dime as it entered the rookie's forehead, but it blew most of the rookie's brain out what was once the back of the young officer's skull. Ant collapsed on the floor reaching for his brother as a large pool of blood formed beneath him. "Jason," he whispered, "I'm sorry."

PREACHER

Two weeks later, police officers stood outside the hospital room, periodically looking in, seeing all the tubes coming out of Anthony Jenkins who was hand cuffed to the railing of the hospital bed. Agent Stevens shook the officer's hand as he asked the condition of the prisoner. "He's still out, Stevens."

"You two just make sure I'm the first to know when he regains consciousness, so I can charge him for killing two officers along with the six other murders."

"I thought the rookie shot Jason"

"What? What did you say?"

"Never mind"

"You're damn right! That never happened, hear me? Stick to the god damn script!"

"I got it."

"You damn well better."

Preacher turned off his television after watching yet another clip on Anthony Jenkins. Disgusted that even though Ant's brother was a decorated officer, the media questioned if Detective Jenkins was a part of his little brother Anthony's organization. Preacher had the boldest idea he'd ever had. "Marla, bring me the phone."

Preacher dialed an out the country number and waited for someone to answer. "Hello."

"I need a sit down" Preacher said then hung up.

An hour later, Preacher greeted his childhood best friend. He explained Ant's situation to him, and what he wanted done about it.

"You must really like this kid."

Preacher nodded yes to his friend.

"Consider it done Preacher."

DC BLOOD BROTHERS

DR. PETERSON

Dr. Peterson checked Ant's vitals. Still shaking his head from side to side surprised. Anthony Jenkins survived 14 shots; one bullet even nicked his heart.

"Paging Dr. Peterson."

The same time the doctor heard his name over the intercom, his pager started going off on his hip. He looked to see his home number. He stopped the Nursing station to find out what his wife wanted.

Ring!

"Hello."

"Darling you called?"

"Yeah, hold on."

"Hello." Dr. Peterson was taken aback hearing a strange male voice.

"Listen closely Doc. I have your wife, two sons, and your beautiful baby girl."

"What do you want?"

"First, Doc I want you to hear this."

The doctor heard a shot fired and his wife scream.

"Doctor."

"Yes, please don't hurt them."

"I just shot your wife in the leg, because you're asking me shit. This is how it goes; I give you orders, you follow them, no questions. Now, I want you to find a way to have Anthony Jenkins on the main floor at 3pm tomorrow."

"But, I…"

Another round was discharged.

"Dr. Peterson, your mouth just cost your nine year old son his life. If you want to save your other kids, have Jenkins down by the parking garage of the main floor at 3pm. And by the way, Dr. Peterson, if for any reason you don't deliver; not only will we kill your immediate family, but I have orders on your mother, aunt, your new born niece, and every person on your family tree."

ANTHONY JENKINS

Three years later, Anthony Jenkins' shadow covered his brother's tombstone. Ant read the stone: Jason Parcell Jenkins, dedicated Husband, Father, and Officer. Rest in Peace. Tears fell from Ant's eyes.

"Jason," he began. "I'm sorry. I swear if there was anything I could do to switch places with you I would. I just got caught up Jay. When dad got killed, I just lost it. Sometimes I check on your kids and wife. You have a beautiful daughter. I'm so sorry you never got the chance to see her face. I never knew Michelle was pregnant, but I have a son too. Though he'll probably never see my face.

I must be the most wanted man on the planet. You just don't know how much I hate myself for what happened. I was even gonna kill myself, but that would have been too easy, so my punishment is to go on living everyday with the guilt.

DE BLOOD BROTHERS

Shit! If it's true what they say, "What goes around comes around." I'll probably get killed anyway. I started going back to church. I think of mom and dad every time I go. They preach that God will forgive you no matter how you sinned. I can't see that when I can't even forgive myself. I just came to say, "I'm sorry." And it wasn't worth it, I realize that all my life I did things to obtain power and control, because I felt so helpless when dad was killed, but there is no such thing.

Power isn't something you obtain; it's an illusion of someone's insecurities for another who has a bit more confidence or influence. Control is the biggest illusion. If we could control things we'd never have to bury our love ones; we'd never have accidents, life would be perfect, or would it? We do what we can in hopes of the best. Humility and Balance, Dad used to say that's what the world needs... to avoid creating monsters like me."

Discussion Questions

1. How did Anthony end up in the streets after having such a well-structured family? Does it matter what kind of family you come from? Does environment have an equal impact?

2. How did Anthony and Jamal's relationship change from the beginning of the book? Was Jamal truly Ant's friend through it all?

3. Is Ant a good or bad person? Were his actions justified by his pain from his father's death? Do you think he should have had a change of heart after dealing with his father's killer?

4. Could Franklin have turned down Bone's a little easier? Could that have saved his life? Even if Franklin had two hundred dollars on him, would Bone's still have murdered him?

5. Was Millie a good wife and mother? Did she curse her youngest son by naming him after a drug dealer she was obsessed with as a teenager? When she thought of getting an abortion, did that make her a bad wife considering decisions without consulting her husband?

6. Was Willie too slick for his own good? Did he take himself off point by believing the undercover cop was so naïve? If Ant didn't take care of the undercover cop, do you think Willie would have killed her?

7. How smart do you think Smiley was for retiring? Was he a true hustler who understood the game or was he a good businessman who knew when to pull out? Why was he so respectable in the streets? And, why was his relationship so open with his girlfriends?

8. Was Ant wrong for trusting Lisa? Why didn't he kill Lisa to make sure she would never talk?

9. Did Ant have Jamal killed for disrespecting him by dealing with Lisa? Was Ant enraged because Lisa had Jamal's baby? Was Ant paranoid because his right hand man had her so close?

10. Should Anthony have been killed in the end rather than Jason? If so, would Anthony have had any change of heart the second before he took his last breathe? Or do you think it's better that Ant lived to regret his mistakes and lost someone close to him after taking the lives of so many people?

11. How do you think the murder of the Daniels family affected Ant?

12. Do you think Mrs. Daniels was wrong for giving information to the police? Would you think she was wrong if she would have remained silent?

13. Do you believe Jason had a good outlook as a police officer with his views on society and crime? Or do you think his views were more focused on violent crime due to the murder of his father?

14. What do you honestly feel Ant's opinions of his actions are now? What do you think he could do to help others not go down the same path as he did?

Lá Femme Fatalé Publishing Division
Order Form

Charge it to the Game by Michele Fletcher	$15.95
DC Blood Brothers by Viyo Lance	$15.95
Fire & Flames by Coco	$15.95
Memoirs of a Bitch by Cecelia Robinson	$12.95
Stripping Asjiah by Sa'Rese	$15.95

Shipping/handling (via U.S. Priority Mail)
$4.05 per Book   Total $_____

Purchaser Information

Name: _____

Reg #: _____

Address: _____

City: _____ State: _____ Zip: _____

Total Number of Books Ordered: _____

For orders shipped directly to prisons Lá Femme Fatalé Productions deducts 25% off the sale price of the book.

Costs are as follows: Shipping/handling $4.05

Lá Femme Fatalé Productions
9900 Greenbelt Road, Suite E-333
Lanham, MD 20706
1-866-50-femme (33663)
www.lafemmefataleproductions.com

L77

Biography

"Viyo Lance" was born Kenneth L. Martin, Jr. on July 15, 1974, in Washington, DC He grew up in the various quadrants of Washington, and Maryland. He is the son of Kenneth L. Martin, Sr. and Gail D. Martin. His grandmother, Annie May Cinada, has always been an inspiration to him. He has two beautiful daughters, Dominique Lee-Martin and Kayah B. Martin. His four siblings are Richard Martin, Edward, Howard and Averie Kearney.

The name "Viyo Lance" is derived from the word violence, because that best describes the things he has seen and been through. He has been invited to speak, and volunteer for various youth programs in the community. He loves to read and is always looking for new and intellectual topics to write and converse about. He always knew that he wanted to be in the entertainment industry. His first focus was on music, but writing always came naturally.

He currently resides in the suburbs of Prince Georges County, MD and is now working on two forthcoming novels.

Made in the USA
Lexington, KY
28 December 2011